Hang a Thousand Trees with Ribbons

Other Novels by Ann Rinaldi

KEEP SMILING THROUGH

THE SECRET OF SARAH REVERE

FINISHING BECCA
A Story about Peggy Shippen and Benedict Arnold

THE FIFTH OF MARCH
A Story of the Boston Massacre

A BREAK WITH CHARITY
A Story about the Salem Witch Trials

A RIDE INTO MORNING
The Story of Tempe Wick

Hang a Thousand Trees with Ribbons

THE STORY OF PHILLIS WHEATLEY

Ann Rinaldi

HARCOURT BRACE & COMPANY
San Diego New York London

Library of Congress Cataloging-in-Publication Data
Rinaldi, Ann.
Hang a thousand trees with ribbons: the story of
Phillis Wheatley/Ann Rinaldi.
p. cm.
"Gulliver Books."
Summary: A fictionalized biography of the eighteenth-century African woman who, as a child, was brought to New England to be a slave, and after publishing her first poem when a teenager, gained renown throughout the colonies as an important black American poet.
ISBN 0-15-200876-4
ISBN 0-15-200877-2 (pbk.)
1. Wheatley, Phillis, 1753–1784—Juvenile fiction.
[1. Wheatley, Phillis, 1753–1784—Fiction. 2. Poets, American—Fiction.
3. Slaves—Fiction. 4. Afro-Americans—Fiction.] I. Title.
PZ7.R459Han 1996
[Fic]—dc20 96-872

Text set in Fournier
Designed by Kaelin Chappell
First edition
A B C D E
A B C D E (pbk.)
Printed in Hong Kong

In memory of my aunt Jo

TO BE SOLD

A Parcel of likely Negroes, imported from Africa, cheap for cash or short credit; Enquire of John Avery, at his House next Door to the White-Horse, or at a Store adjoining to said Avery's Distill-House, at the South End, near South Market; Also, if any Persons have any Negro Men, strong and hearty, tho' not of the best moral character, which are proper Subjects for Transportation, may have an Exchange for small Negroes.

—*From an advertisement in both the*
Boston Evening Post *and the*
Boston Gazette and Country Journal
for July 29, 1761, and several weeks thereafter

Sir You having the Command of my Schooner Phillis your orders Are to Imbrace the First Favorable Opertunity of Wind & Weather & proceed Directly for the Coast of Affrica, Touching First at Sinagall if you fall in with it On your arrival then Cum to Anchor with your VeSsell & go up to the Facktory in your Boat & see if you Can part with Any of your Cargo to Advantage . . . if you Could Sell the whole of your Cargo there to a Good Proffett & take Slaves & Cash Viz. Cum Directly Home. . . . You must Spend as little Time as poSsible at Sinagal & then proceed Down the Coast to Sere Leon & then make the best Trade you Can from place to place till you have disposed of all your Cargo & purchase your Compleat Cargo of Young Slaves which I Suppose will be about 70 or Eighty More or LeSs I would Reacommend to you gowing to the Isle Delos if you Cant Finish at Sereleon . . . be sure to bring as Few Women & Girls as possibl . . . hope you wont be Detained Upon the Coast Longer than ye 1st of May by Any Means, the Consequence you know We have Experienced to be Bad, You & your people & Slaves will get Sick which will ruin the Voyage. Whatever you have left Upon hand after April, Sell it altogeather for what you Can Get if even at the First Cost Rather than Tarry Any Longer . . . be Constantly Upon your Gard Night & Day & Keep good Watch that you may Not be Cutt of by Your Own Slaves tho Neavour So Fiew on Board Or that you Are Not Taken by Sirprise by Boats from the Shore which has often ben the Case Let your Slaves be well Lookd after properly & Carefully Tended Kept in Action by Playing Upon Deck . . . if Sick well Tended in ye Half Deck & by All Means Keep up Thare Spirretts & when you Cum off the Coast bring off a Full Allowance of Rice & Water for a Ten Week PaSage Upon this your Voyage Depends in a Grate Measure . . . by all Means I Reacommend Industry, Frugality & dispatch which will Reacommend you to further BuSsiness. Your Wages is Three pounds Ten Sterling per Month Three Slaves, priviledge & three % but of the Cargo of Slaves Delivered at Boston, This is all you are to have . . .

—From a letter written by Timothy Fitch,
a successful merchant in the slave trade,
to his employee Captain
Peter Quinn, dated January 12, 1760,
dateline Boston, Massachusetts

Chapter One

MAY 1772

"What do you remember, Phillis? What do you remember?"

They are always asking me that. As if I would tell anyone about my life before. The few good memories I have I cherish and hold fast. My people believe that if you give away your memories, you give away part of your spirit.

It was Nathaniel asking now. We were at breakfast before the rest of the family came down. "If you can remember anything about your life before, you should tell these men today," he said, looking up from the newspaper he was reading.

Today I must go to the governor's mansion. To stand before a committee of the most noble men in Boston to prove that the poetry I have written is mine.

Me. Phillis Wheatley. A nigra slave who was taken into the home of the Wheatleys as a kindness. And who responded to that kindness by doing something few well-born white women would do in this year of 1772.

Put her thoughts to paper. Write down the workings of her mind.

Now, because I had made so bold as to do such a thing, I must stand before these shining lights of the colony today and answer their questions. Had I truly written this poetry? Or stolen it from somewhere? Was I passing myself off as a lie? The mere thought of their questions made my innards turn over.

"Don't be anxious, Phillis," Nathaniel was saying.

"I'm not anxious."

"You're touching your cowrie shell. You always do that when you are anxious."

He was right. I drew my hand down from the shell that I wear on a black velvet ribbon around my neck. My mother gave it to me when we were taken from our home. It gives me comfort when I'm distressed.

"You look very lovely in that new frock," Nathaniel said, spooning fresh fish into his mouth, "but must you wear that shell for this occasion today?"

"I always wear it," I said. "It's my good talisman."

He shrugged and went back to his reading.

I'd been bought for cowries. Sold by the people

of my own land into the hands of Captain Peter Quinn for seventy-two of the lovely creamy white shells that serve as currency in the slave trade.

Nathaniel does not know this, though he knows me better than anyone. None of the Wheatleys know it. There are certain things that are just not for the telling.

"Why would these learned men wish to know of the past of a little nigra girl?" I asked.

"Don't be petulant, Phillis."

"I'm not."

"Yes, you are. It won't work with these men. They are all important and busy and are going out of their way to grant you this time today. But, to answer your question, if they consider your poetry in light of what your life was like *before*, it could work in your favor."

"I want them to consider my poetry for what it is. Not for being written by a slave."

"You're not a slave, Phillis."

There is the lie. A convenient one, of course, for everyone concerned.

"I don't see anyone waving free papers under my nose of late, Nathaniel."

"If I knew you were going to be vile this morning, I would have had you take a tray in your room. Has your position in this household ever been one of a lower order, Phillis?"

Nathaniel knows I desire my freedom. He considers it a personal affront, an insult to all his family has done for me.

"No, Nathaniel. My position in this household has always been that of a daughter," I said dutifully.

"Then don't belabor this freedom business. It's tedious."

Unless you don't have it, I thought. "I don't mean to be ungrateful, Nathaniel. Yet . . ." I stopped.

"Yet you would rather be free. Is that it, Phillis?" He said the word with grievous hurt in his voice.

"Yes."

"To do what? What would you do with this precious freedom that you cannot do now?"

But I had no answer for that. For I do not know what I would do with it.

"None of us is truly free, Phillis," he said languidly, "but if you wish it so much, then I put forth to you that you will someday be like Terence. Do you recollect who Terence was?" He was playing the teacher now, a role he cherished.

I knew I must answer. I did so sullenly. "A Roman author who wrote comedies. African by birth. A slave. Freed by the fruits of his pen."

"As you will someday be. If you follow the course we have set for you. Pray that day does not come too soon. For you will regret it."

My bones chilled. But I challenged him. "How so?"

He expected to be challenged. It is the way of things with us, the way he taught me everything I know. By argument, open discourse. "Because then all this"—and he waved his fork to include the polished dining table, the sparkling silver, the shining pewter—"will be lost to you. And you to us. You thrive only under our protection, Phillis. Free, you will perish."

"Terence did not perish."

"True. But that was Rome. This is Boston." There was a twinkle in his blue eyes. He was enjoying himself.

But he was right, and I knew it. He is always right. That is the tedious thing about him.

"I just thought it might go well for you this morning if these esteemed gentlemen knew what you had been through. With the middle passage, for instance," he said.

I glared at him. He was debonair, self-assured, the only son in a well-placed family, wearing a satin and brocade waistcoat and a velvet ribbon on his queue, but his question sat ill on me. "What do *you* know of the middle passage?"

"Don't take umbrage, Phillis."

"If we're going to fight, give me fair warning, Nathaniel. I've the mettle for it. But don't pretend kindness and speak to me of such things as the middle passage."

He lowered his eyes. "So it was as bad as they say, then?"

"That depends on who is doing the saying."

"No matter. Some men on the docks."

"If they work on slavers, then they know, Nathaniel. Everything they say is true. But I have no need in me to speak of it."

He raised his cup of chocolate. "A proper answer from a proper young woman."

"I'm not a proper young woman and you know it."

"My, we're contentious this morning."

"I wasn't when I came to the table. You've made me so."

He smiled. "No, you are not a proper young woman, Phillis. No proper young woman writes poetry."

Well, he spoke no lie.

"Don't look so distressed. Proper is tedious."

"Your sister, Mary, is proper, and you think her wonderful."

"I think her tedious. And prissy and foolish."

"She loves her reverend."

"Yes, and likely the loving will kill her. Here she is being brought to bed of a child twice in one year. Such a lot is not for you, Phillis."

"What is my lot, then?"

"Grander than that . . . If you succeed with these fine gentlemen this morning."

"And if I don't?"

"You will, Phillis, you will."

His words brought tears to my eyes. When all is said and done, Nathaniel always has believed in me. When I first came to this house, ten years ago, he befriended me; while his pious and prissy sister, Mary, his twin, tormented me so.

I was seven then and they were seventeen. I thought Nathaniel was a god. Or at least a roc, which is the name we give the huge birds that, in our stories, swoop down and fly away with elephants.

In his own way, Nathaniel swept down on me. And saved me. And now I hate him for it, no-account wretch that I am. In part because I have come to depend on him so.

And in part because I love him.

I love him because he is sharp, smart, and not lazy. Because he sees beneath the pious claptrap of Boston and says things we should not speak of.

Things I think all the time. I love him because there is an excitement about him that bespeaks things about to happen. Or makes them happen, I don't know which.

I love him because he had a hand in making me write my poetry.

He does not know I love him, of course. If he did, it would be the end of any discourse between us. Certainly it would be the end of me in this house. Bad enough that I write poetry. To profess love for the master's son would be unforgivable.

Soon Nathaniel will *be* the master, with Mr. Wheatley sickly with gout and about to retire. Nathaniel is buying out his father's holdings now, and running things.

He smiled dourly. "Surely you could share a memory from your past with *me* one of these days, couldn't you? Haven't we known each other long enough?"

I nodded. "What would you know?"

"I'd be most honored, someday, if you would tell me of your mother. That is, if you have any recollection."

Do I remember my mother, he wants to know.

I not only remember, I can still *see* the deck of the ship we came on. I can *smell* the salt air, and the hot vinegar the crew uses to clean up the stench belowdecks.

I can still *hear* the clamor as the male slaves are being exercised, the fiddle music being played by the crew, the clanking of chains as the slaves commence dancing.

Once again I am with Obour, my friend. We have

just finished our first meal of the day, our boiled rice and millet.

And I can still hear my mother's screams as she was thrown overboard. Dashed into the sea because, as I was told later, the sailors had found a sore on her face. And they thought it was smallpox.

"You could not bear my confidences, Nathaniel. I can scarce bear them myself," I said.

He nodded. "Don't underestimate me, Phillis. This meeting at the governor's mansion this morning could never have come about if you and I did not have an understanding of one another."

What is he saying? My eyes went moist. *Does he know my feelings for him?*

There is no telling what fool thing I would have said if Aunt Cumsee hadn't come into the room then, like some dark conscience, come to refill our cups with chocolate.

Come to hover over me, was what she was doing. I met her amber eyes.

Remember yourself, those eyes said. *Don't hold him in higher esteem than he holds you. Sweet talk is all it be. He is dallying with you because it amuses him to do so. You're only a slave to him—chattel. Dally back, but no more. Or it will come to grief.*

Aunt Cumsee knows I love him. I could never keep anything from her.

I glared at her. "No, thank you, no more chocolate for me. Excuse me, Nathaniel, I must make ready."

He stood as I rose from my chair. "Ask Prince to bring around the carriage, won't you?"

"He's cast his spell on you again," Aunt Cumsee whispered to me in the hall, "just like those witch doctors where you come from."

"Hush." I pushed her along into the kitchen. "What do you know about witch doctors? You've been here so long, you've forgotten the old ways. All you know is Massachusetts."

"We gots our share of witches. An' I know what he's doin' to you."

"He's doing nothing," I said. "And for your information, the witch doctors where I come from don't cast spells. The only magic they do is with herbs. To make people well."

"But he's castin' his own kinda spell over you. Always does."

I kissed her. "Don't scold. I know what I'm about. I know that right now, even as we speak, there is some noodleheaded white woman out there who is setting a snare for him."

She nodded. The look in her eyes was so old it unsettled me. "Still, he's castin' somethin' on you. An' you sit there, dumb as the sundial in the garden, waitin' for him to favor you with his light."

"Silly," I told her. And I ran for the door. "Wish me luck now, won't you?"

She shook her head and sighed. "Luck got nuthin' to do with it. Prayers do. An' I done all my prayin'."

I ran outside. "Prince," I called. "Prince! Master Nathaniel wants the carriage! We're going to Province House!"

Chapter Two

"You goin', then, is you?"

"Yes, Prince."

He was bringing out the horse and hitching it to the chaise. I stood and watched.

"Sure she's goin'." Sulie pushed past me with a pan of chicken food in her hands and stood in the yard tossing it about. "Can't wait to take her little behind over to that governor's mansion and talk her fancy talk to all those mens." And she mimicked what I'd said to Nathaniel at breakfast. " 'You couldn't bear my confidences, Nathaniel. I can scarce bear them myself! Oh!' " She slapped a hand against her forehead in a mock manner of a white girl about to faint. Chickens clucked around her feet.

"Shut your mouth, Sulie." Prince glowered at her.

"Leave her be. She's doin' what the Lord intended her to do."

"The Lord intended her to scrub pots and iron the master's shirts," she flung back. "An' all her poetry be is a way to get outa doin' it."

"Least she's got a way," Prince replied.

"Ain't natural." Sulie spoke as she flung food at the chickens. "She's gettin' above herself. It'll bring the wrath of the Lord down on us all."

"Leave the Lord outa this," Prince told her. "You is just jealous, Sulie."

"Got nuthin' to be jealous about." She finished her chore and came up the back steps to stand beside me. Hatred runs deep in Sulie. She is thirty and blessed with a bosom and looks I do not have. Yet she outright hates me, ever since my poetry writing got me excused from household chores.

"Aunt Cumsee gotta work twice as hard since you ain't in the kitchen no more. Last year or two didn't matter none. Now she gettin' old."

"I said leave her *be*, Sulie." Prince came out from around the horse and chaise.

"*You're* the one best leave her be. 'Lessen you're plannin' on havin' her sit up next to you on the carriage seat agin today. I heard Mrs. Wheatley say you do that agin and you'll be sold off."

Prince moved toward her. I stepped down quickly,

between them. It wouldn't have been the first time they'd come to blows. Both would be punished if that happened. The Wheatleys do not hold with servants fighting, as do many other families in Boston.

Yesterday I'd been sent to call on Mercy Otis Warren, who wrote plays. The weather took a turn for the worse and my mistress sent Prince to fetch me home.

"It was my idea to sit up on the front seat next to Prince," I told Sulie.

"Then you should know better." She spit at me. "Fool girl, got him in trouble. You heard what the Missus called him. 'Saucy varlet.' 'Impudent,' to have you sit next to him. You git him sold off and you'll answer to me," she hissed. "I'll kill you. I'll put poison in your chocolate. I know where to get it. I know Robin on the wharf."

"You crazy, you!" Prince lunged for her. "Doan even say such!"

To make matters worse, she was smitten with Prince. And he not with her. So she was jealous of me on that score, too. She hated me because Prince and I were friends.

Sulie pushed past me and went into the house.

"Doan mind her none," Prince said. "She's crazy!"

"Does she know Robin?" My voice shook.

"Everybody does. Doan mean nuthin'. Robin learned his lesson."

Robin does odd jobs for Dr. Clark, who owns the apothecary shoppe on the wharf. In the fifties, when the notorious slaves Mark and Phillis murdered their master, John Codman, it was said they got the arsenic from Robin.

Mark and Phillis were hanged and burned. People still talk about it in Boston. Mark's skeleton still hangs in a cage on Charlestown Common.

Robin has never been brought to trial. He still roams the wharves, dressed like a dandy. *What lesson has he learned?* I wanted to ask.

"She just takin' on 'cause she be jealous," Prince said. "You please these mens this mornin' wif your white people's learnin', and your words be in a book. She heard Aunt Cumsee say it."

"Maybe she's right, Prince. Maybe I am getting above myself. And it will bring the wrath of the Lord down on us all."

"She don't care a fig for the Lord, 'ceptin' when it please her."

"Surely Sulie's right about Aunt Cumsee. She *is* getting on." I minded how cumbersome she'd seemed while serving breakfast this morning. "Threescore and ten Aunt Cumsee is now. All that lifting and carrying could kill her."

"Only thing that'll kill her would be if'n you didn't make use of your mind. It's all she talks 'bout,

Phillis, you makin' this book . . . An' I do the liftin' and carryin' for her."

"If I make this book, everything will change, Prince."

He moved back to the horse and chaise. "I know. No more you'll be plain ol' Phillis. You'll be miss Fancy Phillis then, and you'll never talk to Prince no more."

He was making sport of me. But tears came to my eyes just the same. "I'll always be friends with you, Prince. And I'll always speak to you. I promise."

"Phillis!" Mrs. Wheatley came out the back door. "I slept late. Come, let me wish you well."

I ran to her. She embraced me in the folds of her sky blue morning gown. Her delicate face, like a flower about to open to the sun, closed with distress at seeing me talking with Prince. But all she said was, "Phillis, dear, do your best this day. My prayers are with you."

I smiled. "I'll make you proud," I said. Then I got into the chaise with Nathaniel, who had just come out behind his mother. And, two-faced wretch that I am, I did not look at Prince as he hopped up front to drive.

"I noticed you were conversing with Prince," Nathaniel said to me as we rode through Boston's busy streets.

"Prince is my friend."

"Be careful. For one thing, it displeases Mother. For another, he has unsavory friends. Need I say more?"

"No." I've long known that Prince is running with the Sons of Liberty. We all know. The Wheatleys do not question him about it. Though they keep their own counsel, it seems to me that they have leanings toward these new Patriots and countenance Prince's activities.

Nathaniel does not. As an upcoming merchant, stepping into his father's shoes, he is still not declaring himself.

"He's my friend," I said again.

Nathaniel sighed. "Just don't hurt Mother," he said.

Chapter Three

Province House. The sight of it made me weak with fear. It is three stories built of brick, laid in English bond. It has great dormers and is topped by a tall weathervane that is a statue of an Indian with a bow and arrow. There is a brick walk in front. And sentries standing guard.

There is power here. The power of wealth earned through accomplishment and strength.

Yes, I thought as the carriage drew up on the roundabout, *I want to be part of that power. I want my poetry published, so I can be a true daughter of Phoebus, Greek god of the sun. And not a shadow, existing forever only by the leave of someone else.*

Nathaniel helped me from the carriage. A servant came rushing forward to see us down the path and through the English gardens.

Right into a courtyard we went, where there was much greenery and flowers. Never had I seen such a garden! I cried out with joy. And in the middle of it, a fountain. Water gushed. I started toward it.

Nathaniel put a restraining hand on my arm.

There were benches and a table nearby. All that was missing was the sun, for though it was mid-May the day was overcast.

The servant bade us sit. Another brought a silver tray of tea and cake.

"Are they ready to receive us?" Nathaniel asked the servant. I could tell he wanted me out of there, away from that fountain.

At that very moment a tall, elegantly turned-out young man came from the house. "Nathaniel!"

"John!" Nathaniel got to his feet. "Phillis, you remember Mr. Hancock," he said to me.

Indeed, I did. I stood up and curtsied.

He is tall, elegantly dressed, and possesses such grace of movement that the very air around him seems rarefied by his presence.

He is very rich. Everyone in Boston knows him on sight. He had been most kind to me on past visits to the Wheatley house. He took a chair and gestured that we should sit. "Phillis, how has this rogue friend of mine been treating you? Kindly, I hope."

I smiled and said yes.

"And are you ready, then, to walk into the lion's den?"

"I am ready in the most humble manner, sir."

"Are you." He leaned forward, resting his elbows on the knees of his satin breeches. "Phillis, before you go inside I would advise you of something."

His face is lean and has about it that look of quiet strength that bespeaks breeding. I have learned, by now, that it is a commodity only money can create, yet that no money can buy.

"Phillis, since the sixteenth century, Europeans have wondered whether or not the African species of man could ever create formal literature. Or master the arts and sciences. If it is determined that they can, then it will also be determined that they belong to the same family as the European variety of man."

"And if not?" I asked.

"Then it will be ascertained that they are destined, forever, to be slaves."

I studied my hands in my lap. His gaze was fixed on me. I raised my eyes to meet his. They were warm and brown.

"So you can see that a lot rides on your answers to us this day, Phillis."

I thought of Sulie, mean as a hornet, ready to kill me if I caused Prince to be sold. I thought of Robin, dressed in satins and roaming the wharves; Robin, who sold the arsenic that killed a man, and thrived from the doing.

Could *they* create formal literature? Master the arts and sciences?

For I am doing this for them, as well as for everyone else of my race.

"These men inside have power and far-reaching influence," Mr. Hancock was saying. "Mayhap, before you decide to come inside, you should have more time to reflect on whether you want to go through with this examination."

I looked at Nathaniel. He returned my gaze. "Whatever you wish to do, Phillis," he said. "No one is pushing you."

What I wished to do was throw up. My head was swimming. I felt nauseous.

Mr. Hancock stood up. "I would suggest we leave her alone to think, Nathaniel," he said.

It is not fair! Not fair that the whole future of my race should be put on my shoulders. I am only seventeen! How did it come to this?

I put my arms over my middle as I sat in the chair and bent over, as if taken with gout of the stomach.

All I ever wanted to do was write some words down on paper. The fact that I could do so never ceased being a matter of incredulity to me.

I love the way the words look, all of a piece on

the parchment beneath my hands, weaving my thoughts into a tapestry, like a spider weaving a web.

I love the way I can make them rhyme. I love the smell of the very ink I use.

Most of all, I love that when I write I am not skinny and black and a slave. My writing has no color. It has no skin at all, truth to tell.

When I write I am the real me.

I am whole, beautiful, alive, filled with a sense of pleasure and worth. Why can't they all just leave it be?

I was supposed to come here just to answer questions about those poems. Show these men that I do, indeed, know Greek and Latin. And all the other lessons Nathaniel has taught me.

Now they have turned it all into something else.

Now the future of my race depends on my answers this day. Oh, it isn't fair!

Mother! Suddenly I wanted her so badly I felt the hole inside me I always feel, wanting her. Because my best memories cut sharp. And they make me bleed.

The morning I was taken. The vision of her pouring out water before the sun each morning. And the bittersweet memories of what happened on the ship.

"Mother," I said to the hole, "tell me what to do . . . As you told me on the ship to stay quiet and make myself small and sleep anywhere and eat what I was given and never make a sound."

Mother, what shall I do?

I am ashamed to admit it, but I cried, sitting there on that bench in that lovely garden. And then, after a moment, something happened.

The sun came out for the first time that day. A clearing came to the sky and the sun shone down, sparkling on the greenery around me. And on the water in the fountain.

I knew what I must do. I stopped crying and stood up.

On the table was a silver teapot. I picked it up from its silver tray. The tea was cold by now. Slowly I poured it out into the grass. Then I took the teapot over to the fountain, knelt, and filled it with water.

And, as I had seen my mother do so many times as a child, as I had done in the fountain the Wheatleys once had in their garden—before Nathaniel tore it out to stop me—I poured the water out, slowly, back into the fountain, while facing the sun.

Something else happened then. *I felt like my mother.* I was her for a few minutes as I poured the water. And when it was all poured out of the teapot, I felt becalmed and strong. Back to the chair I went. I set the teapot on the tray.

My mind was clear now, cleansed. And I let the thoughts pour into it, like water into the fountain.

Chapter Four

JANUARY 1761

We lived near the River Senegal on the Grain Coast. And if the leopard hadn't come, I would still be living there.

But he came, to steal the antelope my father had killed for us, and that hung outside our house.

My father was known as a great hunter. We never lacked for food. Mostly he was known for hunting the black-legged mongoose. These creatures plagued us. They seemed tame and children would try to catch them. But they would bite, and many times the bitten child would die.

Other people in my village depended on my father to catch these creatures. Also he hunted the African wild dog. And the bat-eared fox.

My father's brother, Dahobar, was jealous because

of the name my father had gained as a hunter. And because both brothers were rival chiefs. Dahobar had slaves. Not only that, he sold his own people to the traders for the white man's presents.

From the River Senegal to the River Congo, the slave traders' great ships came with brightly colored cloth, beads, rum, and most of all, cowrie shells.

A man's standing as a chief depended upon how many cowrie shells he had.

My father had no slaves. We were farmers. He and all the people in our tribe raised rice and maize and cattle. But we had muskets, even like the Wheatleys have here in Boston. Muskets and gunpowder we had, brass pans and kettles, red cloth, scissors, needles, colored thread. My father bartered for these things at market in exchange for what he raised.

Well, what happened is that the leopard that took our antelope had to be shot. So my father, the great hunter, went out to shoot it one day, took aim, missed, and shot a man instead.

My father had never missed his mark. Nobody knows what happened. To make matters worse, the man he shot was from Dahobar's tribe.

My father was brought up before one of Dahobar's tribunals and sentenced to be sold into slavery.

A ship with great masts lay riding at anchor in the

River Senegal. White slavers had rowed ashore to visit Dahobar.

My father was taken away from the tribunal to be sold, but he escaped and came back to our village. His warriors were placed on guard. The ship left the River Senegal without him.

We children were not allowed to venture from our home for fear the slavers or, worse yet, Dahobar would seize us.

My friend Obour lived not far away, near the rice fields. To be together, for sport and to earn a few cowries ourselves, we sometimes worked at scaring the birds away from the grain.

But now I was not allowed to leave my home to meet Obour anymore. Kidnappers hid in the thickets along the creeks and they kidnapped children as well.

Obour worked hard chasing away birds to help her family. And I knew she would be in the rice fields early of a morning. So one morning I sneaked out before the sun was up and made my way along the familiar paths and roads just to see Obour.

I would be back before the sun favored us. Before my mother poured the water out of the stone jar to honor the sun.

There Obour was in the rice fields, busy chasing birds, laughing and enjoying herself as she always did. When I splashed through the creek, she saw me coming and raised her arms.

It was still not light, but I could see her clearly. And she could see me.

Then, as I ran to her, another figure leaped out and grabbed her.

Before I got to her, she was struggling in the grip of the strong arms of a large dark man, a kidnapper. Likely one of Dahobar's men.

I fought him for Obour. And for myself. I scratched and bit, hit him with sticks. All I knew was that he was hurting my friend.

Soon, without my understanding it, another person was fighting him. My mother. She had seen me leave the house and had followed me.

The man pushed me and Obour aside. He hit my mother in the head with a big stick. Then, even while we clung to his legs and still attacked him, he tied my mother with grass rope, and then he tied us.

Some other children who had just come into the fields to work saw what was happening and ran for help. But it was too late.

By the time help came the three of us were gone. The man who captured us took us a distance, to meet with evil companions.

One was my father's brother, Dahobar. He grinned when he saw us. "The great hunter," he scoffed. "He may have run from me, but now I have hunted what is his. And he will never see you again."

We were taken on a long walk with Dahobar and

his men, through the green forests to the ocean, where a great ship waited in the distance with its sails furled.

And the man I was to come to know as Captain Quinn.

Chapter Five

I had never seen the ocean before. I wept when I saw it. Fear swooped down upon me like a great bird, like a roc. Its talons clutched at my heart.

I was accustomed to the river. It went by us silently, in one direction. You knew what it was about all the time. Rivers play no tricks on you.

The ocean was a two-headed beast. It went both ways. First it came at us, attacking like the leopard, making great roaring noises and threatening to eat us alive. Then it retreated, creeping backward, making smaller hissing noises. Only to return with even greater force.

So much openness! The sun on the white soil hurt my eyes. Where were the friendly green trees of the forests that always protected us?

Obour and I clung together beside my mother.

We had marched for near a whole day to get here, tied one to the other. We had been given only some thin meal and tepid water. And I was tired.

Twenty others were with us, men, women, and children. Some we knew, some we did not know. But when we got to the ocean, the men in our group started snapping their fingers.

This was a bad sign. It meant there was no hope. And then Dahobar ordered those men who had snapped their fingers to be put in irons.

Soon we saw the great canoes coming toward us on the water.

"Kroomen," one of the men with us whispered. The word went round and round amongst us.

Kroomen were a tribe that lived on the Guinea Coast. They made their living by fishing. Until they found they could make a better living carrying people who were sold into slavery from the shore to the ships. They were the only tribe who knew how to get their canoes out over the great crashing waves, which even the sailors on board the ships could not manage.

They were very big and powerful, these Kroomen. They rubbed their bodies with palm oil. And their canoes were dug out of the trunks of cotton trees.

They brought the man I now know as Captain Quinn to shore. With some others.

"Koomi," someone murmured.

Murmurs of fear went down the line. Koomi were white men who lived in a land across the water. They would eat us!

There was much haggling then between Captain Quinn and Dahobar. Much pointing to us. Much shaking of Koomi heads.

Men were separated from women and children. Captain Quinn made us take off our clothes. I shudder to remember how we stood there naked while he opened our mouths, and made us jump up and down and move our arms, and pinched our skin and felt our muscles.

Some of Dahobar's captives he pushed aside. He did not want them. I heard him say a word I did not understand. "Diseased." He also pushed the other children aside. Not me. Dahobar insisted I be taken. And Obour clung to me, so they took her, too.

When Captain Quinn was satisfied with the rest of us, he ordered the Kroomen to bring Dahobar's reward from the long canoe. Hogsheads of rum. Barrels of cowrie shells. Stacks of new muskets.

Those of us selected were then branded.

I was so frightened I think I have chased the memory of it from my mind, as Obour and I had chased the birds from the rice fields. All I recollect is seeing Captain Quinn's men come forth with the hot brand. Then I fainted.

Mother was holding me when I woke up. They

let her put a cloth of cold water against my hip, as was being done to some others. While she did this, she took her cowrie shell off her neck and put it around mine.

"No matter what happens," she whispered, "stay quiet, keep yourself small, eat what you are given, and never make a sound. This cowrie shell will protect you. It is a giver of life."

Soon the pain from the branding subsided. It was not a deep brand, but it brought blisters. And to this day I have the initials T. F. on my hip. Timothy Fitch, the merchant who owned the slave ship.

It was years before I could bring myself to look at it.

We were given back our clothes and herded into the canoe. All around us the great two-headed beast of the ocean screeched and gnashed its teeth at us.

I hid, hunkering down into the side of the canoe. I screamed. I vomited. I clutched Obour. I yelled for my mother, who was at the other end, so far away I could scarce see her.

"Keziah!" I heard my mother calling my name, even above the surf crashing around us as the canoe rode the waves. I heard her voice as from a great distance though a giant of a Krooman was standing in the middle of the boat and directing the rowers.

"Mother!" I screamed until my throat was raw.

But no one heard me. The time for hearing me was past.

Two men jumped out of the boat. We could hear their screams as they were eaten by sharks.

When the canoe finally made it through the waves to the ship, there was great turmoil to get us up the rope ladder. Another jumped into the sea, a woman. Sharks were circling around, waiting. As one of the Koomi carried me up the rope ladder I looked down to see the swirling waters below filled with blood.

The men were immediately shackled and hauled off 'tween decks. We could hear their cries from below as they were packed into the hold.

The women were put in another part of the ship.

Later, I learned many things. My mother had only sixteen inches to lie on. But since the *Phillis* was a loose-packed slaver, Mother had two and a half feet of space overhead, instead of only twenty inches, as she would have had if we were tight packed.

This was considered lucky.

Obour and I were the only two children. We were also put in the hold, shackled down. All I recollect is a Koomi man over me nailing down my chain, the cries and wails of those around me, the stench of those who had already dirtied themselves. And the dimness.

There was no air in the hold. Even the candles

could not live there. They went out. And then, so did I.

The next morning we sailed. I learned later that slave ships must leave immediately. Sickness can break out on board. If the crew takes sick, the cargo can mutiny.

Slaves are more likely to form an uprising within sight of shore than out at sea. Once at sea, they are helpless.

So we sailed. I cried, feeling the ship move under me. Because I knew I would never see my home again. All because I disobeyed my mother and went out alone. All because Dahobar hated my father.

All because the leopard came.

But again, I was lucky. The gods favored me. Or mayhap it was the cowrie shell I now wore around my neck.

The second day out, I came down with a dreadful sickness. I was brought abovedeck. In my delirium, I did not know how or by whom. But I woke with the smell of salt air in my nostrils and a man shoving boiled rice down my throat. I was gagging.

Captain Quinn stood over me. "You will eat!"

I told him I wanted my mother. A nigra crewman who knew some of my language translated for him.

"Your mother is with the women. She will soon be brought on deck for exercise. Eat!"

I told him no. I was not hungry.

"Do you think you have a choice? Do you want to be thrown to the sharks?"

Wanting to show him I was brave, I said yes.

"Do you want to be flogged?"

I was not that brave. But I stared hard at him, holding my ground. "I want my friend, Obour," I said.

The nigra crewman who was translating told Quinn that Obour wouldn't eat, either. Then he conferred with Quinn in their own language. Quinn looked thoughtful, as if he were pondering some great matter.

"I shall have you both flogged," he told me. "My first mate, Kunkle, is good with the cat. Two small girls. You are of no profit to me, anyway. I was told to bring no young girls. They are useless. One whip will do. Fetch her!" he ordered the crewman.

The man went to obey him. An idea came to me then, as Quinn stood before me, smiling and rocking back and forth on his heels.

"I will tell Obour to eat," I said, "and I will eat, if you leave us both unshackled. Here on the deck. And not send us below again. Two small girls. What can we do?"

"Tell me what she is saying," Quinn ordered the crewman when he came back with the struggling Obour. "She babbles."

I said it again. The crewman translated. Then he and Quinn conferred again.

Then I was told by Quinn to keep my part of the bargain. And he would keep his.

So Obour and I ate our rice and millet.

The next day I learned something.

Quinn could have used a great tool he had to feed us. They called it the *speculum oris*. They forced it into a slave's mouth, then turned a screw, and the device opened, forcing the jaws apart. Then food was pushed in. I saw them do it the next day to a man who wouldn't eat.

Obour and I stared at each other in wonder. And from that day on, I knew we would be all right.

Why we were all right, I do not know. Quinn was not a man of good parts.

He had his first mate, Kunkle, flog the slaves with a whip that he called "the cat." Once he had Kunkle flog one of his own men. The crew was a scurrilous lot, so I wasn't sorry when one was flogged.

As for Kunkle, he didn't have to be pushed to carry out such orders. He was a small man, but mean and filled with venom, like a snake waiting to strike. He took special delight in setting the crew against one another. He enjoyed their bickerings.

Kunkle roamed the deck with a whip. A large, ugly mastiff dog was always with him. We knew he would set the dog on us if we did not obey. If a slave went mad belowdecks, Kunkle had him brought above, hit over the head with a club, and tossed overboard.

Quinn had Obour and me put in the storeroom on days when storms came and the sea was boiling. On nice days we were allowed to stay quiet in a small corner on deck. Betimes we had a canvas over us.

From this corner we saw all the goings-on.

We saw the men and women brought up from 'tween decks for exercise. Which meant they were made to "dance" while some crew members played fiddles. And other crew members washed away the stench of blood and feces and vomit from 'tween decks. And the stench of vinegar in the sun was almost as bad.

On these days I saw my mother. And I would stand up, weak as I was, so she could see me. I saw her dancing with the others. But she was not well. Her movements were clumsy.

My mother. So close to me, yet so far away. Jeered at by the crew. *They couldn't treat my mother like that.* I wanted to kill them!

I wanted to run from our corner and throw myself into her arms. Obour was hard put to stop me. She held me back, weak as she herself was.

I lay, crying, against her. "I want my mother."

"I want mine, too," she said. "And she isn't here. Be good and you'll have yours again. I never will."

We saw the bodies of the dead thrown overboard.

We saw the seamen sneak out in the middle of the night to the hogshead of beer Quinn had lashed to the rail, fill their mugs, and sneak off again.

Obour had told me some hard truths, the day she was brought on deck at my request.

"Too many are sick below. They will die," she said. "You were right to stand up to Quinn. He must treat us well. He is losing too much of his cargo."

Was that why he was good to us? Or was it, as I found out later, because he had two little girls of his own at home?

Or was it because I was so skinny and gap toothed that not even he, a hardened slaver, could have me flogged or used the terrible tool on me to make me eat?

We moved up the coast. Captain Quinn had to work the slave markets of Sierra Leone and the Isles de Los before he could set sail for home.

In two months he was finished and we had a full hold. We set sail from the Isles de Los.

A week out, I awoke one night to my mother's screams.

The night had been becalmed. Obour and I were sleeping on deck, under our tarp in our corner, to escape the terrible heat of the storeroom. The screams pulled me from my sleep. I sat up and shook Obour.

In the half-light of the moon and the eerie glow of the ship's lanterns swinging on their gimbals, we saw two crewmen dragging something across the deck. At first we thought they were making off with the hogshead of beer.

Then we knew this could not be. Because Kunkle was with them. And behind him came the mastiff.

The thing they were dragging was a woman. My mother. I recognized her voice.

My mother was begging for her life. I heard her begging. "No, please, I am not sick. I am well."

"Throw her over!" Kunkle ordered.

"Oughtn't we to ask the captain?" one crewman asked.

"Throw her over!" What was Kunkle yelling? "He's drunk as Jonah in the belly of the whale! I'm giving orders here. You want her to infest the rest of them by morning?" What did it mean?

Then I saw them heave my mother over the side. And I knew what it meant.

I sat transfixed. My mouth opened, but no scream came out. Then I got up and ran across the shadow-flickered deck, Obour behind me, calling me back.

I got there in time to see my mother clinging to the taffrail at the stern of the ship. The first mate cursed, calling her a vicious name. I did not understand the language yet, but I understood the viciousness of it.

Then he gave more orders. And I saw one of the men climbing over the taffrail with a large knife in his hand.

"No, no," I screamed. "Mother, Mother!" I began to beat at the man with the knife, just as he was climbing over.

The mastiff growled and started at me. I felt his hot breath at my heels. Kunkle had him pulled away, then grabbed at me.

I could hear my mother's screams as she clung for dear life onto the taffrail. I kicked Kunkle. I bit him so I could run to the rail and see my mother's face again. Her eyes were large and round.

"Keziah!"

Then the seaman was over her, chopping at her hands. The chopping sound was like that of fish being cut.

I flung myself at him, attacking. Again Kunkle grabbed me, and then I felt a blow to the side of my head. The last thing I heard was my mother's terrible screams, muffled by water. Then, like the candles in the hold, I went out.

My head resounded with pain. There was a ringing in my ears. Someone bandaged my head and the ringing stopped. Then it was worse, because all I heard was my mother's screams.

They did not think I would live.

I was exhausted and weak, but every time I fell asleep I saw the horrible sight of my mother clinging to the taffrail and that man chopping off her hands. So I lay awake on the deck at night, hearing the sound of the sea, the low talking of the crew, the ship's bells, the scrambling of rats in its belly, the creaking of the capstan, the loud snapping of the sails. I stared up at the stars and thought of my mother.

She was somewhere up there now. But where? The emptiness inside me was as large and as dark as that nighttime sky.

Daytime, I just lay staring into space. And I did not eat.

Obour nursed me as best she could. Sometimes all that meant was that she clung to me while I sobbed. Then when my tears were spent there was nothing else to do. So she talked.

"Captain Quinn would tie Kunkle to the yardarm if he could," she told me.

"Then why doesn't he?"

"He can't spare the man. Kunkle keeps the crew in order."

Another time she told me, "Kunkle told Quinn your mother had signs of the smallpox. But a woman brought abovedecks for air yesterday told me Kunkle had her thrown overboard because she would not allow him to take liberties with her."

I did not answer, because I could not speak.

"Your mother was a handsome woman," Obour said.

Again I could not bring myself to speak.

Quinn had a new pallet sent to me. It was clean and not wet and smelly like my old one. He also had special foods sent to Obour and me. Better food than rice and millet. Betimes yams. Betimes meat or pudding.

From the few Koomi words we had picked up we learned that the crew was complaining about rancid meat and moldy biscuits. But everything brought to us was in good order.

Still, I could not eat. I lay in a delirium of disbelief. Each morning as I woke from my nightmarish sleep, when I remembered what had happened the world came crashing down on my head.

"You must eat," Obour said, "or you will die."

"I want to die."

"You can't."

"Why? Give me one reason."

"I have no reason. Except that it is better to live."

"Who said this?"

"Your mother would say it if she were here."

"But she isn't here. And I'm responsible. So unless you have any other reason, I'm going to starve myself until I die."

"Quinn won't let you."

"I'm half-dead already. No good to him. I'm damaged."

She left me and I lay alone under my canvas, planning my death. In a little while, she came back.

"I have thought of a reason," she said.

I listened.

"I told the crewman who speaks our language what you said. He told Quinn. He sends me with this message. If you die, he will kill me."

I just stared at her.

"So you must stay alive for me, Keziah. Please! Do you want to be responsible for my death, too?"

I roused myself. I ate. I did not want to be responsible for my good friend's death. There was weight enough on my heart.

Living was harder than dying. I found that out soon enough. There is always something out there waiting to get you. Some unseen thing, like the leopard.

At night I still had nightmares. But Obour helped me. We comforted one another. We became accustomed to the rhythms of life aboard the ship. Because if we did not, we would surely die. And we both had to live. I knew this now, though I did not know exactly why.

I learned much later that Kunkle was charged with the murder of my mother. In Massachusetts. But he ran off and could not be found. They say Captain Quinn is still looking for him. A crewman told Quinn she had no sore from smallpox, but that she would not let Kunkle take liberties with her. It seems by the rules of the slave trade that you are allowed to throw overboard the mad, the sick, the dying. But you are not permitted to murder a slave woman for your own reasons. It is not good business.

Chapter Six

My first view of America was of dirt and grime.

The place we were kept when we were taken off the ship was like a pen. It had a high fence around it. We heard voices, laughter, the sound of movement, children playing, people calling in greeting to one another, the shouting of people who sold fish, hammering and building going on, even music betimes. But we could see nothing.

We were kept to ourselves inside the walls of a building at night and brought out into the pen in the day.

After two days of this a man came to see us. His name was John Avery. Those men amongst us who had picked up enough of the Koomi language on ship interpreted for us. They also told us he worked for the man who owned our ship.

The man named John Avery stood in the middle of the pen with Captain Quinn, looking at us and sniffing something out of a gold box.

"Meanest cargo I ever saw," he said.

We were to be sold the next day!

Word went around our compound and fear broke out like dysentery. We trembled from it. Obour and I clutched one another on that last night together. Tomorrow we would be separated. Likely we would never see each other again.

It was midsummer and the nights were hot. So those of us who wanted to, slept outside in the pen. I remember looking up at the stars in the sky and wondering if they were the same stars that shone over our home in Senegal. How could the stars I had always considered so beautiful grace the sky over this land called America? Where people were sold like cattle.

The next day, early, we were awakened and given some meal, and the women and men were washed. This was done by having buckets of water thrown at them. Then they were given osnaburg garments to put on.

Those set to the task of making the slaves look presentable did not bother with me or Obour. John Avery came by and scowled at us as we sat in a corner on some hemp.

"You want them brought out?" one of his men asked.

He shrugged. "Two small girls. What can they bring?"

All this was translated to us after they passed us by. And we breathed sighs of relief. We would not be sold this day!

But then, later, when the sale started, they brought us out anyway. All was confusion and fear and noise as, one by one, the nigras were put on a block for display and John Avery turned them around and talked about them. Men came to stand around them, to touch and feel them, to open their mouths, to pinch and peer. Then the bidding commenced.

I clung to Obour. What would I do if they put me up there with everyone gaping at me?

I should have starved myself to death, I decided. *And Obour with me.*

The slave market was next door to John Avery's distillery. And the sale had been advertised. So people came not only to buy but also to see what manner of cargo Captain Quinn had brought this time. And they came for entertainment.

One by one the cargo of Captain Quinn's ship was sold. Money exchanged hands. The satisfied customers left with their purchases in tow.

The sun was high. Obour and I cringed in a corner in some shade.

Then, of a sudden, a man stepped forward. "How much for that child?"

John Avery was taken with surprise. He made no reply. "Which? There are two," he replied.

"The smaller one. My wife is in need of a domestic."

John Avery laughed. "She'll not get any work out of that one. All skin and bones, she is. Now, if you'll come back tomorrow, I'll have another lot for sale. More costly, of course, but better suited to your purposes."

I did not understand much of this, of course, but I did know the stranger was gesturing at me. Tall and well dressed he was. And I, who knew nothing of the manners or customs of this America—even I sensed that he had dignity and kindness. And something else.

Power. Not the kind Captain Quinn had, where he shouted things and had men quivering. Not like first mate Kunkle's, either, whose power was in his whip.

This man had no need to either shout or carry a whip. There was power in his demeanor. People stepped aside for him. Yet his voice was soft.

"I want that one," he said. "How much?"

"Two pounds sterling," Avery told him.

"Bring her forth," the man said.

John Avery fastened a rope around my waist.

"No," I said in my own language, "I don't want

to leave Obour." Our hands reached out to each other.

And, strangely, then Obour smiled. "Go," she said. "You'll do well. He is a man of good parts."

"But I want to stay with you!"

"Don't worry for me. I'll find a master. And someday we'll see each other again. Be of good heart. Don't dishonor your family."

I was turned around then by John Avery. "Mind your manners," he said sternly. "Here is your new master." His words meant nothing to me. His gestures did.

I looked, for the first time, up into the blue, smiling eyes of John Wheatley.

"What's her name?" he asked.

John Avery shrugged. "Don't know. But she and that other one over there are the last of the lot from the *Phillis*."

"Phillis," John Wheatley said. "Her name is Phillis, then."

John Avery shrugged.

"I'd like to see the other one," another man said.

"You'll find plenty of work in her," John Avery said.

Then my new master held out his hand. I heard the other man say Tanner. They knew each other. They talked for a while. I heard the man who had said the word Tanner now say the word "Newport."

I was shivering from fear, though the sun was hot. My lips were parched. My head throbbed. I was hungry and dirty. And I shrank in shame before these well-turned-out men who moved about with such ease and grace in this fearful place called America.

The men parted with smiles and good words. Then my master called out to someone. And my fear vanished. Out of a fearful thing with wheels pulled by creatures I'd never seen before came a young man with skin the color of mine.

"Prince, look what I found. She looks starving. Come, carry her into the carriage and we'll get her home."

"Lawd awmighty," Prince said.

He looked to be about seventeen. He was garbed in Koomi clothing and he seemed very much at home in this place.

In a moment Prince scooped me up in his arms. "Lawd awmighty," he said again. "She be light as a feather. But shakin', Mr. Wheatley. This child shakin' like a leaf."

"Get the blanket," came the reply.

I was put in the thing with wheels by the one called Prince, who then climbed up on a seat and yelled at the creatures. They started off.

I sank into the seat in my blanket. I couldn't stop shaking, it seemed. But one good thing: Obour had been sold, too. She would have a home. But where? Then I remembered two words. Tanner. And Newport.

I kept repeating them over and over in my mind as I fell asleep.

Chapter Seven

"Jesus loves you, chile. Hold still now, while I make you presentable."

I didn't know who this Jesus person was that the large woman spoke of as she scrubbed me in a copper tub in a corner of the kitchen. But her skin was like mine. Her language was peppered with some words I could understand. And some I couldn't. So I thought Jesus was the name of Mr. Wheatley.

He had turned me over to Aunt Cumsee immediately. I heard the words "feed her" and "evening prayers." Did that mean he loved me? I was too spent to care. So I allowed Aunt Cumsee to wash and dry me. Then came the soft cotton garment. It had a fluffy neck. All the while, Aunt Cumsee told me about Jesus. And how he had died for me.

How could he have brought me home from the

slave market if he was dead? I put it down to weariness and drank the warm milk she put in front of me. There was ham, too, and bread. I ate hungrily. If this Jesus could manage all this and live in this big house, it was all right with me. Even if he was dead.

"How is our little newcomer faring, Aunt Cumsee?"

The woman who came into the room was buxom and ever so pretty. She wore a gray gown with rose fluff on it. She had a round face and her skin was like ivory. Her lips were the color of the fluff, and always ready in a smile. But it was her eyes that held me.

They were of the bluest blue, and made you think she was just about to tell you something wonderful.

"She be just about ready, Miz Wheatley."

Wheatley. This was the wife of Jesus, who loved me!

"Oh, she's just darling. Poor little thing. We're going to have prayers now. Bring her in."

"Yessum."

I was led across the wide hall, past drawings of people that hung on the wall, windows covered with shining cloth, tall doors trimmed in heavy wood. There was another high arrangement of wood that curved upward. Where did it go? Surely these people were gods.

"Come along, chile." Aunt Cumsee tugged my

hand. "You must look sharp and learn some manners."

"Well, what a difference! Bring her in!" Mr. Wheatley, or Jesus, stood up and held out his hands as I walked across the soft floor. I looked down. *It had flowers on it.* I reached down to pluck them, but they lay flat. I knelt, staring at them.

Everyone laughed.

"Silly thing. She's trying to pick the flowers off the carpet." The girl said this. She was young and not as pretty as her mother.

"Hush, Mary. You never know when to keep a still tongue in your head, do you?"

I looked up. The boy was sitting with a flat object that had leaves in it in his lap. When he set it aside I saw the leaves had squiggle markings on them. His voice was deep and sure. He came over to me and raised me up to stand. "What's her name?" he asked.

"Phillis," Jesus told him.

"Come, let us start prayers," the lovely woman said.

The boy took me on his lap. "Hush," he told me. "These are evening prayers."

I did not understand the words, but I understood that I must be quiet and still. It was not difficult in the protection of his arms. He had white fluff at his neck and wrists. He wore breeches the color of the sun when it goes to sleep. He smelled very good. And when no one was looking, he took something out of his pocket and slipped it into my mouth.

It tasted so lovely and sweet!

I fell asleep in his arms. Vaguely, I heard the family's murmurings to their god. And I heard the mention of this Jesus who was so important to them. But I saw no water, no fountain. So I could not figure out how they could pray.

Then their murmurings stopped and the boy carried me out of the room. I opened my eyes for a spell. The house was getting dark. There were blazing candles set around, on tables and in holders on the walls. Then we started going up the piles of wood. Climbing.

I whimpered in fear.

"Hush, it will be all right," the boy said. The sureness of his tone becalmed me. So I closed my eyes and drifted again to sleep.

It was the first time I'd felt safe since I slept on my pallet at home. Now I was set down on another pallet. It was very soft. And I was covered.

"Sleep well," the boy said.

In the morning he was gone. I thought I had dreamed him. In the morning there was only Mary, the girl. And she was angry.

"She cries at night, Mother. She wakes in fits and

yells. I can't have her in my room! I tried to put her on the chamber pot and she wet the floor! Do something else with her!"

I was shamed. I had done wrong. I had not known what the chamber pot was for. My soft garment was wet and smelled.

Aunt Cumsee had to take me in hand and wash me again and give me clean clothes. I stayed with her in the kitchen.

By the time of the next full moon, I knew what the chamber pot was for. And I'd also learned the other important things I needed to learn to survive.

The blocks of wood that went upward were called stairs.

The boy and girl were in their seventeenth summer. And they had been born at the same time. In my land this was considered great good fortune. And benevolence from the gods.

Here it was called twins.

The boy's name was Nathaniel. He went out of the house every morning to a place called Latin School.

"His mother wants him to be a man of God," Aunt Cumsee told me. "But I think he wants to be a merchant."

Daily, I was learning their language from her. One

word at a time—but everyone seemed surprised that I was learning so fast.

Mary did not want me back in her room.

"Someone must train her, Mary. I want to make a Christian of her," Mrs. Wheatley said.

"I'll take her only if you give her to me as my personal servant. All my friends have Negro servants."

Mrs. Wheatley looked perplexed. But she agreed. "Remember kindness, dear. Her little soul belongs to God."

As far as Mary was concerned, my little soul, and my body, belonged to her. From that moment on I was at her beck and call. And kindness had naught to do with it.

All day I fetched for her, picked up her discarded clothing, held her things, followed her around. By the time of the next full moon, I learned that not to do what Mary asked, when Mary asked it, earned me an immediate slap.

She washed away all her meanness, of course, when her mother was in view. But her mother was not often around. And Nathaniel came home from school late in the afternoon. After the evening meal he retired to his chamber to pore over his books.

I knew they were called books because Nathaniel told me.

It was he who taught me to climb the stairs. And to eat properlike, with a pewter spoon.

I was no stranger to some of the food they ate—fish, chicken, pork. But I knew naught about potatoes, cider, frothy syllabub, cakes. Or tea. They seemed absolutely demented about their tea.

Their customs were strange to me. They sat at tables to eat. Bells called them to their place of worship. They had a small leopard that slept in the barn and betimes came into the house. Mary picked him up and stroked him. He was part of the family. They called him Caesar.

When Mary went out with her mother, I was put to small tasks with Aunt Cumsee. There was another woman with skin like mine in the house, called Sulie. She was mean and sour, and I think she was jealous of me.

Aunt Cumsee said that Sulie didn't love Jesus.

By the time of the next full moon I was learning to do small stitches on a sampler. Mrs. Wheatley taught me.

I sometimes followed Prince around in the yard when he cut wood or harnessed the horses. "Lawd awmighty," Prince would say, "you so little, you likely be stepped on. Mind yourself."

I discovered that Prince's Lawd awmighty was the same as Aunt Cumsee's Jesus. And neither one of them was Mr. Wheatley.

Jesus was another name for their god. And he needed, very badly, to be loved.

I felt a kinship with this Jesus. Especially when Aunt Cumsee told me he'd been born in the middle of the animals, because he was poor. And I had been brought here, to America, so he could save me.

"Save me from what?" I asked.

"From the devil," she said. "From hellfire." She proceeded, then, to tell me about hellfire. And how I would burn in it if I didn't love Jesus. She spoke so plain, I started to cry. And I was hard put to stop. I didn't want to burn in fire.

She took me on her lap and quieted me.

"Why couldn't I stay home and be saved?" I asked.

"Because then you wouldn't have known about Him."

Well, I could have foregone the knowing. Especially when it meant seeing my mother thrown overboard, and seeing grown men be eaten by sharks, others go mad, and still others be flogged. I could have done without all the sickness and fear I'd suffered. I slipped off her lap.

"Where you goin'?"

"To the barn. I want to see where this Jesus was born."

Aunt Cumsee laughed then and slapped her knees

with her hands. "Can't see, chile. He was born far across the sea."

I was astonished. "He wasn't born here in America?"

"No."

"Then why was I brought here to be saved?"

She had no answer for that. So I asked her another question.

"If he wasn't born here, if he was born poor, why are these people so rich? Why does everyone say they are favored?"

Again she had no answer. Instead she told me she was born across the sea, too, a long time ago.

"What sacrifices must we make to him?" I asked Aunt Cumsee. "Goats? Or will small animals do?"

She looked at me with tears in her eyes. "In time, chile, you'll see," she said. And she said it sadly.

By the time of the next full moon Mrs. Wheatley told me she was pleased with me. Never had anyone learned their language so fast. "I will make a true Christian of you. You don't have to fear Jesus," she said. "Do you understand?"

I understood. The only ones I had to fear were Sulie and Mary Wheatley.

Chapter Eight

We were in the front parlor. It was one of the first cold days of the year. At home we would be in the rainy season.

It was raining now, but Aunt Cumsee said the rain had snow in it. "Wait till you sees snow, chile," she said, "just wait."

Mrs. Wheatley was out, "making calls." Mary and her giddy friends were taking their ease in the back parlor.

"Where's Nathaniel?" one of the girls asked. "Shouldn't he be home from lessons by now?"

"At the Salutation, likely," Mary said, "having a cup of flip."

Another girl had a book.

"Oh, a novel!" Mary squealed as her friend

showed it around. "Don't tell my mother! She won't allow me to read novels."

I did not understand what a novel was. But I did understand the words "Don't tell my mother." Mary said them often when with her friends.

How I envied her her mother. How I ached with longing, seeing them together. How I wished I had my mother to tell things to. How I missed my father, the great hunter.

I was trained up by now to help when Aunt Cumsee served tea. She poured it into cups for the girls. I was expected to walk around and offer a little tray of cakes. And another of purple grapes.

Aunt Cumsee left the room and I walked from one to the other, offering the cakes.

"Curtsy when you do that," Mary said sharply.

I just stared at her.

"You know how. I showed you."

"Nigras can't curtsy," one of the girls said.

The others giggled at the very thought.

"She knows how," Mary insisted. "She's just lazy. And spoiled. Curtsy, I say, Phillis. Now!"

Still holding the tray of cakes, I grabbed my skirt with one hand. Then I tried to bend my knee. But I lost my balance and the cakes went toppling off the tray to the floor.

"See what you've done!" And there was a sharp slap on my arm from Mary. "Pick them up!"

I did so.

"Are you allowed to hit her, Mary?" one young woman asked, wide eyed. "My mama doesn't hold with hitting the nigras."

"My mama says you shouldn't belabor a point with them," another chimed in. "They are, after all, like children."

"She's mine," Mary said. "She was given to me. And it's my job to train her. Mama wants to make a Christian of her. To what aim, I don't know. The little noodlehead can't even follow simple directions." She sighed. "I try with her. I know I shouldn't hit, but I am so vexed with her. She keeps me awake, crying at night. And during the day, she's useless. But there is one thing she can do, isn't there, Phillis?"

My heart fell inside me.

"Dance," Mary said. "Like they made them do on the ship. My mama is friends with Mrs. Fitch, whose husband owns the ship. She told Mama about it. They whipped the slaves if they didn't dance." Mary's eyes glittered with mischief. "Dance for my friends, Phillis."

Tears came to my eyes. *Dance*. All I could think of was my mother, dancing with the others, jeered at by the crew. Obour and I had never been made to dance. But I knew how. Twice, Mary had made me dance for her, holding a little switch in her hand to threaten me. I had resolved I would never dance for her again.

"Dance!" she ordered.

I shook my head. "No," I said.

"What mean you by that?" Mary's voice was shrill. "Do as I say. Now!"

I shook my head no. Her friends gasped.

"I'll teach you to say no to me, you little savage." She reached for me, but I ran. I dashed across the room.

"Come back here!" she ordered.

But I wouldn't.

She stamped her foot. "Go ahead, run, you little varlet. You'll be sorry you ever drew breath when I get hold of you! And I will! Go ahead, run! I'll find you. You can't go far!"

But I did go far. To a place where Mary couldn't find me. I went to Nathaniel's room. No one would look for me there. I went there often to hide from Mary. The door was closed but not locked. I crept inside. Rain slashed against the windows. But a fire had been started in the hearth for his return.

I closed the door carefully behind me and, as I'd seen Aunt Cumsee do so many times, I lit one candle on the desk.

Its flickering light brought everything to life. The books, the long feather he used for writing, his papers and maps.

I climbed up and knelt on the chair and drew a book toward me. I opened it. Oh, it smelled lovely! Musty and old and spicy and new, all at the same time. I stared at the markings on the page. And something happened to me.

I became both chilled and feverish. I fair trembled at the touching of the pages. The markings leaped off the paper at me.

These books said things to Nathaniel. And he understood. If only I could understand these strange markings! I would be smarter than Mary then. And she could no longer treat me so shabbily. She would have to respect me. For then I would know more than she did.

Mary and her silly friends did not care for books. Except for novels, whatever they were. All they talked about was boys.

I settled down into the chair. I tucked my feet under me. All around me were Nathaniel's things. There was an ivory chess set, on a small table. There, on a wall peg, were a linen coat and a tricorn hat. On still another peg was slung a set of pistols.

A clay pipe, a water pitcher and bowl, a razor, a linen towel that he had likely used that morning. A pair of slippers on a small rug by the bed. A discarded ruffled shirt.

The fire crackled in the hearth. The candle flickered. I put my head down on the desk. Beyond the closed door, from belowstairs, I could hear Aunt Cumsee's voice. And Mary's. Then sounds of the harpsichord. I breathed a sigh of relief. Mary and her friends would be taken with their music now.

For a while, at least, I was safe. I fell asleep.

"So here you are, you little minx."

A hand on my shoulder. I roused myself and looked up to see Nathaniel.

"What are you about in my room? They're all looking for you. I heard you're in trouble with Mary. What did you do?"

His kindness was too much. I burst into tears. Next thing I knew he was holding me in his lap, and with halting words I told him how I would not dance for Mary.

He frowned. "And you say she struck you? I hope this is not a thing she often does."

I twisted my apron in my hands.

"The devil, you say. I'll not have it. Have things come to such a turn in our house that we have to strike the servants? I'll speak to Mother about it." He set me down in a nearby chair, got up, and began to pace.

But something else was bedeviling him. "Yes, I'll speak to Mother. I have other things to speak to her about. And the time has come to have my say."

He stood, hands clasped behind his back, and looked at me. "Autumn's here. A time for making decisions. I'm supposed to go to Harvard. But I have decided that I don't wish to be a minister, as Mother wants. But a merchant. Like Father."

He sat down again and peered at me. He was very agitated. "This is the time to be a merchant, Phillis. The French war ended last year. Canada is ours. The old king is dead. Money is flowing. There is a boom in building, in shipping. Ships from around the world crowd our wharves. They can't be unloaded fast enough!"

I sat entranced, listening.

"Why, there are eighteen thousand people living in Boston alone! Do you know what Father is selling in his King Street shoppe? Lisbon wine, spermecetti candles, and the ordinary staples. Do you know what a woman came in asking for today? Lavender kid gloves from Paris. Tincture for the teeth! A silk umbrilloe!"

I did not understand all his words, but I understood well his fervor.

"Here," and he took a paper from his coat pocket and laid it on the desk. "Here is a page of the *Lively Lady*'s manifest. She docked just yesterday. Look what she carried. And the lot of it was purchased by Joseph Rotch the merchant."

My eyes fell on the paper, on the neat, scrawled writing that listed things. I pointed to a long word. "Umbrilloes!" I said.

"Father must expand! He must start to carry paints, oils, varnishes. Even farm people are tired of floors made of clay and fish oil. I must learn Father's business and forget the ministry. There's a fortune to be made."

Then he stopped short. "What's that you said?"

"Umbrilloes."

"Where? Show me."

I pointed to the long word.

"By god," Nathaniel said. "You can read!"

I grinned at him. I had pleasured him and I liked that. No, I could not read, but it was such a long word. It stood, then, that it must be the longest piece of scrawled writing on the page, didn't it?

"Phillis! You can read!"

I shook my head. "No," I said. "But I wish to, Nathaniel. Teach me."

"Teach you! Yes!" He picked me up off the chair and whirled me around. "Yes, why not? Why shouldn't you read? Why shouldn't I become a merchant if I so wish? We've a new king on the throne! George the Third. Only twenty-two he is. Anything is possible!"

Chapter Nine

That very evening, in the parlor, right before prayers, he told his parents he did not want to go to Harvard College.

His mother wept at his announcement. "Is this what you want for him, Mr. Wheatley?" she asked her husband.

"My dear, it would warm my heart to have my son take my place when I am old. But if the Lord wants him for a minister, I am willing to make that sacrifice."

"How did this *happen*?" Mrs. Wheatley looked at her son.

"It's all that drinking of flip he does at the Salutation," Mary said. "If you ask me, he's allowed too much freedom."

Mary had little freedom. Her formal schooling was

finished, but she was expected to stay close to her mother, learn the feminine arts, stitch a fine seam, and discourse only on women's subjects. Yet she was as clever as Nathaniel. Even at my young age, I knew she envied him. And that if she had been allowed to use her mind, she might not have been so mean.

"Nobody's asking you," Nathaniel growled.

"Children, don't fight," Mrs. Wheatley admonished.

Mary glared at her brother across the Persian carpet. "How can you turn down a chance at Harvard? You fool."

"Enough, Mary!" Mr. Wheatley spoke as sharply as I had ever heard him. I trembled at his anger.

"I don't need any advice from anyone who strikes the servants," Nathaniel said.

"Who has struck a servant?" Mrs. Wheatley asked him.

"Ask Mary, why don't you?" Nathaniel mumbled.

"Mary?" her mother asked.

Mary wouldn't answer.

"Ask Phillis, Mother," Nathaniel urged.

All eyes were on me.

"Phillis, has Mary struck you?" Mrs. Wheatley asked.

My lips went dry. Tears came to my eyes. Mary's gaze was fixed on me. If I said yes, I would pay for it later. If I said no, I would make Nathaniel a liar. He did not need that now.

"Yes," I said.

Mrs. Wheatley gasped. "Mary, how could you?"

"We don't strike servants in this house, Mary," her father reminded her.

"Is she a servant?" Mary asked. "Nobody treats her like one. Aunt Cumsee coddles her in the kitchen. Sulie has to do twice the work because she's not doing her share. She's a spoiled little piece. Insolent and spoiled. I can't make her do anything, Mother. She refuses to learn."

"What did she do that earned her a slap?" her mother persisted.

"Everything." Mary glowered. "Ask her, why don't you?"

Again all eyes were on me. I was expected to tell.

"Go ahead," Nathaniel urged me gently. "Don't be afraid."

Mrs. Wheatley nodded at me in encouragement. So I told.

"Dance," I said. "Mary wanted me to dance. I wouldn't."

"Dance?" Mrs. Wheatley's face went white. Would there be no end of agony for her this night? "To what end?"

Mary shrugged. "They did it on the ship."

And then her mother knew. "The *ship*? You mean the onerous business Mrs. Fitch told us about?"

Mary bowed her head. "I just wanted to show my friends, that's all, Mother."

"Heaven preserve us!" Mrs. Wheatley looked about to faint.

At once her husband was at her side, comforting her. His face was set and resolute.

"This is intolerable," he said. "I'm ashamed. Mrs. Wheatley, I fear your daughter needs more instruction in the sober Christian virtues. This is what comes from allowing her to attend Old North Church with her friends."

"Don't blame Reverend Lathrop. He's a good man. Mary is taken with his sermons," Mrs. Wheatley told him.

"She's taken with the Reverend Lathrop," Nathaniel put in.

"Hush, Nathaniel!" Mary's face went red.

"Be that as it may, you go to Old South with us from here on in," her father announced. "Those sermons of Lathrop's are too agitating for young girls." Then he crossed the room and stood before me. "Phillis, I apologize for any ill-usage Mary has made of you. You are no longer her servant. You are to sleep, henceforth, in the room with Aunt Cumsee at night."

"Father!" Mary protested. "I need a servant. All my friends have personal nigras."

"Well, you no longer have one," he said severely. "You have abused your authority. So keep a still tongue in your head. As for you, Nathaniel, I have a plan. Mrs. Wheatley, I would hope you agree."

She smiled weakly. "Whatever you say, Mr. Wheatley. It seems my methods with the children have failed."

"Nathaniel, you have six months to prove to me you should not attend Harvard and become a minister as your mother wishes. In those six months you shall continue your studies."

"But I've completed the sixth form at Boston Latin, Father. What do you expect me to do?"

"A tutor will come to the house every day to further prepare you for Harvard. Reverend Mather Byles, perhaps. Or Reverend Ebenezer Pemberton of New Brick."

"Puffing Pem? I'd sooner perish," Nathaniel said.

"Don't be disrespectful!" his father boomed.

"To what end, all this?" Nathaniel asked. "And how can I prove to you I shouldn't be a minister if I'm studying with one?"

"You will study two hours a day. The rest of the day you will devote to showing me why I should allow you to become a merchant. If you do not convince me by spring, you will start at Harvard next fall. Is this fair?"

Nathaniel slumped down in the settee. "Yes, sir."

"Mrs. Wheatley?" He looked at his wife.

"I think it entirely fair," she said.

"Good. Now there will be no more arguing. I will not tolerate it."

"I'll go have Phillis's bed moved into Aunt Cumsee's room," Mrs. Wheatley said, "and I'll be back for prayers."

She left. Mr. Wheatley went to throw another log on the fire. "Beastly night," I heard him say.

"Father," Mary said.

"Yes? What is it now?"

"If Mother allows it, may I sit in on some of Nathaniel's tutoring sessions?"

"In heaven's name, to what aim? You know it's unladylike for a young woman to have too much learning, Mary. You'll scare away all your beaux."

"I don't have any beaux. And likely, I never will!" Mary burst into tears. "Even Nathaniel's friends think that."

"Who thinks it?" her brother demanded.

Mary wiped her eyes. "Josiah Thornton, John Hitchbourne, all of them. Hitchbourne even said once that I was not likely to come to much. That I was not pretty enough."

"I'll call him out for that," Nathaniel said.

"You'll do nothing of the sort," his father told him. "You know I despise dueling. Do you wish to break your mother's heart even more?"

Mary commenced weeping again. Her father did not know what to do. He turned back to attend the fire.

In that moment I felt a mixture of sorrow and fear. Sorrow for Mary. And fear for myself. For if Mary, the daughter in a well-placed family, was not allowed to learn, why should I be? A slave?

Clearly, Nathaniel was moved by his sister's distress, too. "You'll have beaux, Mary," he said huskily. "I promise." Then he looked at his father. "I think I'd like to have Reverend Lathrop tutor me. He's nearer my own age, he's known to be a masterful tutor, and he could use the extra money."

Mary looked up, surprised. She dried her tears.

Their father scowled, seemed about to object, then softened. "Very well, Nathaniel, I'll speak to Lathrop tomorrow."

"And I don't mind if Mary sits with us. Part of the time, anyway."

"Didn't you just hear me?" his father asked. "I've forbidden Mary to go to Old North to hear Lathrop's sermons."

"Greek and Latin aren't sermons, Father." Nathaniel grinned. "If Mary can abide Greek and Latin, I can abide her being there. It will make it more pleasant, Father."

"Study is supposed to be not pleasant but serious."

Nathaniel stood up, walked to his father, put an arm on his shoulder, and whispered something in his ear. Mr. Wheatley turned to look at Mary, then turned quickly back to the fire.

"No," he said in disbelief.

"Yes," Nathaniel whispered.

"Very well then, providing everyone behaves," Mr. Wheatley agreed.

Chapter Ten

Reverend Lathrop came every afternoon to tutor. And I was allowed to sit in on the sessions, too, as long as I completed my kitchen chores.

He was a tall, amiable man with a long nose, blazing blue eyes, a ruddy complexion, and a passion for speechifying. I thought him most wonderful. His voice was deep, yet becalming. It rose and fell with passion as he paced: the passion of Greek and Latin, of poetry and truth. I might not understand all the words themselves, but I understood the feelings behind them, as the candlelight cast his shadow, larger than life, on the wall, the fire crackled cheerfully, and the cold wind howled outside.

Sadness, power, death, betrayal, loss, fear, guilt.

All these things I had witnessed, was still witnessing. But I was astonished to realize they had been felt by others, hundreds of years before my time.

Reverend Lathrop's measured New England cadences were like struck flint lighting a spark in my soul, awakening its rhythms, its moods; setting its juices flowing.

He obviously affected Mary, too. She sat there and gazed at him with a look of pure rapture on her face.

"She's smitten with him, Phillis," Nathaniel told me. "And he feels about her in kind. But he knows I am the only one who can help him make progress with Father. Because Father isn't sure about him yet. So I am going to enter into a pact with him. If he will convince Father I would make a terrible minister, I will convince Father to allow him to press his suit. Isn't that brilliant?"

I said yes, it was.

"Then I will become a merchant. And when I do I will buy you a new frock. Many frocks. And you are going to read. I am going to teach you. Do you know why?"

I waited.

"Because I have some things to prove to Father. I believe in the common man. And his ability to take part in the current boom, to better himself. Why, he's doing it now! Which means he will soon need to buy more things to live in a proper manner. My father can sell those things. And get richer!"

I did not understand all this; I heard only one thing. I was going to learn to read!

"And as part of all that, I believe in you! That you can be taught. You are going to be my proof that people can better themselves. By spring you will be reading."

I jumped up and down.

"Of course, I must do more to convince Father I can be a merchant. I must do something clever. I'll think on it."

He started me with the *Lively Lady*'s manifest. By that Christmas I could recognize the words "scented soap," "gold watch chains," "scarlet silk."

We told no one. It was our secret.

He brought home many ships' manifests, including that of the Wheatley ship, *London Packet*. By February I could read "ladies' toupees and braids," "silver-plated shoe buckles," "Bohea tea."

Nathaniel was so proud of me he was ready to burst. We told no one but Aunt Cumsee.

Now Sulie started to bedevil me in earnest. Not because I could read. She did not know that. But because I was being favored so by Nathaniel.

If I swept the hearth clean, she would mess it again, so it looked as if I had not set myself to the task.

Once Aunt Cumsee asked me to fetch the dry

clothes in from the gooseberry bushes in the yard. Sulie tripped me. I fell, and the clothes got dirtied on some muddy ground.

She laughed so hard, she near cried. "That'll teach you! Who do you think you are, you little skinny black worm, sittin' up there wif' Master Nathaniel?"

I had to be wary of Sulie. She was out to do me harm.

By February Nathaniel had taught me about Jupiter, king of the gods. And Lathona, the moon goddess. I learned that Apollo was born on an island in the eastern Mediterranean. Nathaniel showed me the place on his globe. By March he was so proud of my progress that he decreed I must learn to hold a pen.

This was no mean feat. Using his quill pen in itself was a chore that I labored over. But as I learned to write, first my letters, then my name, it came to me that the words looked like birds. The black trail of the ink made up their wings.

They carried me outside myself. They released me from my ignorance.

I could fly.

One day, when I had finished my recitation, Nathaniel jumped up and pounded the fist of one hand into the palm of the other.

"I know what I am going to do, Phillis. I have a plan to convince Father I should be a merchant."

Again his plan was brilliant. He had some money

of his own, left to him by his grandmother Wheatley. He would purchase some merchandise from a ship that had just docked, advertise it in the *Boston Evening Post*, and get one of his father's trusted workers to stock it in the shoppe on King Street.

"Come on, Phillis, put on a warm cloak. I'm taking you with me to the wharves."

Besides the thriving shoppe on King Street, Nathaniel's father owned several warehouses on the docks, much wharfage, other fine houses over on Union Street that he rented, and a two-hundred-ton merchantman, *London Packet*.

So Nathaniel knew his way around the wharves. Workers and merchants greeted him. He knew what coffeehouse to drop into to get information, what ships were due and from where, and who would be at what alehouse.

"Likely, Prince, this time of day young Hancock is at the Cromwell Head on School Street, having a late repast of fish and chips and striking a deal to split the cost of a cargo of South Carolina rice."

Prince drew the chaise up outside the Cromwell Head.

"Wait here," Nathaniel told us.

Across the street was Hancock's Wharf. There were things to see aplenty, and Prince pointed them out to me.

"There's old Mr. Hancock's countinghouse. He's uncle to John. They say he's worth seventy thousand pounds."

"Is that a lot of money?" I asked.

Prince laughed. "Enough for him to have bought Clark's Wharf and have plenty left over . . . There's a lady there on the wharf what makes waxworks. She makes kings and queens and dresses 'em like they was real. Name of Mrs. Hiller. Ask Master Nathaniel to take you there someday."

I nodded solemnly. Prince knew everything.

"Old Mr. Hancock just gave young Mr. Hancock a three-masted schooner, the *Liberty*. Young John be only four-and-twenty and they say he gonna inherit everythin' . . . There's another shoppe owned by Mr. Fletcher. He has toys. A little town wif houses you can fit in your hand. And he has little moons and suns and he shows how they go 'round. It takes four shillings sixpence to get in there."

For an hour, Prince pointed out sights to me. I felt the excitement, the bustle, the mystery, and the sense of purpose. Then suddenly my fancy was caught by a young nigra dressed in a blue satin suit trimmed with yellow. He even wore a wig.

"Who is that?" I asked Prince.

"Robin. You doan wanna know 'bout him. He's a bad one."

"He looks like a peacock." The Wheatleys had

peacocks in their yard. The birds made noises when intruders came around.

Prince chuckled. "Fine feathers doan make fine birds." And then he told me about Robin and how he'd supplied the arsenic to Phillis and Mark, ten years ago.

"One of these days I'm going to have fine clothes, too. Nathaniel said he'd buy them for me when he becomes a merchant."

His face went solemn. "What you want fine dresses for?"

"So I can be somebody."

"You ain't never gonna be nobody, little one. You is always gonna jus' be little Phillis the slave."

"That's not true, Prince. I'm learning to better myself. Master Nathaniel said I could."

"You kin strut around in fancy clothes like Robin there, but it won't matter none. You still be a nobody. No matter what you do."

Even if I learn to read? But I couldn't ask that. Because that was our secret, Nathaniel's and mine.

"Only way to be anybody is to be free," Prince told me. He seemed so sad. This was not like him. He was always happy, cheering everyone else up. He took life as it came.

"How can I do that, Prince?"

"They can do it. It's done alla time. Master writes a paper and you is free. You wanna better yourself, get them to write that paper and make you free. If'n they don't, you be like Robin all your life, a slave struttin' 'round in fancy clothes."

A cloud seemed to darken the sun of a sudden. I shivered. "Does Robin still work for Dr. Clark?" I asked.

"Uh-huh. Dr. Clark still owns the apothecary shoppe. It be bad, that apothecary shoppe. Dark. Damp. He mixes things. They smell. Like eye of cat and tail of dog. But people go there and he knows what to give 'em when they be sick."

"Do you think he'll ever free Robin?"

"He'd sooner drink his own remedies," Prince said.

I pondered all this as we waited for Nathaniel. *Masters can make their slaves free. All they have to do is write a paper.*

I pondered it in silence until Nathaniel came back. He returned jubilant. "I'm in luck. The *Liberty* just dropped anchor this morning. I had some flip with young John and he's agreed to sell me some merchandise. And to use his influence to get me good space to advertise in the *Post.*"

I just stared at him. I felt betrayed. Why had he never told me it would do no good to read if I would never be free?

Chapter Eleven

"You want to be what?" Nathaniel scowled fiercely.

We were in his room the very next day. He was overseeing my reading.

"Free." I had displeased him. He was angry. He was fearful when angry, but his anger had never yet been directed at me.

"Wherever did you get such a notion?" Then he laughed. And it was worse than anger. "Free! Of all the flapdoodle! Do you know the *meaning* of the word?"

"Yes."

"Then tell me."

"It means that when you buy me my lovely new dresses, I'll be someone. And not just poor little Phillis the slave forever. Because fine feathers don't make fine birds."

He was peering at me intently. "Go on."

"Only way to be anybody is to be free. Even if I learn to read, there's no profit in it, unless I'm free."

"You can read now. Is there no profit in it?"

I hung my head. "Yes, sir, there is."

"Who told you this nonsense?"

I should not have said, but I did. "Prince."

"Well, if that's the kind of folderol that rascal is filling your head with, then I say you are no longer to speak to Prince!"

Fear gripped me. "But he's my friend."

"No friend counsels a little girl to such sentiments. Tell me, Phillis, what you would do with this freedom if my parents were to give it to you? Where would you live? For then you would be free to leave here."

"I don't want to leave." My voice shook.

"Ah, but you would have to. Did Prince tell you that?"

"No, sir."

"Did he advise you of how you would earn your living? How you would buy your bread? Where you would sleep at night?"

I was near tears. "No, sir."

"Well, that is what being free is all about, Phillis." He knelt in front of me and dropped his voice to a whisper. "Being free means you must take responsibility for yourself. And ofttimes for others. Are you ready to do that?"

Tears streamed down my face. "No, sir."

"Do you see me running about these days, doing everything I can to plan my future? I'm free, Phillis. I want to be a merchant. I'm well placed, schooled—and yet, I'm near daft trying to get out from under the yoke of my parents. How do you think *you* would fare?"

I did not answer.

"Phillis"—his voice grew even more gentle—"my parents will be panic stricken. Is this what my teaching you to read has wrought?"

I shook my head no.

"You have so much to learn, Phillis. And you have such a fine mind. I thought this was an agreeable arrangement. But if you persist in this nonsense about being free, I shall have to stop teaching you to read. Do you want that?"

I told him no, I didn't.

"Then let me hear no more of the matter," he said.

It was May, and Mrs. Wheatley's birthday. I was in the kitchen. Aunt Cumsee was helping me ice the golden cake.

"Come, Phillis," Nathaniel said. He stood in the doorway, holding out his hand. "It's time."

I was in a frenzy of excitement. Aunt Cumsee took

off my apron and kissed me. "Do me proud," she said.

"Give me the cake, please."

She handed it to me and I carried it carefully, walking with Nathaniel into the dining room, where Mrs. Wheatley, in rose silk, sat ready to pour the tea. Her husband, Mary, and Reverend Lathrop had all given her presents. Now Nathaniel and I were about to give ours.

They looked up, smiled, and clapped for the cake. I set it down. "I made it myself," I told Mrs. Wheatley.

"It's lovely, dear."

"And we've another surprise for you," Nathaniel said. "Phillis can read. We'd like to show you before we have dessert."

"Read?" Mrs. Wheatley's hand flew to the lace kerchief at her throat.

"Surely you jest, Nathaniel." His father's face went grave. "Don't use the child in this manner. Not even for jest."

"You sly fox," Mary said. "John, I told you they were up to something."

"The child has extraordinary abilities. I told you, Mary," Reverend Lathrop said.

Nathaniel held up a hand for silence, then produced a copy of the *Lively Lady*'s manifest. "Read, Phillis."

So I read. I recited the items. Not once did I look up. But I heard their gasps; heard the polished floorboards creak as Aunt Cumsee came in with a platter of fresh fruit. I felt Prince come into the room to pour some wine for the men.

Sulie came in next to clear some dishes. I kept reading.

Finally, I finished and looked up. For a dreadful moment there was such silence that I could hear my own heart.

Were they displeased? Angry?

"Phillis!" Mrs. Wheatley said. "How ever did you learn?"

"Nathaniel taught me."

"By heaven!" his father said.

"I told you the ordinary person could better himself, didn't I, Father?" Nathaniel asked. "It's what I have based my whole theory of selling on. Times are changing. We must change with them or be outdistanced by other merchants."

Thanks to the advertisements in the *Post*, the merchandise Nathaniel had stocked in the shoppe had sold. Mr. Wheatley was hard put to keep up with his customers' demands. And, as Nathaniel had said, they were all the common man and woman.

"You've done fine, son," Mr. Wheatley said. "You have proved yourself. But let's not talk selling now. The child has a brilliant mind. And you were the one to see it."

"Phillis, come here and give me a hug," Mrs. Wheatley said.

I ran to her to be embraced.

"She can say some Latin, too," Nathaniel boasted. "Phillis, what does *Post nubile phoebus* mean?"

"After clouds, the sun," I answered.

"Par nobile fratrum."

"A noble pair of brothers."

Nathaniel looked about to explode with pride. *"Pulvis et umbra sumus."*

"We are dust and shadows." I caught Prince's eyes as I said it. Silently, he left the room.

"She can write, too, Mother," Nathaniel boasted.

Tears were streaming down Mrs. Wheatley's face. "Dear child! And to think they were selling you on the block. Mr. Wheatley, I am confused. What are we to do?"

He was not confused. "For now we are to sit and enjoy the lovely cake," he said, "and Phillis is to sit at the board with us. Aunt Cumsee, another plate and some sterling."

"Yes, sir!" She left the room.

Of a sudden I was frightened. *Sit at the table with them?* "I'm supposed to fetch in the cider punch," I said.

Nathaniel was pulling out a chair for me. "Sulie

will fetch it. You are to sit with us, as Father says."

"*Hhmph,*" Sulie said. And she pinched me as she passed.

Nathaniel lifted me onto the chair. I looked around. The board was shining and polished. White linen was under each plate of delicate china. Crystal goblets, silverware, blazing candles in candelabra. From here I could see the sideboard, where sat the silver coffee urn, Baltimore chocolate pot, punch bowl.

Mr. Wheatley stood at the head of the table. "Henceforth, you will take all your meals with us, Phillis. You need special nurturing. And I say you shall receive it. What say you, Mrs. Wheatley?"

"That you are right, Mr. Wheatley."

Then there was Prince again, hovering over me, setting down a gold-edged plate, a fork, and a spoon. He took a white linen napkin and set it, just so, in my lap.

"You mind your manners, now," he said softly. Then he was gone.

Chapter Twelve

FEBRUARY 1764

"I'm not happy with your Latin today, Phillis. Tell me one reason why I should take you to the wharf."

"Because you promised."

"Did I, now? Tell me of it. I disremember."

He was going to be vile. In almost three years I had become well acquainted with his moods. Times he was given to melancholy. And when the notion took him he could be surly, even mean.

"You said that if I made no more mention of being free, you would take me to the wharves whenever a ship arrived from the coast of Africa."

"What kind of ship?"

He would have me say the word. "A slave ship."

"And? Has one arrived, then?"

"The *Belisarius* is due this morning." I took the

latest copy of the *Boston Post* and turned to the page of marine news. "It's listed under arrivals."

"So you are reading the newspaper every day as I asked. And not only Scripture."

"I read Scripture for your mama. The newspaper for you."

"And what pleases you most, Phillis?"

"The newspaper," I allowed.

My answer satisfied him. "Let's go, then. But I still expect improvement in your Latin. You can do better than that with your translations of Virgil."

Nathaniel drove the chaise himself. I think he did not want Prince to know we were going to the wharves for the arrival of a cargo of slaves.

I liked it when we went places together, just the two of us. And he always kept his promises. It was part of being a successful merchant, he said, to honor your agreements.

And he was a successful merchant now. More and more he was taking over his father's interests. He had the respect of everyone in town. He was making money faster than he could spend it. Last summer he'd had a fountain put in his mother's garden. She had always wanted one.

There were days we did not see him at all, he was so busy. On such days I sorely missed him. On such days Mrs. Wheatley stepped in, instructing me in Scripture. She was of a mind that a girl couldn't know too much Scripture. Then, just as I felt mired in it, Nathaniel would stop home unexpectedly in the middle of the day, as he had just done. To check on my progress.

Hancock's Wharf was crowded with nigras come to see the arrival of the slave ship. They came to see if anyone from home was aboard.

Nathaniel had promised me that if I saw anyone from home, he would purchase them. We had come once or twice before. But I never saw anyone.

The Boston nigras would stand bearing mute witness while the cargo was unloaded and the dirty, stunned wretches, some still in chains, were led to the warehouse.

"Why I indulge you in this, Phillis, I will never know," Nathaniel said.

I was about to give a saucy reply. I had found that sauciness pleased him more than humility at times. But the words never got past my lips.

"Mr. Wheatley! Ho there, sir!"

A young man came running out of the Hancock countinghouse. "Message from Mr. John."

Nathaniel read it, swore softly, then handed the young man a shilling. "Are the Hancocks all right?"

"Yes, sir. Mr. Thomas has the servants readying things to take his wife to the country. Miz Lydia, she's in a awful tizzy. Says she won't go unless he goes with her. So young John is staying to take care of things."

"Thank you, my good man. Give the family my regards. I must get home." And with that, Nathaniel turned the carriage so fast it near toppled over.

"Home? Nathaniel, what about the *Belisarius*?"

"We're going home, Phillis. Now."

"What's happened?"

"Smallpox."

Smallpox!

That word was as dreaded as the word *fire* in Boston. By the third week in February it had spread through town. Seven well-known families had it. The Glentwoods, the Flaggs, the Gylers, the Deans, the Jenningses, the Reveres, and the Hitchbournes.

I was not allowed out. Neither was Mary. Shoppes and markets were closed, but Nathaniel and his father went to their countinghouse. Business fell off. Carriages and carts rumbled outside in the streets as people fled town. The lieutenant governor adjourned the General Court. Everything was in a state of mayhem. And the Wheatleys were no different.

By the last week in February, the pesthouses were full. And it seemed as if every other house on our street flew a smallpox flag.

Aunt Cumsee sprinkled sulfur all over the house.

It smelled horrible. Then she took to smoking a pipe and puffing smoke all over the place.

"Things can't get much worse," Mr. Wheatley said. We were taking our main meal—at two during the winter, because the light was better. "Isn't the pox enough? Now we hear that Harvard Hall has burned down."

"Things can and will get worse if we don't get inoculated," Nathaniel said.

"Inoculated?" Mrs. Wheatley dropped her spoon. "You heard what Reverend Sewall said about that. If God sent the pox to scourge His people, what He desired was not inoculation but repentance!"

"With all due respect for the good reverend, Mrs. Wheatley," her husband said, "if God gave us the intelligence to discover inoculation, I am sure He wishes us to seize the remedy and use it."

I had heard the Reverend Sewall's passionate sermon. I shivered, knowing I was one of the sinners for whom God had visited the disease upon us.

I had taken too readily to the Koomi ways, too easily forgiven them for enslaving my people. I had fallen prey to their soft words, their riches, their gifts.

I had never repented for disobeying my mother and running off to meet with Obour that morning. My mother was dead because of it.

"We must pray," Mrs. Wheatley was saying.

"We can do that better if we live than if we die,"

her husband answered. "And apparently many others agree. They are pouring into town for inoculation."

"The selectmen have agreed to let the inhabitants try it, Mother," Nathaniel said carefully.

"But it's dangerous!"

"What choice do we have, Mother?" he asked. "Boston fought against inoculation in the epidemic of twenty-one, but we are now ready. Dr. Sprague has agreed to come to the house and do it. He and Drs. Warren, Kast, Perkins, and Lloyd are wearying themselves to the bone, inoculating people all over town. Dr. Clark is doing it free for the poor."

Of a sudden Mary gave a choking sob. "What about John?"

"Reverend Lathrop has already been inoculated, Mary," Nathaniel told her. "He sent word to the countinghouse that he did it to give good example."

"Then I can do no less," Mary said.

"Brave girl," Nathaniel told her.

Mary nodded, white faced.

"Then you have made arrangements?" his mother asked.

"Sprague comes tonight," Nathaniel said.

At that moment we heard a yowl and a great crashing sound. It came from the kitchen. We got up and ran.

Aunt Cumsee lay on the floor. Sulie stood over her, screaming.

Prince, Nathaniel, and Mr. Wheatley lifted Aunt Cumsee to bed. By the end of the day we knew she had the pox.

Mr. Wheatley went to the selectmen for a flag to put out in front of our house. And a guard.

I went to my room and closed my door. I would not be inoculated. I was not afraid, no. It was more than that. God had sent the disease to scourge me. He wanted repentance! And now Aunt Cumsee was sick. I must repent and save her.

Chapter Thirteen

In a little while I heard the Wheatleys come upstairs. They were arguing.

"It is the work of the Lord to attend the sick!" Mrs. Wheatley wailed.

"It is the work of the devil to expose yourself to disease! No one is to go near Aunt Cumsee! Even she knows better. You heard her ask Nathaniel to send for her sister. She's had the disease already and is in no danger."

I whimpered.

"Poor dear," Mrs. Wheatley moaned. "I knew we shouldn't have sent her out for food. Oh, how will we manage without her?"

"Sulie can do for us. She is in charge of the house now. Go and rest until Dr. Sprague comes."

I heard her door close. He went back downstairs.

I stood looking out the window of my room as the town crier went by.

"Distemper spreading through town! Inoculation at Province House! Inoculation! With the blessing of all the clergy!"

His voice faded. I went to open my door. The house was full of strange shadows, creakings, and murmurs. It had an unnatural light about it. Footfalls were heavy, voices muted. Aunt Cumsee's sister, Cary May, was already belowstairs. Aunt Cumsee's room was below mine. If I put my ear to the floorboard, I could hear the two sisters. Cary May's voice was sharp and strong, Aunt Cumsee's low and familiar.

"If the Lord wants me, I's ready," I heard Aunt Cumsee say.

"Lord gonna have to git by me first," her sister responded. "You there, Prince! More heated bricks! More blankets!"

From outside came the sound of carts rumbling by on the street, taking away the dead. Then I heard a rap on the front door. Dr. Sprague! I stepped out into the hall and peered over the banister.

"Good to see you, Doctor," I heard Mr. Wheatley say. "Good of you to come. You look weary, man. Have you eaten?"

"I've had naught but a piece of bread and a cup of wine all day."

"You shall sit by the fire, rest, and eat."

"My requirements are modest. Anything will do."

Nathaniel summoned Sulie to get a dish of meat and bread. "And some claret!" he ordered.

"Tell me," Mr. Wheatley urged, "is the danger yet past?"

"All who wish to be inoculated will be obliged," the elderly man said. "The scourge has spread across the River Charles. Mayhap it is God's blessing that Harvard Hall burned. The students were sent home."

Mr. Wheatley, Nathaniel, and the doctor went into the dining room. I heard Sulie's quick footsteps crossing the hall, her sharp voice ordering Prince to come with the claret.

There was a back way downstairs and out of the house. It was used by Sulie and Aunt Cumsee when the Wheatleys did not wish to be disturbed by the comings and goings of the servants.

I put on my heavy cloak, for the night had turned raw. I crept down the back stairs and ran.

I dozed, covered with an old horse blanket, under a barn window. I dreamed of Robin on the wharf in his fancy blue suit, of Prince telling me I would never be any good unless I was free. Of a sudden I felt myself falling, and I knew it was because Sulie had tripped me. I heard her evil laugh.

I dreamed of my mother pouring out water before

the morning sun. She was telling me something. What? I could not hear her words. Someone else was speaking at the same time.

"Phillis. Come with me."

I opened my eyes. Oh, how cruel! I was not at home by the spring with my mother. I was still here in the barn. Nathaniel stood over me, wrapped in a heavy cloak. Light spilled out of a lantern in his hand, blinding me.

I stared stupidly up at him while my head thudded with ache and I felt a sour taste in my mouth.

"We've been looking all over for you!" He was angry. "Haven't we enough trouble on this damnable night without you running off and causing more? What in God's name are you doing out here? I will have an answer from you, Phillis."

"Hiding," I said.

His scowl deepened. "From what? The pox? You needn't be afraid. No one will fault you for that. Everyone's afraid. Dr. Sprague is waiting to inoculate you. The poor man is exhausted and wants to go home. Now come along, I say."

I shook my head and sank back in the straw.

"What the devil?" Nathaniel set his lantern down on a barrel. "What mean you by that? Enough nonsense. Come along."

But I would not move.

His eyes narrowed. I knew the look. He was not

to be trifled with. Now that he had taken on more and more of his father's business concerns, he was accustomed to having his words heeded. "Come with me now, Phillis. If you don't come now to be inoculated, you can't come back into our house. I shall tell Father to sell you."

Sell me? I stared up at him.

"I mean what I say, Phillis. If you think I don't, you're sadly mistaken. I'll take you to the auction myself. *For God's sake, Phillis, come!*" He shouted his words. They boomed off the rafters.

Some barn swallows took flight. I heard the flapping of their wings as they fluttered about in fear.

"I can't come." I sobbed. "I can't be inoculated!"

"You won't, you mean. Because you're stubborn and spoiled! Everyone's been inoculated! My mother, Mary, everyone!"

"Please, Nathaniel, I can't."

He reached for me. I dodged him. He cursed. He said something about what came of treating servants like family and pulled me by my wrist from the straw.

"I can't," I yelled. "God sent the pox to scourge me! I must repent!"

His mouth fell open. "What's that you say?"

Tears were streaming down my face. "It's what Reverend Sewall said. The disease is God's curse on us. On me. For what I did. So I can't get inoculated. I must repent or Aunt Cumsee will die!"

He released my wrist. "God sent the pox to scourge *you*?"

"Yes. Because I've sinned. And I've not made amends."

"So has most of Boston. And with more imagination than you, Phillis, believe me. Explain to me, then, what have you done to bring such chaos down on Boston?"

I felt foolish when he put it that way. As he meant me to feel. "There's no profit in the telling."

"Have you stolen something? Look here, Phillis, I won't have theft. Did you take something from the market when I took you last week?"

I shook my head no.

"Then what? Out with it. I'm weary of this game."

I looked up at him. He could sell me off if he wished. Or strike me. It was his right. In the state his parents were in, he was likely in charge of the house. I took a deep breath.

"Back home," I murmured, "I sinned. Because of my actions, my mother was kidnapped with me. And she died."

He let out a sigh of relief. "Oh, that." He waved the thought away with a hand and picked up his lantern. "God isn't angry with you for that, Phillis. Take my word for it. He has lots more to be angry about. Now come along. Not taking inoculation and getting sick won't save Aunt Cumsee. If God wants to take her He right well will. He doesn't enter into bargains with little girls."

I felt properly rebuffed and diminished. But I stood my ground.

He turned to leave. "Did you hear me? I've run out of patience, Phillis. Come! By all that's holy! I swear to you, I can abide no more!"

With that he leaned down and swooped me up under one arm, like a roc. He strode through the barn with me in his grasp. All my protests were of no avail.

"I'll sell you off before I'll have you stuffing your head with this religious folderol, Phillis. Half the females in Boston are taken with hysteria because of it. Haven't I taught you anything these last three years?"

His angry words were measured out in cadence with the purposeful steps of his boots in the mud. "I'll hold with no damned religious nonsense, no dark or ancient suspicions. Haven't we had enough of that in this province? The days of witchcraft are over. What do you think learning is all about? To dispel all this flapdoodle."

His anger saved me that night. From myself. It was the only weapon he had. And it was sufficient.

Chapter Fourteen

I opened my eyes the next morning feeling in the grip of the devil's own talons. My head throbbed. The house was very quiet, although I heard some moans from Mary's room next door.

My door opened. "How be's you, chile? I brought some nice hot broth."

"I want some cold milk." She was a stranger.

"No milk allowed. Doctor say so. No bread, pudding, or meat. You take this nice broth now."

"Is Sulie sick?"

"She ain't feelin' too bad. I come to help."

"Who are you?"

Her laugh was rich. "They call me Bettie. I works for Dr. Sprague."

"How is Aunt Cumsee?"

"She jus' got the miseries from the pox, is all. Here, you take this nice broth."

"She's going to die, isn't she?"

"No. It ain't her time yet."

"You're lying to me. Where is Master Nathaniel? He'll tell me the truth." I started to get up.

She put a hand on my arm. But it was the look in her eyes that stopped me. It was solemn yet becalming. Her eyes had an amber light in them. Never had I seen such eyes on a nigra.

"Nobody dead, chile. Ain't time yet fer any of 'em to die. Old Bettie here to make sure everybody gets well. But nobody gonna get well 'lessen you let 'em rest and stop all this talk 'bout dyin'. Never did I see such a sorry chile as you."

"How do you know nobody will die? Just because you work for a doctor, you don't know everything."

"You is a right saucy little piece, ain't you? No, chile. I doan know everythin'. But I had the pox. An' I ain't dead."

I took her measure. Only then did I mind the pox marks on her face. "Is that what it did to you?"

She laughed. "I's alive, chile, ain't I?"

"Will I be like that?"

"If'n you doan take this broth and get back to sleep."

I stared at her, hard, then I drank my broth and lay back and slept.

The second day I was both feverish and chilled. Once again I heard old Bettie creeping about. Outside it was still raining. Rain poured like tears down the windows. Wind blew. Even the candlelight flickered.

I dragged myself out of bed to look out the window. The light outside had an eerie yellow about it that seemed otherworldly.

"What you doin' up an' about?" Old Bettie came in, set down a bowl of broth, and took me by the shoulders, leading me back to the bed.

"We had such light as this at home, before hurricanes," I said.

"Where's that?"

"Senegal. I come from the Grain Coast."

"All the way from Africa? Little thing like you?"

"Yes. Where do you come from?"

"Oh, around an' about. My people been here for a hunnert years. I gots lotta friends. How many friends do you have?"

I swallowed the broth. "None."

"Oh, come now. All little girls have friends."

"Mrs. Wheatley doesn't allow me to have nigra friends. Not even Prince. And I don't have any white friends. Except Nathaniel."

She frowned. "The master's son." She made a

sound of dismay in her throat. "How long you been here, chile?"

"Near three years."

"Smart little girl like you? Writes? Reads? Treated like one o' the family? Surely you know some friend in this country."

I told her of Obour then. And how we came over on the ship together. And how I hadn't seen her since.

"You should find out how she's keepin'," Bettie told me. "Not right you shouldn't have friends of your own kind. You should ask after her."

She left me then. The house was so quiet. I sat thinking of Obour. *Not right,* Bettie had said. No, it wasn't. How was Obour faring, I wondered. Was she taller than I was? Prettier? Could she read and write? Did she think of me?

I felt the loneliness creep over me then, worse than my fever. Was I the only person, besides old Bettie, alive in this house? I had to find out.

I opened the door of my room, crept into the hall, and peered over the banister. I heard muted voices belowstairs. Mr. Wheatley's. And Nathaniel's. They were comforting. I went back to bed and slept.

I dreamed of Obour. I saw her in my dreams as clear as day, chasing the birds in the rice fields. "Obour!" I called out to her. She turned and scowled at me. "Not right," she said, "not right." I ran to her, but she seemed to get farther and farther away. She seemed to disappear, right in front of my eyes. "Obour! I'm sorry! Come back!" I screamed.

Then I dreamed of my mother.

She was standing before the morning sun, pouring water out of a stone jar. She smiled at me. Her smile was so radiant and so filled with peace that I knew that she was not dead. Nobody who was dead could be that happy.

Then she told me what to do for Aunt Cumsee. Her presence was so real. *My mother was not dead.* She was somewhere else, she was happy. And she'd come to me when I needed her.

After she finished telling me about Aunt Cumsee, she said what Bettie had said. "Find Obour." Then she disappeared.

I didn't cry out when she faded away, because she left me with a sense of peace. I slept. Long and deeply.

When I awoke it was early morning. My fever was gone; my head no longer throbbed. Outside the sun was peeking over my windowsill. Quickly I dressed and, with my shoes in my hand, I crept into the hall and down the stairs.

Everyone must still be sleeping. I tiptoed into the kitchen. The fire in the hearth burned brightly.

Things bubbled in pots over the fire. Outside I heard Sulie calling to the chickens as she fed them.

On the wooden table I saw a bowl of warm biscuits. I took one. No bread, Dr. Sprague had said. But I was inordinately fond of my bread. On the table, too, was a pitcher of fresh milk. Prince must have just brought it in. I poured myself a cup, quickly, then reached for what I had come for. A pitcher of water on the table.

I escaped the room just as Sulie was coming back toward the house, her apron gathered up, full of fresh eggs.

I went through the center hall and out the front door. There was the smell of spring in the air. Perfect. I put on my shoes, then went around to the side of the house.

There it was. The fountain in Mrs. Wheatley's garden. It spouted no water now. It had been stopped for winter. It was on the east side of the house. The sun was just coming over the tops of the trees. I lifted my face to feel its warmth.

This is what my mother had told me to do for Aunt Cumsee in my dream. And it would tie me to my mother. Here, in this country, I could do as she had done on the coast of Africa.

It was the same sun.

Nobody was that far away. Nothing was that

impossible. I had become well after inoculation, hadn't I?

I held the pitcher of water above my head, facing the sun. And I poured out the water into the fountain.

Once again the peace of my dream came to me. I felt one with the sun, the water, and the vaulted blue sky. Mama had always said that the sun was the instrument of order in the world. That it would heal us and restore us and quiet our chaos.

There was chaos in the Wheatley house right now. Sickness. There was chaos and sickness in all of Boston.

I stood with my eyes closed and the empty pitcher in my hand, my face still turned upward.

"Phillis, what are you doing out of the house?"

Nathaniel came across the lawn to me. "You'll catch your death." He had a blanket in his hands. He threw it over my shoulders.

"Nathaniel, I'm well. My head is clear."

"What are you doing out here?"

I laughed. "I'm making my morning offering."

"Your what?" He put his hand on my brow. "No fever. Child, you *are* well." He scowled. "Phillis, in heaven's name, this isn't some heathen thing you're about, is it?"

I looked into his face. "The Greeks did it, Nathaniel. An offering to the sun. To Apollo, or Phoebus, as the Greeks called it. Or Sol, according to the

Latin. You know how the Greeks and Romans felt about the sun. You taught me."

"Yes, yes, but come along now. People can see you from the street. And this isn't Greece. Or Rome. It's Boston. People will be hard put to understand."

"Isn't this a beautiful morning?"

"Yes."

"Aren't you gratified that I'm well?"

"Yes, and I'd like to keep you that way. We're all feeling a lot better. We'll be glad to have you at the table with us for breakfast. We just couldn't find you."

I started to walk back to the house with him. "Did old Bettie make breakfast?"

He turned to me. "Old who?"

"Old Bettie. The lady who took care of me when I was sick."

He stopped and felt my brow again. "Sulie looked after you, Phillis," he said. "She sailed through the inoculation with little or no affliction. She's as strong as an ox, that girl. I know no old Bettie."

I stopped in my tracks and gazed up at him. Tears came to my eyes. "Dr. Sprague sent her around."

"Dr. Sprague sent no one. You must have conjured her in your fever."

The vaulted blue sky seemed to explode above me. And in an instant, I knew what I must do. I ran after him and grabbed the soft velvet of his coat sleeve.

"I'd like you to do something for me, Nathaniel."

He sighed. "Very well. What is it?"

"I'd like you to write to my friend, Obour Tanner, for me. I'd like to know how she is. Would you do that for me?"

"No, I won't." His mouth curved downward in a dour smile. "I won't because you can do it yourself. You know how to write. I think it's time you wrote your first letter. Don't you, Phillis?"

Chapter Fifteen

Letter writing was not as simple a task as I'd supposed it to be. How often had I sat watching Nathaniel scrawl a note on expensive vellum and finish it with a flourish?

Now I sat at the table Mrs. Wheatley had set up for my studies in my room, laboring over the effort.

"Dear Obour," I wrote.

I wrote it three times before I got it right. The first two times I dribbled ink on the paper. Oh, I'd learned to write with a quill pen. Nathaniel and Mrs. Wheatley had both seen to that. But now it was different. This was a *letter*. It would take my words across miles to my friend.

I labored all evening. I told Obour how we'd all had the inoculation and were now well. I told her about how I saw my mother in my dream. And my mother had sent old Bettie to me to tell me to correspond with my friend. "She also told me to pour some water out before the sun in the morning for Aunt Cumsee, who is still ill," I wrote. "So I rose early again this morning and did so. Oh, Obour, now I know that though I am learned in the Koomi ways, my mother wishes me still to remember the old ways, too."

I told her about my lessons and how Mrs. Wheatley said we might plan a trip to Newport soon.

"Can you read and write?" I asked her. "Oh, if you can, please tender the kindness of a return. Your dear friend, Keziah. Oh yes, they now call me Phillis, Phillis Wheatley."

At the end of the evening Nathaniel came into my room and asked to see the letter. I gave it to him. He read it and scowled. "You must write it again."

I felt dismay. "Why?"

"This business about old Bettie being sent to you by your mother. It puts forth a belief in expired souls and their ability to have an influence on events in the natural world."

"We believe that," I said.

" 'We'?" he asked.

"My people."

"You don't belong to those people anymore, Phillis. You belong to us. You are studying to be a

Christian. We expect you to act accordingly. My father has a position to keep in the merchant community. So do I. Mr. Tanner is a business associate. We can't have it bandied about that we allow you to believe such things. And as for the water ceremony—well, we can't have you writing about that, either, Phillis. And you must not perform it again." He set the letter down.

It sat there on my desk like some unclean thing.

"As for the rest of it, you have done well. I told you you could write a letter, didn't I? Writing is a privilege. A freedom not allowed to most of your race. Don't abuse it, Phillis. Write the letter again, and I'll post it for you tomorrow. Come now, don't give me that face. You want Obour to know how learned you've become, don't you?"

And with that he turned and left the room.

Something was not right. I sat at my desk and mulled the matter. Then I got up, letter in hand, crossed the hall to Nathaniel's room, and knocked on the door. It opened.

In the flickering candlelight I looked up at him. "You know how you always say I should think problems through until I have a satisfactory answer?"

He nodded.

"And that if I keep getting questions, it isn't thought through?"

"Yes."

"Well, I keep getting a question, Nathaniel."

"Go on."

"If writing is a freedom, then why must my words be approved by you?"

"Because you are a child, still under our jurisdiction."

"Well, remember when you told me how your father was one of the merchants who petitioned the Massachusetts Court against the writs of assistance?"

"I recollect, yes."

"Remember how James Otis got up there and said the writs were against the fundamental principles of English law? And that man's right to liberty is inherent and as inalienable as his right to live?"

Nathaniel sighed deeply. "I'm tired, Phillis. To what aim is all this?"

" 'And so it is with his right to property,' Otis said, 'be it only the eel, the sculpin, the smelt he takes from his net. Bond servants have these rights, Negroes have them, even the poor slave against his master.' That's what Otis said, didn't he, Nathaniel?"

"Otis is a troublemaker. He's also a bit mad."

"He said Negroes have rights, Nathaniel."

He ran his hand through his hair. "In heaven's name, Phillis, don't go about saying such things. Massachusetts has five thousand Negro slaves and thirty thousand bond servants. You'll start a panic. And it will be the end of your learning and my teaching you."

"But why give me the freedom to write if I can't properly use it?"

"I'm granting you a privilege, you little simpleton. One does not abuse a privilege. Can't you understand that?"

I just stared at him.

"Negroes shouldn't be taught to read or write, Phillis. And they have no rights under English law."

I felt slapped. I reeled back, as if under a blow. My lips trembled. "I'm sorry, Nathaniel," I said. "I forgot myself. Please forgive me."

I turned and walked back across the hall.

"You will make me say these things, won't you, Phillis?" In the flickering shadows he looked agitated. "You can never accept a favor with grace. Always you must push for more. It isn't enough that my parents gave you a home. You want freedom! It isn't enough that I am teaching you to correspond. You want to write troublesome things!"

"You taught me to think. I'm thinking."

"Well, there's a proper time for it!"

"I'm sorry—I haven't learned the proper time to exercise that right!"

He swore under his breath. I slammed my door.

Then I wrote the letter over again, the way he wanted it.

It was the way of things with us. We had moments of excitement when he opened the whole world to me, when he laid it out before me on his desk.

He had taught me about the writs of assistance. And all about James Otis's wonderful speech in the old Council Chamber upstairs in the Town House three years ago. He had been there with his father.

He told me about the Proclamation of 1763, in which the Crown determined that no British subject could settle or purchase land beyond the Allegheny Ridge.

He told me about the new Sugar Act and how it reduced the tariff on sugar, but made stricter laws against smuggling.

"The king is my sovereign," he'd said, "but Parliament is bottling us up between the mountains and the sea. The Sugar Act will ruin our trade with the islands, and if we look west for goods to barter in a world exchange, well, they've shut that door in our faces!"

Now he was bottling me up. As Parliament was bottling up the colonies. Yes, he was teaching me. My mind was growing. And I had nowhere to go.

Because I had nowhere to go, I went inside myself.

If I did not take such a course of action, I fair would have died.

The next morning, again, I awoke extra early, dressed, and went into Mrs. Wheatley's garden to pour water before the sun.

Aunt Cumsee was still behind the closed door of her room. I'd paused outside that door before going to the garden. But there was only an ominous silence.

"She's improving," was all Mrs. Wheatley said at breakfast. "You must continue to pray for her, Phillis."

"I do," I said.

Nathaniel cast me a dark look. "Tell my mother how you pray for her, Phillis."

My heart turned to a cold clump of ice. *Oh, Nathaniel, to think that you are so angry that you will betray me.*

"Very well, if you don't speak, I will. She's been going to your garden every morning, Mother, to perform some heathen task. Some ritual from Africa."

"What are you saying, Nathaniel?" It was his father who asked, not Mrs. Wheatley. She was too taken with shock.

"Tell them, Phillis," Nathaniel said.

I twisted my apron in my lap.

Nathaniel never took his eyes from me as he went on. "She takes a pitcher full of water from the kitchen and pours it out before the sun. It's called sun worshiping. It's often practiced by African tribes."

I heard Mrs. Wheatley gasp.

"Is *that* what my friend Jonathan Cripley was talking about?" Mr. Wheatley's voice was disbelieving. "He said the fishmonger saw someone praying in our garden yesterday."

"Likely half of Boston saw it," Nathaniel said. "I've spoken to her about it, but she won't stop."

"How could you, Phillis?" Mary asked. "When Mother is teaching you to be a Christian?" Then a thought seized her. "Mother, Daddy, if John hears about this, I'll be mortified."

"Phillis, what have you to say for yourself?" Mr. Wheatley's voice was gentle.

I cared not for what Nathaniel thought of me. Right now I could kill him with my bare hands. And Mary was acting like an insipid little hen. But I ached at having hurt my benefactors. "I was praying for Aunt Cumsee," I said. "When I was sick I dreamed of my mother. And she told me to make the morning offering. The way she did every morning at home."

Mrs. Wheatley gasped. "But I taught you to pray as a good Christian, Phillis. And you said you believed."

"I do," I whispered.

"But you cannot be a good Christian and keep the old practices, dear. We cannot hold with such."

I burst into tears.

Mrs. Wheatley became distraught then. She pushed back her chair and held her arms out to me. "Poor child. It was the sickness and dreaming of your mother. We still hear you cry out for her at night. I know you are sorry. And you won't do it again, will you?"

"I should hope not," Mary said.

I ran to Mrs. Wheatley. She held me on her lap and patted me while I cried.

"When people have been in such a dolorous situation they take a notion to do strange things," Mr. Wheatley said. "It's over now, forget it. The child isn't going to do it anymore."

"No, she isn't," Nathaniel said. "Because I'm going to have the fountain removed."

"Don't you think that a bit severe?" his mother asked.

"No," Nathaniel answered. "I don't."

I still made my morning offering. In my own chamber. Only now I used the pitcher of water placed there every morning for washing. I stood in front of the window when the sun was up, and I poured water from the pitcher into the bowl.

I suppose I should thank Nathaniel for bottling me up so that I turned inside myself to find what was there.

I started to write.

At first I just started writing fragments of thoughts down on paper as they came to me in the middle of my studies. I suppose I did it in rebellion against Nathaniel. Because he wouldn't let me write what I wanted to Obour.

I wrote how angry I was at him. And how, at the same time, I missed him, my old friend—because though he still oversaw my lessons, we could never be friends in the same way again.

I kept the paper with my thoughts on it in a special drawer in my desk. Then, after I got rid of the bad feelings, I wrote the good ones.

I wrote about the sunset. And the sounds of the street that filtered in my window of a spring night, when all was quiet and peaceful in the house and the sound of Mary's harpsichord drifted from belowstairs.

I wrote about my happiness at seeing Aunt Cumsee well. And my delight in the first letter I received from Obour. And my surprise and happiness at finding that she could write. My own letter, from Obour, come all the way from Newport!

When I wrote, I felt better, as if I had remade the world all of a piece, the way I wanted it to be, not the way it was.

So I wrote some more. And the paper piled up in the drawer of my desk. Oh, what a delicious feeling to know that all my thoughts did not have to be approved by Nathaniel!

I could scarce contain my own excitement. The more I wrote, the more excited I became. I felt like Columbus must have felt when he just discovered America. Only the land that I had sighted was myself.

In a way, my own way, I was free.

Chapter Sixteen

AUGUST 1765

Mrs. Wheatley, Mary, and I were returning from a morning's shopping and a midday repast at the house of family friends.

All morning we'd shopped for linens and laces for Mary. For the past six months, she'd been stitching her dowry.

Mary and John Lathrop were betrothed. But no marriage date had been set yet. And from the way the two of them argued these days, my mistress was fearful none ever would be.

Mary was not much for politics. And John was fast becoming known as a firebrand Patriot preacher.

Mrs. Wheatley bade Prince stop the carriage at a small shoppe next door to the Old Colony House.

"Come, girls, I want you both to see something," she said.

Inside, before a large multipaned window, sat a young nigra man at an easel. "Mrs. Wheatley, how good to see you!" He put down his paints and stepped forward to draw up chairs.

"This is my daughter, Mary, Scipio. And my young ward, Phillis. Girls, this is Scipio, an African painter."

The young man smiled, showing gleaming white teeth. When he bent to kiss our hands, I saw Mary draw back in badly concealed revulsion. Scipio winked at me. And we became immediate friends.

"I'm thinking of asking Scipio to draw both your likenesses," Mrs. Wheatley told us as he showed us around. "What think you, Mary?"

Mary did not think much of it. Not at all. She sniffed. "Where did you learn to draw?" she asked.

"In London, Miss Mary. And my good wife, Sarah, also instructed me. She does work in the Japanese style. She paints in lacquer on glass."

Mary flushed. She had not been to London.

"And you earn your keep this way, then?"

"No, Miss Mary. I am servant to the Reverend and Mrs. John Moorhead of Long Lane Presbyterian Church."

Mary smiled. This pleasured her. "I think that at some future time I may allow you to draw my likeness," she told him.

"Of course," Scipio said, bowing again. And he winked at me as we went out the door.

Mary was a snob, I decided. She didn't deserve John Lathrop.

We went home by way of Boylston Market. A new shipment of coffee had come in this morning from the islands. Mrs. Wheatley wanted to sample some.

Of a sudden, Prince drew the horse up sharp. We bolted forward and near fell.

"What is it?" Mrs. Wheatley rapped on the window.

"A crowd, ma'am."

"Crowd?"

"More like a mob."

"To what aim?" my mistress asked.

Prince opened the small window between the driver's seat and us. "They've hung Andrew Oliver in effigy."

Oliver was secretary of the province. All around the straw figure a crowd had amassed, jeering at it.

"How distasteful," Mrs. Wheatley said. "Drive on, Prince. Take us home. I have just lost my taste for coffee."

Prince clicked to the horse and we swerved down an alley, away from the crowd. But I found myself looking back.

White people say *we* have strange practices. But what could be more sinister than stuffing a figure with straw, painting its face, giving it a name, and screaming at it? Does this not bring bad medicine down on the person it represents?

As if she could read my thoughts, Mrs. Wheatley began to fan her face and look distressed. "I fear for Mr. Oliver. Boston crowds get so ugly."

"Then he never should have taken the position of stamp master," Mary said. She sighed. "John is likely home this minute writing another seditious sermon."

"The man must preach what he believes, Mary," her mother said. "Have you two been quarreling again?"

"We did have high words, Mother. I just don't see why he can't be content to preach the Word of the Lord. And not be so influenced by the Sons of Liberty."

"Don't question his judgments, Mary."

"Oh," Mary complained bitterly, "those pernicious stamps!"

Those pernicious stamps were all we'd heard about since May, when a coastal vessel had brought the news that Parliament would soon demand a stamp duty, from half a penny to twenty-five shillings on any skin or vellum or parchment or sheet of paper on which anything should be engraved, written, or printed.

I thought of all the papers in my drawer. How priceless words seemed now. How precious!

The Boston summer had been restless. People gathered in small groups on street corners in the sweet dusk. And you could see them raising their fists in anger. Small boys ran waving copies of the *Gazette* and yelling about the latest published letter by John Adams. Ships anchored in the harbor would all fly their flags at half-mast, as if on some sudden agreement. Or church bells would toll when it was not the Sabbath. Everyone was waiting for the pernicious stamps. They were to arrive in November.

Aunt Cumsee laid a cold supper for us that night. Meats and pickles, relishes and fresh fruit. When Mr. Wheatley praised her, saying it was too hot for anything else, she apologized.

"All I could do," she said. "I had no firewood."

"Where is Prince?" Mr. Wheatley looked around.

"Not been here all afternoon," she said.

"He'd best be back before dark," Nathaniel said. "The town clerk has ordered that no mulatto or Negro servants be abroad after nine at night. I heard Prince was running messages to the Sons."

"What is the nature of the messages?" Mr. Wheatley asked.

"Every post for the last day or so is bringing messages of encouragement from other colonies," Nathaniel said. "All we hear is 'Resolved,' from the citizens of Annapolis, Plymouth, Newport."

"What have they resolved?" Mary asked.

Nathaniel sipped his cold cider. "That with submission to divine Providence, we can never be slaves. And the Virginians passed a set of resolutions that are absolutely daring."

"And what makes them any more daring than our Braintree Instructions, written by John Adams?" Mary challenged.

"The Virginians are men with money. Landed proprietors."

"So, since men with money are against this Stamp Act, you're against it now, too." Mary's tone was snide.

"It will ruin our economy," Nathaniel said.

Mary grimaced. "If something affects trade you care. My John is preaching against the Stamp Act for the good of all."

"The good of all is his business," Nathaniel said; "mine is trade." Then he grinned. "Did John not tell you how it affects those contemplating marriage?"

"Don't jest, Nathaniel," Mary said.

"I don't. The *Gazette* said today that many young people are joining in wedlock earlier than they intended, because after the first of November it will be difficult to have the ceremony performed without paying dearly for stamping."

Mary flushed. "Mother, make him stop."

"Enough, children," Mrs. Wheatley chided. "You know we encourage intelligent discourse. But let's not let it divide our family."

I looked at Nathaniel. *It affects us all,* he'd said. *We can never be slaves.* I liked the ring of it.

When Aunt Cumsee brought in the whipped syllabub, we heard the clamor outside. Dusk had fallen; candles flickered on the table. We ran to the windows. A crowd had appeared.

Mary gasped. "Where did they come from?" She was afraid.

I was not. I was seized by a sense of excitement.

"Crowds come from nowhere these days," Mr. Wheatley said. "I suggest we close all the shutters."

We went about fastening the shutters on the inside.

Nathaniel secured all the doors. "Mary, play your harpsichord so Mother and Father don't hear the noise." And he ran up the stairs.

Mary sat to play. Aunt Cumsee served the syllabub. I lighted more candles. Nathaniel came back down and took his place at the table. Inside his frock coat he had a long pistol stuck in the waistband of his breeches. Was I the only one to notice?

After dessert Mr. and Mrs. Wheatley sat in chairs before the empty fireplace. Mrs. Wheatley took up some petit point.

I slipped out of the room and followed Nathaniel across the hall into the parlor. He had one shutter open. From outside there came the dull murmur of many voices as more and more people surged down King Street, waving their arms, one great body driven by their anger.

High above them they carried the straw Andrew Oliver on a bier.

Nathaniel stood watching, hands behind his back.

"What is it?" I whispered.

"A mock funeral procession."

"What are they chanting?"

" 'Liberty, property, and no stamps!' "

I listened, making sense of the chant then. Over and over they said it. Louder and louder. There was a rhythm to it, a sense of purpose. They were coming right by our house.

"Are you afraid?" Nathaniel asked.

"Mary is. But no, I'm not. I think it's exciting."

He grunted.

"And besides, you have a pistol."

"How do you know that?"

"I saw it."

He reached out his hand and brushed my cheek. "You'll fare well," he said. "You don't miss much and you're not afraid."

I flushed under the praise.

He put an arm around my shoulder and drew me toward him. I smelled the tobacco and strong-scented soap he used. I leaned next to him, happy, watching the crowd go by chanting, stomping, orderly, yet fair to bursting.

"Take notice of them, Phillis," he said. "These are the common folk, the tradesmen, the town artisans, cord wainers, carpenters, farmers, shopkeepers, printers. These are the people who helped make me a merchant. Never underestimate their power."

"Women, too," I said, looking up at him.

He smiled down at me. "Yes, women, too."

"Where do they go?" I asked.

"Likely to Oliver's office. Even to his residence."

"For what purpose?"

"To do mischief. To smash windows. Tear his garden. Drink his wine. Scatter his papers."

I felt a thrill of joy. I felt the cadence of their words pounding in with the blood in my veins. *Liberty! Property! No stamps!*

And we will never be slaves, I thought. *We will never be slaves.*

The next morning Prince was back, bringing wood in for Aunt Cumsee, waiting on the table. No one called him to account. But I heard Nathaniel chide him quietly as Prince fetched Nathaniel's hat.

"I hope you know what you're getting involved in, Prince. Most of our miseries we bring on ourselves. And they're the sum of our own stupidity."

"I know," Prince said. "I know."

Chapter Seventeen

SUMMER 1766

A year later I wrote my first poem.

I was twelve years old and of a sudden I hated the way I looked. I was skinny as a beanpole. My skin was as black as if I'd been rubbed with fireplace ashes, and I was starting to know that no matter what I did, no matter how smart or amiable I managed to be, I was still not white folk. And I never would be, either.

I hated my hair, which would lend itself to no brush but stuck out every which way on my wretched head.

I would watch Mary brushing her long silken hair at night and hate the sight of it. And her.

Mary was not pretty, but she had two commodities I lacked. She *acted* pretty. And she had a bosom.

Generally those two virtues were of great account in Boston in 1766.

Oh, I could recite from Shakespeare and Alexander Pope. I read Plato and Homer. I read the *Iliad* and the *Odyssey*. Nathaniel drilled these things in my head.

Mary did not even know what they were. "Would you like to come to a musical with me and Thankful Hubbard this evening?" she asked one day as I stood watching Sulie doing up her hair.

"No thank you. I've got the *Iliad*," I said. I meant that I had to study the *Iliad*, for Nathaniel would be asking me about it that night.

"Oh?" Mary frowned. "Well, in that case you'd best lie down and take a powder. You know how Mama frets about sickness."

I just stared at her as I left the room. Was she that much of a noodlehead? Or was she just not paying mind to me?

She was a noodlehead, I decided. And yet she was the petted only daughter in the family. Nathaniel abided her, teased her, but when all was said and done, took her interest to heart. Her parents provided her with every frippery and forbearance.

Mary's afternoons were filled with teas, jaunts with friends, rides in the countryside, and bookshoppe lectures.

One afternoon when she had just left for such a lecture, I looked up from my newest sampler at my mistress. "Why do I have to sit here doing stitches? Why can't I go to a bookshoppe lecture like Mary?"

"Mary is courting, dear. This is her time to do frivolous things. Soon enough, she'll marry and be burdened with responsibilities."

"Will I marry?"

"Mayhap, yes, someday. But you are different, Phillis. Surely you know that."

"Because I'm a Negro?"

"No, dear, no. There are Negroes aplenty in Boston. Because you have a good turn of mind and we have educated you. So you must prepare yourself, school yourself, discipline yourself, for what lies ahead."

"What lies ahead?" I asked.

Her eyes went soft. "I don't know, Phillis. We none of us know what lies in the future. But we want you to be prepared. So you must work harder, pray more, and watch with whom you form alliances. You must be above reproach at all times."

While Mary has all the sport, I thought dismally.

I wrote my poem. If Mary thought the *Iliad* was a disease, I would write poetry. I would write about virtue.

I had memorized and recited so much poetry for

Nathaniel that spring that writing one of my own came as easy as breathing. And it looked so pleasing, written out in my fine script.

My words, mine. I felt filled with a secret satisfaction I had never felt before in my life.

Oddly enough, it was Mary who discovered my first poem. And it was all because of hair.

My hair.

I was reciting for Nathaniel one evening. He was absolutely daft about my reciting. He said it would give me esteem, and I needed esteem.

"Don't fidget," he scolded. I was reciting a Shakespeare sonnet. He made me do it again.

I commenced.

"Don't tug at your hair!" he scolded. "Why must you always tug at your hair?"

"I hate my hair."

"What in God's name has your hair got to do with poetry?"

I started to cry. "I hate my hair. It makes me look like a Negro."

"You are a Negro."

"But some Negro women have pretty hair, all short and fluffy. Why can't mine be short and fluffy?"

He lounged back in his chair, scowling. "There's a Negro man named Lewis who has a shoppe. He styles hair. You recite this sonnet better for me tomorrow and I'll take you there and have him make you pretty. What say you?"

I said yes.

"Very well, then study." And he put on his linen coat and strode out. Likely to meet friends at some coffeehouse.

Two days later I sat in the shoppe of Mr. Lewis.

"She wants it short and fluffy," Nathaniel told him.

Mr. Lewis smiled. "Short I can give her. Fluffy the good Lord already gave her."

"Do your best, my good man," Nathaniel said.

"I know what she wants," Mr. Lewis said mildly. "I know what all the pretty young Negro girls in Boston want to do with their hair."

"Do it, then," Nathaniel urged. "I'll be back in half an hour."

I sat dwarfed in the large chair and wrapped in a great piece of flannel. Mr. Lewis stood over me, grinning, with gleaming scissors in his hand.

For half an hour he worked on me, snip, snip, snipping. I could scarce breathe, I was so frightened. I felt the hair getting shorter and shorter. All the while that he worked, he talked to me about the nigra women in Boston whose hair he had cut. "Did the maidservant at Mr. Hancock's," he said, "also the personal serving girl of Peggy Hutchinson. She's the daughter of the lieutenant governor. The maidservant, Petula, stayed with Peggy that night last August, when the mob went through his house and tore it down. They destroyed everything. Next day was the first day of Superior Court. And since Hutchinson is chief justice, he had to make an appearance. Petula told me he walked into court in shirtsleeves, with tears coming down his face. He had no other garment. Nor did his family."

Because he cut the hair of the maids in all the best houses in Boston, he was filled with stories and gossip.

"There," he said finally. And he held up a silver-handled mirror. "What do you think?"

I squealed in delight. My hair was cut short, cropped around my head in hundreds of tiny curls. "It makes my face look . . ." I stopped just short of the word.

"Saucy," he said.

I touched the curls. "Oh, it's beautiful."

Nathaniel returned, beaming when he saw me. "Who is this dazzling creature, this daughter of Zeus?" he asked.

I blushed. "Don't mock me."

"Would I do such a thing?" And from his frock coat pocket he withdrew a square of paper, unwrapped it, and handed me the most dainty bit of scrimshaw fashioned into a brooch.

I fingered it lovingly. Tears came to my eyes.

Nathaniel did not see them. He was paying Mr. Lewis for his services.

"Thank you, Nathaniel," I whispered as we walked out of the shoppe. "You're so good to me."

"Until the next time I scold."

But my heart was filled with love for him. True, he scolded, and true, we argued. But always it had been Nathaniel who sensed my hurt and pain and rescued me from it.

"Don't thank me," he said gruffly. "I did it for myself. Now I won't have to see you tugging at your hair anymore. You women are so vain about your hair."

"Not half as vain as you men are," I returned, "with your powdered wigs."

He expected the retort from me. I had to have the mettle to stand up to him, always, or I would not have been worth the bother to him. I knew that.

Chapter Eighteen

When we arrived at home, I was so anxious to show my mistress my new hairstyle that I ran right through the center hall to where I heard her voice in the kitchen.

I did not see Mary standing in the front parlor with a paper in her hand.

In the kitchen Mrs. Wheatley was taking inventory of the larder. Aunt Cumsee gave me a piece of pie and some milk.

"Phillis, come here." Nathaniel's voice boomed through the house. I ran to him.

He looked up from a chair in the parlor. Mary stood behind him. "This poem—is it of your making?"

I stared at the paper he held as if it had suddenly taken on a life of its own. *How did it come to be in his hand?* That was the paper I'd hidden under my pillow. Then I saw the smugness in Mary's face.

"You've no right to go poking around my things when I'm not here," I flung at her. At the same time I went to Nathaniel and reached for the paper.

He held it aloft. "Hold your tongue! And answer the question."

There was nothing for it but to say yes. So I did.

Nathaniel began to read it then. When he got to the line *"Wisdom is higher than a fool can reach,"* my face went red. And I wanted to run from the room.

How could I make so bold as to write such words? They were so high sounding, so false. What did I know of wisdom? Oh, I wished Nathaniel would stop reading. He was saying, aloud, all my innermost thoughts, dragging them from the dark reaches of my soul and pouring them out into the sunlight.

"Stop!" I shouted.

Nathaniel stopped. And then the silence was worse. We just stared at one another, he and I. The clock in the corner ticked loudly. I minded that others had come into the room. Mrs. Wheatley and Aunt Cumsee.

"Please don't read any more," I begged. "Please give the paper to me." I reached out for it.

Nathaniel held it away from my grasp. "You *wrote* these words, Phillis? On your own?" He was truly taken aback.

"I won't do it again," I said.

"Mother, did you *hear* it?"

"I did." My mistress stepped forward. Her eyes were filled with a dull confusion.

What had I done?

I stood helplessly while they all stared at me. I felt time passing, moving across the face of the sun, slowly, inexorably, toward eternity.

They were angry with me. I had written something in secret, something Nathaniel knew naught of. Writing was a freedom, he'd told me. But because I was still a child, I was still under the Wheatleys' jurisdiction. And my words must be approved by them.

"I won't do it again. Give me back my work, please. I won't do it again. I promise."

Again I reached for the paper. This time he handed it to me. I turned and started to walk from the room.

In that instant everyone came to life.

"Don't go," I heard from Mary. "I won't poke about your things again, I promise."

"Phillis, dear"—at the same time, from my mistress—"*dear child*. To my knowledge, no Negro has ever written a poem."

"Lord be praised," from Aunt Cumsee.

But it was Nathaniel who stopped me. I felt his hand on my arm. I could not see for the tears of shame in my eyes. For it came to me, then, what I had really done.

I had broken some long-honored rule. I had stepped over some line. I had disrupted the normal workings of the universe.

"Phillis," Nathaniel said, "you had best do it again if you know what is good for you. And again, and again, and again."

After that my life changed. My writing was no longer mine. It belonged, after that day, to the Wheatley family, even as I did. Mary made me copy my poem over and over again to show her friends. When they came for tea, she made me recite it for them. Mrs. Wheatley announced there would be no more chores for me, not even shelling peas or helping Aunt Cumsee make beaten biscuits.

I did not care overmuch for that decision. I missed my time in the kitchen with Aunt Cumsee. She had a steadfast earthy wisdom that I needed to balance my daily diet of Greek and Latin.

Mrs. Wheatley had a new cherrywood desk brought to my room. Mary gave me a bowl of potpourri to set on it and two silver candleholders with beeswax candles.

I was supplied with expensive vellum, a new inkpot, two new quill pens, very sharp. The fire in my grate was kept up all night against the chill. In case

I was "seized by a thought and wanted to write it down," Mrs. Wheatley said.

Mr. Wheatley contributed a hunt tapestry to be hung on one wall. It was old and valued. I had always seen it in his library. It was from England.

Aunt Cumsee gave me a special shawl to wear around my shoulders to ward off drafts if I "had the notion to write in the middle of the night." She kept me supplied with trays of tea and cooked special things for me. Cream soups. Apples in chocolate sauce. The lightest of pastries.

I was to keep my usual schedule of a morning: breakfast with the family, then read the Bible with Mary and her mother for half an hour and devote an hour to doing my needlework. Then I was to accompany Mrs. Wheatley on calls.

After a noon meal I was to rest for an hour, then study lessons for an hour and spend the rest of the day at my desk, writing.

Lessons were shortened by Nathaniel. I was no longer required to do sums or geography. But I was to read Mather Byles, Thomas Burnet, Jonathan Edwards, and more Shakespeare, Milton, and Pope.

Yes, my life changed. But I preferred it the way it was before I became "Mrs. Wheatley's nigra girl who writes poetry." When my writing was mine alone, to be held close and cherished.

Chapter Nineteen

FALL 1767

If I did not produce great works in the next year, no one complained. They urged me to take my ease, read, think, and study. But always I sensed them waiting for me to write my next poem.

How often I tried! But nothing happened. The words turned to dust under my pen.

I cried in secret. I brooded. I sulked. One evening when Nathaniel was being especially hard on my Latin translations, I cried.

"I can't think," I said. "I can't do anything."

"The poetry will come, Phillis," he said.

"Then why haven't I written anything?"

"It will come."

I covered my face with my hands. "I'm a fraud," I said. "The first poem was only an aberration. Everyone will say that!"

"If anyone dares, I'll call him out for a duel."

I looked at him. He meant it. He believed in me.

"You've been working too hard," he said, getting up. "You're only thirteen, for heaven's sake. Give yourself time. Now get some rest. The poetry will come when you least expect it."

Nathaniel believed in me. Somehow I found that worse than anything.

It was Pope's Day, November 5. I did not quite understand what it meant. But it originated in England and had something to do with hating Catholics. Enough reason for Boston to celebrate. It was a day of bright blue skies. Since Parliament repealed the Stamp Act in March of '66, a dubious peace had descended upon Boston. Still, all day the students had been taking on in the street below my window, blowing conch shells, drinking in public, shouting saucy things to women, and in general making nuisances of themselves.

I found them an annoyance. I had a headache. Virgil evaded me. I looked at the dry pages and wondered how I could ever do the translations Nathaniel wanted. And why I must do them when all of humanity seemed to be doing as they pleased.

When did I ever do as I pleased? The last time was the morning I'd run off to meet Obour in the rice fields.

I wanted to run free now. Why did I have to be inside studying on such a golden autumn afternoon, when those spoiled boys from Harvard were out there making sport?

Because they were rich, white, and male. And their place in life was certain. While I, who likely had more brains and wits than any two of them combined, had to sit confined and behave because I wrote poetry and I was a nigra girl.

I set my book aside and started to write.

For the next two hours, while the fire spit in the grate and the noise of the revelers continued outside my window, I wrote. From somewhere belowstairs a clock chimed. I heard Mrs. Wheatley's voice, heard a door slam, a dog bark in the distance. I lost all track of time. When I was finished, I stopped and read what I had written.

I liked the last stanza the best. *Improve your privileges while they stay, ye pupils, and each hour redeem, that bears or good or bad report of you to heaven.*

Yes, it was good. I sat back, unbelieving. I had done it! I had written another poem! My headache pressed hard against my temples. I was spent.

Footsteps in the hall, a knock, then Nathaniel came in. "I hope you've been studying, Phillis. Is that tea hot?"

I could scarce contain myself. "Yes."

"Pour a cup for me. I couldn't get anyone in the

kitchen to even pay mind to me. The place is in turmoil, what with the gathering Mother is having tonight for Reverend Occom and Messrs. Hussey and Coffin."

"And your friends," I reminded him.

He shrugged. "Business acquaintances. They must be fêted if I'm to serve as financial exchange agent for them. They are all powerful merchants. Are those pastries fresh?"

"This day Aunt Cumsee made them."

"They spoil you rotten, Phillis." He took a pastry and devoured it hungrily. "Pope's Day. It was hell out in the streets. Captain Macintosh and his boys. I rue the day the North and South End gangs ever buried the hatchet."

"I've written a poem," I said.

He stopped chewing and stared at me. "The devil you have."

"I've been working on it these past two hours."

He set down his cup and held out his hand.

I gave it to him.

He leaned back in his chair and read. Darkness was gathering outside. The fire was getting low in the grate.

He set the paper down. "It's very good."

"Thank you."

Then, of a sudden, he jumped up, grabbed me, and whirled me around the room. "I told you you could do it, didn't I?"

"Yes!" I shouted. "Yes. Oh, stop, you're making me dizzy."

He stopped, but he could not be still. He paced. "Wait until Mother hears this. Let me have it. I must show it to her before the guests arrive. And you will recite it tonight."

"Oh, Nathaniel, no!"

"Yes!" He was jubilant.

My face clouded. "I'm worried about something, Nathaniel."

He was rereading the poem.

"I wrote my first poem because I was angry with Mary. And this one because I was annoyed at the ruckus the Harvard boys were making. What does that mean?"

"That you're a poet," he said.

"Oh, Nathaniel, please listen. Is anger my muse, then?"

He stopped reading. "*Omnia vincit amor, et nos cedamus amori*. What does that mean, Phillis?"

"I don't know."

"It means, 'Love conquereth all things, let us yield to love.' You have anger in you, Phillis. Write it away. It will quit your soul, and other emotions will be your muse. You've done well. It's a good poem. Don't flay yourself."

He left. I sat before the fire. *Let us yield to love*, he had said. Oh, Nathaniel.

Chapter Twenty

I had lost my cowrie shell!

Frantically I scrambled around my room looking for it. *Where had I put it?* I got down on my hands and knees and felt around the rug. I stood up and felt in the pocket I wore around my waist. There was a hole in it! I'd been so busy playing the poet that I'd not sewed it up. *How could I recite in front of all those people?* I must look again for my shell.

"Phillis? You must come down. We're waiting. Supper will soon be served." It was Mary.

"All right, I'll be along directly."

Mary was playing "The Fair Flower of Northumberland" on the harpsichord as I slowly descended the stairs ten minutes later, without the shell. Candles cast brilliant light. Women in French silks moved through the Wheatley dining room and parlor, chattering. Men in powdered wigs and richly embroidered frock coats stood in bunches, sipping wine. Everywhere, silver gleamed, crystal shone, the fragrances of candles and good food mingled.

I stood hesitating in the hallway. The missing cowrie shell cut a sense of loss deep within me. I felt naked, unprotected. And some instinct told me I needed protection. I was nervous.

Sulie and Aunt Cumsee were setting steaming platters and silver urns of food down on the table. Mrs. Wheatley announced dinner. Gentlemen offered their arms to ladies. Chairs were pulled out from the table. People took their places.

Then Nathaniel saw me and straightened up from settling some fair young thing in her chair. "Ah, here she is. Phillis, come meet our guests. Ladies and gentlemen, this is our Phillis."

I recognized some faces. John Hancock, two of Mary's insipid friends. They nodded and smiled. But there were stares from others. I knew what they were thinking.

A nigra girl? To sit at table with us?

Reverend Lathrop stood and pulled out a chair for me. I sat next to him.

"Phillis is going to recite her latest poem for us after supper," Nathaniel said.

Tension broke. It was all right now. I was not just any nigra girl. I was Mrs. Wheatley's nigra who wrote poetry. An oddity at worst, a titillating amusement at best.

I picked at my food. Turtle soup, two kinds of roast meats, salmon en croûte, a new specialty of Aunt Cumsee's. Buttered vegetables. The pleasant chatter, the tinkling laughter of the women, seemed far away.

Then Mrs. Wheatley smiled at me. "What is your new poem about, Phillis?"

I swallowed a bit of roast potato. "The young men of Harvard," I said.

A thin, balding man at the other end of the table laughed. "Ah, her heart is in the right place."

"I've read the poem, Aaron," Nathaniel said. "I promise you that it is not frivolous."

I stared at the man. He wore spectacles. His hands were long and thin, his eyes dark and probing. Why was he looking at me like that? I felt evil in the man.

"Who *is* he?" one of Mary's friends whispered.

"Aaron Lopez, the Jewish slave trader from Newport."

I near choked on my meat. But I recovered myself quickly when Mrs. Wheatley gave the conversation a new turn.

"Mr. Coffin, tell us of the voyage you and Mr. Hussey took down from Nantucket, in which your ship near broke in pieces in the storm off Cape Cod."

Then, in a quiet voice, Mr. Coffin told of the lightning, the howling wind, the boiling ocean, the ship's creakings and moanings, how he and his friend gave themselves up for lost.

Mr. Hussey sipped his Madeira in silence. And I felt the goodness in these two men who had cheated death. Goodness and evil at the same table, I minded.

Then Mrs. Wheatley turned to Reverend Occom. "Do tell our guests about your plans."

Occom was Indian, a converted Mohegan, now a Christian minister from Connecticut. He and his friend Reverend Nathaniel Whittaker were sailing on the morrow to London.

"We will lecture to raise funds for Moor's Charity Indian School of Lebanon. It is where I was educated."

Murmurings of excitement. I settled down, becalming myself. Mrs. Wheatley smiled at me.

"We hope you have a better voyage than Messrs. Hussey and Coffin," the other addle-brained friend of Mary's said.

Silence. Then Mr. Coffin spoke up. "Not all voyages are so unpleasant," he assured the reverends. Then he looked around the table. "Has anyone here been on a sea voyage?"

"Phillis has," Mary said.

All looked at me. I wanted to drop under the table.

"Tell us," Mr. Lopez said in a soft, purring voice. But he knew. I could tell by the look in his eyes that he knew.

It was Nathaniel who saved me. "Phillis was a child when she was brought from Africa to America. She scarce remembers, do you, Phillis?"

My eyes sought his gratefully. "No," I said.

"In your absence," Mrs. Wheatley told the reverends, "I shall endeavor to raise up funds to assist the families you leave behind. We must be mindful of their welfare."

"And I shall be the first to contribute a token of my esteem to the security of your families," Mr. Lopez announced. He named an amount. Everyone gasped, then, not to be outdone, offered to contribute to the largesse. In no time at all I was forgotten.

No sooner had Mrs. Wheatley announced that the ladies should retire to the parlor than Mr. Lopez came creeping toward me. "I would like to hear your poem," he said.

"Phillis will be reciting later," Mrs. Wheatley said.

The man wore yellow silk breeches and a turquoise frock coat, rings on his fingers. He smelled of lavender water.

A dandy, I thought. *A slave-trading dandy*.

He bowed ever so discreetly to my mistress, but he never took his eyes from me. "Could I not have a private recitation?"

Mrs. Wheatley raised her eyes in dismay and nearly embraced Nathaniel as he approached. "Mr. Lopez wants a private recitation from Phillis. I hardly think, Nathaniel . . ." Her voice trailed off.

"In view of Mr. Lopez's generosity to Reverends Occom and Whittaker, I don't see the difficulty. I'm sure Phillis wouldn't mind. We can step into the back parlor. What say you, Phillis?"

"Nathaniel, may I speak with you? In private?"

He sighed, sensing something. "Excuse us, Mr. Lopez. Our little poetess is having an attack of shyness."

Mr. Lopez bowed and smiled. "Charming," he said, "but she needn't be shy in front of me."

I had no notion to be charming. And it galled me, the way he looked at me with his beady eyes. I turned to him. "I'm not as much shy as I am distressed, sir," I told him. "I just realized earlier this evening that I lost my cowrie shell."

His thin eyebrows raised. "Your cowrie shell?"

"Yes. Surely *you* know what they are. The shell money of the slave trade."

Nathaniel pushed me toward the parlor.

"I was sold for seventy-two of them. But this one was especially important to me. It was given to me by my mother."

Nathaniel was pulling me now. The door of the back parlor closed behind us. "What's happened to you? Explain yourself."

"I thought Mr. Lopez would appreciate my loss, since he knows the true value of the shells."

Clearly he was distraught. "That man is a guest in our house!"

"He's a slave trader."

"Are we to ask you now who we may invite to our table?"

"He deals in human flesh, Nathaniel! He makes money from selling people. People like me!"

"He is also rich as a nabob and has considerable influence in the merchant community."

"Are you going to be his financial exchange agent? Is that why he's here?"

"I am not accustomed to answering to you about my business dealings, Phillis. But this time I will make an exception. The answer is no."

"Then why is he here?"

"Because Mr. Joseph Rotch of New Bedford, Boston, and London, for whom I *am* going to be a financial exchange agent, asked that he be here. Is that sufficient?"

"Yes, but I'll not recite for him."

"Phillis, if you don't care about me, think of my parents."

"They haven't asked me to do it. And I don't like the way he looks at me."

"How does he look at you?"

"Like . . . I'm a piece of merchandise."

Nathaniel smiled. "Well, I'm not selling you, Phillis. At least I wasn't planning on it. Until now."

That he could joke nettled me even more. "I have a headache. I can't recite for him."

"Oh, come now, Phillis! Don't give me that fashionable-white-girl fainting business. You're better than that."

"If white girls can do it, so can I. I must go upstairs and rest. Or I won't be able to recite for the others later. And that would upset your parents." I started for the door.

He stood in my path. "Don't run upstairs, if you know what's good for you."

"And what *is* good for me. Pray?"

He spoke quietly. "I know it's an unnecessary request. I know the man is pushy, bold, and hated by many. But if you don't humor him, he's likely to withdraw his goodwill from me and his gold shillings from the fund for the reverends' wives."

"Does his goodwill mean so much to you, then?"

"Mr. Rotch's does. And the money will mean much to the ministers' wives."

I hesitated. "It isn't just the way he looks at me, Nathaniel. He acts as if I'm a *thing*, an oddment, like a bear brought here by a sea captain and displayed on a chain on the wharf. I can't abide it."

"You had better learn to abide it." His voice gentled. "How much does your poetry mean to you?"

"You have to ask that?"

"Someone has to ask it of you. Think on it. My parents are speaking of getting it published."

"Published?" My hand went to my heart. How like Nathaniel to spring something like this on me now. The thought took my breath away.

"They are convinced, after reading your latest poem, that you are a genius. God help us."

"But I've only written two in a year."

"You will write more. And it takes time to publish. Mother wants to start working toward that end. Only they aren't sure yet if you can bear the responsibility. You will be expected to recite on demand, in front of all kinds of people who will likely look at you as an oddment. So you had best become accustomed to it. And I can think of no better way to start than with Mr. Lopez."

From beyond the door there were voices, laughter, music. But between me and Nathaniel was a universe of cold silence.

"What say you, Phillis? Do you have it in you to become the first published Negro poet in America?"

He knew how to work on me, all right. "Oh, Nathaniel," I whispered, "what an honor."

"Yes. But like every other honor, it has its price."

He held his hand out. "You may hate Mr. Lopez. But see the virtue in reciting, Phillis. You do this for your people."

I took his hand and went with him to recite for the slave trader.

Chapter Twenty-one

The last guest was seen out the door. Nathaniel and Mary had left with their friends. Mrs. Wheatley hugged me. "Thank you for the new poem," she said. "And for giving Mr. Lopez, that dreadful man, a private recitation."

"Phillis, we are going to try to get your poems published," her husband said.

I pretended surprise. I hugged them both.

"Wait a moment before you celebrate," Mr. Wheatley said. Laboriously, he sat down on a nearby chair. I propped his foot on a stool, with a silk cushion under it. He had the gout and was in great pain.

"Tell her, Mrs. Wheatley, what publication entails. It is not all punch and cookies."

"Phillis does not expect life to be all punch and

cookies, Mr. Wheatley," she returned. "Nevertheless, you are right. Come sit, Phillis, sit."

I sat.

She explained. "Getting one's poems published costs money. Oh, a printer might be persuaded, betimes, to absorb the costs, but usually that is only to print a goodly supply of broadsides that celebrate some important event. I am perfectly willing to bear the financial burden, dear."

"Tell her the rest of it," her husband urged.

My mistress took a deep breath. "Before we get a printer, we must expose you to the right people. In this case, the most influential lights of Boston. Governor Bernard should bear witness to a recitation of yours, of course. And," she went on placidly, "the lieutenant governor, Thomas Hutchinson; James Bowdoin; the Reverend Charles Chauncy; and other divines. John Hancock already heard you recite this evening. And was much taken with your talents."

I could not speak. It was all too much.

"Are you willing, Phillis?" Mr. Wheatley asked.

They were looking at me, waiting. I looked back into each of their faces. They were getting old, I minded. The gold threads of her hair were near hidden by the white now. His face was getting heavier. Lines showed that had not been there before. Why had I not noticed until now? Their faces, so genteel, so aristocratic, so *hopeful*, had been anchors of kindness and love for me since I had first come here.

My eyes filled with tears. "Yes," I said.

What could be worse than reciting in front of Aaron Lopez? If I could abide him, I could abide anybody.

Once more, Nathaniel had prepared me for what was to come. Once more, he had been right.

For the next two weeks I went out every afternoon with Mrs. Wheatley to call upon some luminary in Boston. Prince drove us through Boston's streets in the ice and snow.

Everyone in the family had given me something for the wardrobe in which I was to make my "appearances."

Mr. Wheatley gave me a blue cloak trimmed with ermine. Mrs. Wheatley had two new gowns made for me.

Nathaniel came home one day bearing a package wrapped in burlap. Inside were the finest pair of delicate yet warm boots I had ever seen.

Mary gave me her best muff, the one I had so often admired when she wore it to church of a Sunday.

Aunt Cumsee had sewn me a fine new pocket to wear around my waist. It was embroidered with the colors of summer.

I should have been happy, but I was not, as we set out the first day. Something was missing.

My cowrie shell. How I wished for it as we drove through a fine, needlelike snow that dusted the housetops and streets! We were to be received by Governor Bernard this afternoon. I was terrified.

As Prince drew the carriage up before the governor's mansion, servants came running to assist us out of the carriage. But Prince was there before them, helping me down. In his hand he had a small package.

"Wif permission, ma'am." And he bowed to Mrs. Wheatley. "I'd like to give somethin' to Phillis, too."

The governor's servants stood waiting. Mrs. Wheatley knew she could not object. "Of course," she said.

Prince and I had not had a decent conversation for months. He didn't loll around much when his chores were finished, for which Mrs. Wheatley was grateful.

He handed the small package to me. "Open it," he said.

Inside was a black velvet ribbon, the kind white girls wore around their necks, usually with a cameo in front.

On the front of mine was my cowrie shell. I gasped. "I lost it! Wherever did you find it?"

"You lost it in the yard. I had a hole bored in it so the ribbon could pass through."

I drew it out of the wrapping. "It's my cowrie shell," I explained to Mrs. Wheatley. "My mother gave it to me and I thought I'd lost it. May I put it on?"

"Of course, dear, but do hurry. We can't keep the governor waiting."

I tied it around my neck. "I'll wear it always," I said. Mrs. Wheatley took my hand and hurried me down the brick walk.

"My dear," Lieutenant Governor Thomas Hutchinson said the next day, when we were visiting his house, "your recitation was perfect. And the poem! I am much taken. Writing is a pastime of mine, you know. I have no talent at describing characters, but I took years to write my *History of Massachusetts Bay*. It was thrown into the gutter the night the mob destroyed my house in north Boston in sixty-five."

He had the bluest eyes I ever saw. "That would have been the Stamp Act mob, sir," I said.

"I see you know your history as well. They destroyed my home, my fruit trees; drank my wine, took my dead wife's jewelry. They ruined every book and paper I owned. We had to move here, to Unkity Hill in Milton."

"It's a lovely home, sir."

"Yes." He stood up and gestured to a far window. "On good days you can see Mount Wachusett. To the east my fields run down to the Neposet River. And there is a wonderful view of Boston Harbor."

I went to the window with him, looking toward the harbor. But all we could see was falling snow.

"Miss Grizzel, we'll have tea now." He turned to the elderly woman in lavender silk who sat doing needlework. She rang a bell cord for a servant.

"See what can be accomplished, Peggy, when one sets one's mind to a task?" He walked back across the room and touched the golden curls of his young daughter. She was his favorite, Mrs. Wheatley had told me. His other daughter, Sallie, was married.

"Billie," he said to his youngest son, "now you know why I would have you keep to your studies. Here we have a young woman who is a slave. Who had no formal education. And she writes like an angel. Would that you take example from her."

I winced at the word "slave." And for just a moment I felt like the bear on the wharf with the chain around its neck, again.

Then Hutchinson turned to speak to me, and his blue eyes were earnest and sincere. "My two older boys are already through Harvard, my dear, and I would be much gratified if either of them displayed an ounce of your talent."

I blushed and curtsied. The man meant every word that he said. Nathaniel called him Tommy-skin-and-bones. But I liked him. He was a Tory, yes, but he had suffered much. And he was gracious and debonair in spite of the hatred directed at him in Boston. There was something here worth pondering. If I ever got the time to ponder anything again.

I did not seem to have a moment to myself these days, to think, read, or study. I was constantly on display. It was wearying.

And it did not matter to Mrs. Wheatley whether we visited Whigs or Tories. Politics had naught to do with her plans for me.

Shamelessly, she pursued both.

On the way to and from our destinations she would have Prince halt the carriage in front of booksellers' shoppes. We visited the shoppe of James Rivington, that of Cox and Berry. And she had an inordinate fondness for newspaper editors.

"Oh, Mr. Boyles, we were just driving by and I wanted to see one of your esteemed new books. On these cold evenings I just love sitting by the fireside and reading."

We hadn't had an idle evening by the fireside in near a month. But Mr. Boyles, printer and bookseller on Marlborough Street who brought out the *News Letter*, was flattered, of course. In no time he had wiped his ink-stained hands, sent an apprentice for a tray of tea, and was listening avidly as my mistress expounded on the merits of my poetry.

Then around the corner to the *Boston Gazette and Country Journal*, owned by Mr. Edes and Mr. Gill.

All the newspaper editors rose from their desks to greet my mistress. All were friendly and encouraging to me.

"Smell the ink, Phillis," Mrs. Wheatley said to me as we walked into Thomas Fleet's *Evening Post* on Cornhill Street, late of a December afternoon. "Look at the press! They set words in print! And someday all of these newspapers will be printing your work. And all these booksellers carrying them."

It was a heady business for a young girl. I felt the strange excitement. Newspapers were powerful and far reaching. They had a voice. And one day soon, they would give me one.

I wrote another poem. On the near-tragic sea voyage of Messrs. Hussey and Coffin.

The day when I was to be given a voice was coming, sooner than I realized.

Chapter Twenty-two

DECEMBER 1767

My poem about Messrs. Hussey and Coffin was published that December, right before Christmas, in the *Newport Mercury*. Unbenownst to me, Mrs. Wheatley worked her magic and it was accepted.

On the morning the paper arrived in the post, they were all waiting for me at the breakfast table, smiling. When I entered the room they stood and applauded. Then from behind me I felt the others come in, Aunt Cumsee, Prince, even a scowling Sulie.

"What is it?" I felt myself blushing. "What's happened?"

Mrs. Wheatley came forward and embraced me. "Nothing has happened, Phillis, except perhaps the greatest moment of your life. Your poem has been published. Look." She held the paper up in front of me.

My eyes scanned the words. *My words*. "Oh," I said again and burst into tears. So taken was I with the sheer joy of the moment that I could not face any of them. I hid my face against Mrs. Wheatley's snow white shawl collar.

The breakfast was festive, with fresh fish, sugared ham, Bohea tea, and lemon cake made with fresh lemons that had just arrived on the Wheatleys' ship yesterday. Mr. Wheatley and Nathaniel raised their mugs of rum in a toast. Twice there came a knocking on the front door and Prince brought in written congratulations, delivered by messenger, from the Wheatleys' friends.

My head was spinning. I coughed. My head felt feverish.

"There will be no calls today," Mrs. Wheatley announced. "You shall sit by the fire and read and be spoiled."

"More than she is already?" Nathaniel asked good-naturedly. But before he left for his countinghouse he leaned over me and planted a cool kiss on my forehead. "Congratulations, Phillis. You have made Mother very happy."

The kiss was cool, impersonal, such as I'd seen Mary give her pet cat. Still, I luxuriated in it. And I felt its imprint on my forehead all morning.

But there was a price to pay. Even for that one poem.

I had the copy of the *Newport Mercury* in my hand. The house was quiet, except for sounds of pots and pans from the kitchen. It was the first opportunity I'd had to really study my words in the newspaper.

And then I saw the announcement that prefaced the poem.

> *Please to insert the following Lines, composed by a Negro Girl (belonging to one Mr. Wheatley of Boston) on the following Occasion, viz. Messrs. Hussey and Coffin, as undermentioned, belonging to Nantucket, being bound from thence to Boston, narrowly escaped being cast away on Cape Cod, in one of the late Storms; upon their Arrival, being at Mr. Wheatley's, and while at Dinner, told of their narrow Escape, this Negro Girl at the same Time 'tending Table, heard the Relation, from which she composed the following Verses.*

I gasped.

Mrs. Wheatley looked up from her reading. "What is it, Phillis? Are you unwell?"

"No, ma'am, I'm fine. It's just that it says here in the preface that I was tending the table when Messrs. Hussey and Coffin came to dinner and told us of their voyage."

"Yes, I know." She smiled.

"But I wasn't tending the table. I was at dinner with all of you. They have made a mistake."

"It's no mistake, Phillis." Again she smiled, then reached forward and patted my hand. "It's the only way the editors would abide to preface the poem."

"Ma'am?"

She sighed. "I wrote the preface myself, Phillis. I said you were at the table with us. The editors said they could not give such an account. That it would be unseemly. The only way they would publish the poem was if I allowed them to say you were *tending* the table. Do you understand?"

My throat constricted. "Yes, I see. It's the price."

"Now, now, Phillis, don't you fret about the cost of getting the poem published. I am happy to bear any financial burden to promote your career."

"Not that price, ma'am. The one Nathaniel told me about."

"Nathaniel? What has he been telling you? I won't have him worrying your head about what all this is costing us. Mr. Wheatley and I are honored to do it for you."

I sighed and settled down to concentrate on my words in the paper. "Nothing, ma'am. Nathaniel hasn't been telling me anything," I said.

Chapter Twenty-three

SUMMER 1770

I had gone downstairs for about the third time to fetch some freshly pressed garment to pack in my large trunk. On my way back to my room, I heard voices behind the door of my master and mistress's chamber.

I know it is not seemly to eavesdrop. But my mistress was saying words that I myself had been thinking.

"Why is it," she was asking her husband, "that all joy is trimmed with pain and all pain with joy?"

"I'm too tired for abstractions, dear. Explain yourself."

"It has been such a dreadful winter in Boston. Yet in spite of it all, there is hope. If the proposals in the *Boston Censor* bring enough subscribers, Phillis's first volume will soon be published."

"I would not count on that, dear. The *Censor* is a Tory sheet. Influential Patriots ignore it. I think it will not last in this political climate."

"Poetry is not political, John. Both Tories and Patriots have encouraged Phillis. They all applaud her."

"You have *pursued* both Tories and Patriots, Susanna. Soon you will have to sort your loyalties out with Phillis's poetry. As Nathaniel has sorted his out with his business ventures."

"I refuse to sort out my friends. And I trust them not to sort out me."

"And then there is the matter of race. A more pressing reason why I think there will not soon be a volume of poetry published."

"Race? Nonsense, John! Genius is genius. It has no need of status or nationality."

"Its promoters do. Especially have they need of money."

"What mean you, John? What have you heard? Tell me."

"Talk is being bandied about that no printer or publisher will bring out such a volume. That none truly believe a Negro girl wrote this poetry."

"Lies! They have all met Phillis. None have told me they do not credit her with the writing."

"They say one thing to you, my dear. But what

do they say to their subscribers? No, I am afraid that her poems must be brought out in London."

"London?" My mistress was unbelieving.

"Yes. You must set your course for London, dear girl. Even as Nathaniel is doing."

"Nathaniel is going to London?" She was incredulous. "Why?"

"He must develop our business interests there."

"When?"

"Not for a while yet, but he is going. You should think of sending Phillis with him. She will be well received there."

"London?" my mistress echoed. Her voice sounded so forlorn. "But, John, Phillis is an American."

"So is Benjamin Franklin. And he has been well received there."

"John, be serious."

"I am. I thought you said poetry had no nationality."

"Isn't it sad to think that her book won't be brought out here?"

"Sadness has naught to do with it. It is simply a matter of there being more than one way to skin a cat, my dear. The concept is absolutely American."

"London," my mistress said. "Perhaps I can write to the Countess of Huntingdon, Selina Hastings. She is part of the international Christian missionary circle that supports Moor's Indian Charity School. And John Thornton, the English millionaire philanthropist. He's part of that circle, too. What think you, John?"

"I say you are wonderfully American, dear. You know many ways to skin the cat. And I say we should get some sleep. We leave for Newport early in the morning."

London! With Nathaniel! I fair trembled with excitement.

But that was far off. Tomorrow we were going to Newport. I would see Obour! I had not seen her since the day we parted in the slave market.

There were many reasons for the trip. I had developed a cough last winter, 1770. It was Mary's last chance to have a "season" before she married her reverend next January. And Boston was in chaos.

Boston was always in chaos, of course, but this time matters were fraught with danger. Troops had occupied the town since September of '68, drilling, loitering, and being boisterous and troublesome. In February some of those troops had shot at Americans, killing five, one a nigra man. The troops had left in March, but the town was still up in arms about the upcoming trial. One could never tell when another fracas would ignite.

Besides, I had written three poems about the trouble. One on the arrival of the ships of war; another about the death, at Tory hands, of the street urchin

Chris Seider; and the third about the massacre. After all, it had taken place on the street where we lived.

I saw no reason not to. People were declaring themselves all over the place. Ministers were shouting from the pulpits God's words to Noah after the Flood: "Whosoever sheddeth man's blood, by man shall his blood be shed."

All this talk about shedding blood made Nathaniel nervous. It was bad for trade, he said. My poetry made him even more nervous. It was getting too inflammatory. I think he thought it, too, was bad for trade. Nathaniel, who had once complained that Parliament was bottling us up, decided to stay neutral. And said that his parents should get me out of town for the summer. So we were going.

"Eat your meat, Phillis," my mistress said.

But I could not eat. How could I, when but a stone's throw away was my dear friend, Obour?

There she was, in the kitchen of the elegant Tanner home. And there was I, at the table with them and my people in the dining room. I could see her, she could see me. But I was not permitted to talk with her. Especially not when she waited on the table.

I felt anguish and confusion. And anger at my mistress, yes, for not allowing me to go and throw my arms around Obour. And at myself, for not defying her.

I had to sit there and pretend interest while Mr. Tanner went on about Newport's wonders. And how the boats the inhabitants used on the Sound were called double-enders.

"After supper I'd like to offer my guests a sail in our own double-ender," he was saying. "The Sound is lovely at sunset."

"You must excuse Phillis," Mrs. Wheatley said. "I cannot permit her to go. She's had a cough. I fear the damp air."

A few moments later, when Obour brought another platter of ham to the table, she leaned over me and I felt something drop in my lap. When she moved on I looked down. It was a folded paper. A note! I watched her glide out of the room, head held high. Mr. Tanner was now talking about Block Island, thirty miles across the Sound, and how its coves once provided hiding places for Captain Kidd the pirate.

I waited in the Tanner library, as Obour's note had suggested. The others had all gone off for their sail. Impatiently, I paced, not even looking at the books. I stood in front of the great window, looking out at the water.

"I've finished my chores. Are you ready?"

She stood in the doorway. I ran to her. We embraced.

"I can't believe it's you." She touched my short,

curly hair, examined my gown. "My, you're fancy. And you've grown up."

"No," I said, drawing back to take her measure. "I'm still skinny and ugly, skin and bones. But you! Obour, you're a woman!"

She was tall, and rounded in all the right places. But more than that, she had an air of practiced calm I knew I never could have. "I'm older by a year, remember?" She laughed. "Come, let's get out of here."

"What is this place, Obour?"

We had run, hand in hand, shoes off, for about ten minutes along the coast, away from the Tanner house. Now we stood on the heights overlooking the harbor. If we turned, we could see the house in the distance, like a great ship rising out of the dunes. Candlelight already glowed in the windows.

In front of us was the Sound. Behind us, a massive stone tower at least thirty feet high, supported by columns, abandoned and overgrown with sea grasses and weeds.

"This is the old windmill. Been here for more than a hundred years. Nobody comes here anymore. I make it my private place. I come here to read. And think. Let me show you."

She took me inside. Here were sand and a mixture of wildflowers and weeds. In a corner were a blanket and an old chest. “I keep some books here,” she said. “I come here to read your letters. Look.”

She pointed. From a crack in the stone wall, you could see the Sound clear across to Block Island. “Do you have a private place?”

“No. Always I am in sight and sound of the Wheatleys.”

“I could tell that. She would never let you talk to me, would she?”

I blushed. “They’re good to me,” I said.

She nodded knowingly. “Tell me about Boston.”

“I’ve told you in all my letters. There are ten printers, eight booksellers, and many newspapers. All near our house.”

“Tell me of the soldiers and the fighting.”

“The soldiers have left. Driven out by the Patriots.”

“They’ll be back. The Patriots are spoiling for a fight. There will soon be one.”

“How do you know?”

“I read the papers. I hear Mr. Tanner talking. And others who come to this house. This is Rhode Island. You think you people in Boston own the anger at the Crown? We have royal schooners patrolling our coast. A year ago the Sons of Liberty rowed out to a customs raider and burned and scuttled her in our waters. Merchants and tradesmen are angry. There is a spirit of rebellion here. Political meetings all over.”

I listened, in awe. She knew things that mattered.

"We have the Free African Union Society here. Negros here are educated. Your own Prince belongs to it."

I gaped. "You *know* Prince?"

"Everyone in our society does. He and other Boston nigras are establishing a relief society for nigras who wish to take their freedom. He writes to us all the time."

"Prince? I didn't know he could write! Oh, Obour, I feel so humble of a sudden. Prince is doing something of worth for his fellowman. What have I ever done for anybody?"

"You can't do for others unless you do for yourself first," she said. "First you must get free."

"Prince isn't free."

"Says he's going to be when the fighting comes." She sighed. "I wonder how our race will fare when the war starts. We have a stake in it. Do they speak about drawing up your free papers?"

"No."

"My master has promised me freedom when I reach twenty-one. What about you? What's going to become of you when your master and mistress get old and die?"

"I haven't thought of it, Obour."

"You should. Are you laying aside for it?"

"Laying aside?"

"Money, silly. The king's shillings. Don't you get paid when a poem gets published?"

"No. Mrs. Wheatley has to bear the expense of publishing it."

She sighed. "So you're even more in her debt, then."

"I don't think on it that way, Obour."

"How do you think on it, then?"

"Someday soon I'm going to have a book of poems published. The first Negro in America ever to do so! And I'm going to London. With Nathaniel."

"This is all good," she said quietly, "but only because they allow it. By their leave you do these things. They're playing with you, Phillis. They're making something out of you that you can never be. A Negro woman poet."

"Why can't I? It's what I am."

"By their leave," she said again. "What will you do when they tire of you? You'll be cast aside. No woman gets published in America. Especially not a Negro woman."

"Nathaniel would never let me be cast aside."

"Tell me about this Nathaniel who won't let them cast you aside. You're besotted with him, aren't you?"

We were sitting on the blanket inside her tower. When I didn't answer, she smiled.

"I thought so. In all your letters, it was 'Nathaniel this' and 'Nathaniel that.' To what aim is this love of yours? He's the master's son, Phillis. No good can come of it."

"I don't expect anything to come of it, Obour. Good or otherwise."

"But you still love him."

"I can't help that. If not for Nathaniel I wouldn't have learned to *read*. I wouldn't have started writing."

"I read and write. And no Nathaniel brought me to it."

"You don't understand, Obour."

"You haven't let him play free with you, have you?"

"Don't be silly. He isn't even sensible of my feelings. And he's a man of honor."

"Honor, is it?"

"Yes." I met her gaze. "Please don't worry about me on that score, Obour. I will die before I ever let him know I harbor such feelings. And as for Mrs. Wheatley, she is doing so much for me. They love me. I'm like a daughter to them."

Silence inside the old stone walls. A seagull cried somewhere. It was getting on to dusk.

She stood up. She pulled me to my feet and put her arms around me. "I'm happy," she said, "and you have it in you to do much for our people. But hear me now, won't you?"

I nodded.

"When we were on the ship and your mother was

thrown overboard and you were sick, you wanted to die. I told you you must live. You said there was no reason."

"Yes."

"Then you rallied and ate. Do you recollect why?"

"Because you told me Captain Quinn would kill you if I died. I couldn't abide that."

She smiled. "I lied."

I drew back. "You jest."

"Captain Quinn never said such. I lied to give you a reason. Was I right? Isn't there good reason to live?"

Tears came to my eyes. "Yes."

"And I'm right now, too. There is a reason to be free. Think on it. Promise."

I hugged her. "I promise," I said.

Chapter Twenty-four

JANUARY 1771

"For a Scotsman, you surprise me, Mr. Mein," my master said.

The bald-headed John Mein, notorious publisher of the *Boston Chronicle*, was not offended. He turned from his great cherry desk in his office on King Street. "How so?"

"You had the courage to publish the names of those who were violating their own nonimportation agreement and importing from the British, yet you won't bring out a volume of poems by a Negro girl."

"I'm stupid," Mein said, "not crazy. And every time I feel another attack of courage coming on, I mind the pain in my shoulder for being beaten by the Liberty Boys. That's what publishing those names got me."

"I don't think you need fear the Liberty Boys if you bring out a book of Phillis's poetry."

"I fear my subscribers. I need three hundred signatures to bring such a book out. My subscribers will not agree that the poems were written by a Negro girl."

Silence in Mr. Mein's office, except for the sound of snow falling against the multipaned windows. It was the end of January. Mary had been married two weeks ago and, as he had promised, Mr. Wheatley had visited every publisher and printer in Boston, with me in tow, to try to convince them to bring out my first book of poetry.

At every place we stopped, the answer was the same.

No.

Their subscribers would not believe the poems were written by a Negro girl.

The *Boston Chronicle* was the last stop on our list.

"This is America," my master said. "Why are these Patriot publishers so fired up about things if they fear bringing out a book of poems by a Negro girl?"

"Don't ask me, I'm a Tory," Mein said, "and proud of it." He sipped his tea and gestured that we should partake of ours. "I thought your Captain Calef was engaging a London printer?"

"He did. Our merchantman dropped anchor only yesterday. Calef engaged one Archibald Bell. He's a little-known printer of religious works in London."

"Then you don't need me," Mein said.

"Bell sent word he will bring out the book only if we have some kind of written verification that Phillis wrote the poems," my master told him.

"In heaven's name, man, get the verification and go with a London publisher," Mein advised. "These are bad times in America."

He turned to me. His gaze narrowed on me like that of a hawk on a field mouse. "Did you write those poems, girl?"

I started in my chair. "Yes, sir," I said.

"You aren't lying? With all the talent of your race?"

"One moment, Mein!" Mr. Wheatley leaned forward.

Mr. Mein held up his hand. "Let her reply, John."

I saw a look pass between them. Then Mr. Wheatley sat back.

"I wrote them," I said. "You never doubted it when you published my elegy on Reverend Whitefield."

"It was published first elsewhere. Philadelphia, New York, Newport. I thought it only proper it be published here in Boston. Where you claim to have written it."

"I *claim* nothing, Mr. Mein. I did write it."

"Why should anyone believe you?"

"I don't lie, sir."

"Like Crispus Attucks, the mulatto killed in the massacre? Came into town claiming to be a crewman off a Nantucket whaler. When, in fact, he was brought here as an outside agitator and did more rioting than any man in Boston."

I felt anger pounding in my veins. "Attucks is a martyr," I said. "He's dead. You should let the dead rest in peace."

"There's a martyr on every street corner in Boston these days, willing to die for what he believes in. Every time I bring out another issue of the *Chronicle*, I'm a martyr. But I have no fancy to be tarred and feathered or have my presses destroyed for bringing out the poems of a little nigra girl. Especially one who is such a saucy little piece."

He sat back, spent by the speechifying. And pleased that he had given me my comeuppance.

"I've no intention to be rude, sir, but you did push me. And you hurt me grievous much."

"You listen to me, girl." He shook his finger at me. "How do you think you're going to get this written verification that you wrote the poems?"

"I don't know, I'm sure."

"Well, I'll tell you, then. You'll have to appear before some kind of examining body. And be questioned about this poetry of yours. And if you think what I just said hurt you grievous much, wait until you hear what *they* will say to you!"

He took up his teacup, drank, and smacked his lips.

I was trembling. I looked at my master.

His face was white, and from the way he was leaning forward, favoring one leg, I knew his gout was giving him trouble.

"I'm sorry, John," Mr. Mein said. "But you should tell your little protégée that when she does appear before this examining body, she should mind her tongue. And affect some Christian humility. Artists *need* humility, John. Their gifts are too great. They encourage envy."

My master nodded and stood. The meeting was over. They shook hands, and Mr. Wheatley helped me into my cloak and guided me outside to our carriage.

"Don't pay mind to him, Phillis," Mr. Wheatley said inside the carriage. "He's gone a little daft. He's turning his newspaper into a Tory propaganda sheet. The Patriots will soon run him out of town, you'll see."

"He was right, wasn't he, sir? About what I must expect from an examining body?"

He cleared his throat. "If he was right about anything, Phillis, it was about your gift being great." He patted my hand. "Your poetry will be published. Don't worry."

Chapter Twenty-five

MAY 1772

And so I come to sit in the garden of the governor's mansion, waiting to appear before the esteemed gentlemen who will decide if my poetry is, indeed, mine.

As I wait, I know I can do it. They may be the leading lights in Boston, these men, but I know I have the mettle to stand before them.

Until I think of what Mr. Mein said to me.

If you think what I just said hurt you grievous much, wait until you hear what they will say to you.

I trembled, waiting. The sun disappeared behind a cloud. Then I heard footsteps on the brick walk and turned to see Mr. Hancock approaching.

"Well, Phillis?" he asked, smiling down at me. "What have you decided?"

"I shall do it, sir," I said. "I am ready."

"Phillis, you know some of these people," Nathaniel said.

As I walked into the vast enchoing chamber, they all stood. Eighteen of them sitting before a long polished table, sipping tea. Dressed in silk breeches, some of them, wearing wigs. Others in the plain broadcloth of the ministry.

"Yes, sir." I curtsied.

Nathaniel said the names. And each man gave a little bow.

"Gentlemen, let's not keep Phillis waiting," Mr. Hancock said. "Phillis, you may sit if you wish."

I was given a chair. But I stood.

Reverend Cooper stood up. "Are you a Christian, Phillis?"

"Yes, Reverend. You were in attendance at my baptism. You recollect, don't you? It was done hastily, after services. Because I am nigra."

The good reverend blushed. So did some others. Not Nathaniel, though. He scowled at me.

I supposed I was being what Mr. Mein would call a "saucy little piece."

"Of course, I was just as glad it was done then, Reverend," I amended, "being as you wouldn't have been able to come if it had been done sooner. Since your own services at Brattle Street Church wouldn't have been over yet."

He nodded and sat back down.

Reverend Mather Byles was next. "You claim to know the classics, do you not?"

Well, now, never did I hear such tomfoolery! And from Reverend Byles! Who had so often been a guest in our home and who had, on several occasions, tutored me in the classics. I was about to ask him if he had taken leave of his senses when I again caught Nathaniel's eye.

"Yes, Reverend Byles," I answered demurely. "I have studied the classics."

"Who wrote the *Iliad*?" he asked.

"Homer."

He sat down, satisfied.

"Who is Terence?" And none other than Andrew Oliver, the lieutenant governor, stood now.

I had felt to this moment as if I could not breathe. Now, of course, I could. Very easily. Surely he knew who Terence was. These esteemed gentlemen, these foremost lights of Boston, were playing some kind of game here.

Very well, then, I would play along with them.

"Terence was a Roman author of comedies," I replied. "An African by birth, he had long been a slave. But he was freed by the fruits of his pen."

"Do you wish to be free, Phillis?" Governor Hutchinson himself questioned me now.

I drew in my breath. Every face in the room

was turned on me. My head buzzed. I looked at Hutchinson. I had been to his house. He had slaves. Likely so did all the others. Except Councilman Harrison Gray, who was what they called an abolitionist. He did not believe in slavery.

Again I glanced at Nathaniel. He seemed to be holding his breath. His face was about to turn blue.

"I would aspire to be free, yes," I said softly. "God has implanted the principle of freedom in every human breast. I have an abiding interest in freedom. But I should willingly submit to servitude to be free in Christ."

I could tell that Nathaniel was breathing again.

The men all looked at each other. There were murmurings and whisperings.

John Hancock stood. "Who is Phoebus, Phillis?"

"The Greek god of the sun. He is often called Phoebus Apollo."

"Why is it that you make such frequent references to him in your poetry?"

"Sir?"

"You make much of the sun, Phillis," Hancock said. "Why?"

Again I hesitated. Across the room, Nathaniel nodded.

"Because one memory I have of my mother is of her pouring water out of a stone jar, every morning, before the sun at its rising," I told them.

Silence. Several heads nodded.

Would they ask me now about my mother? My past? What would I do?

They did not. Reverend Moorhead stood up. "Who is your favorite poet, Phillis?" he asked in his Scotch accent.

"Alexander Pope," I said.

"Ah, yes, Pope." He shuffled some papers. "Dinna you not write a poem called 'To Maecenas'?"

"Yes, sir."

"Who is this Maecenas?"

Moorhead, you old Presbyterian, you well know, I thought. But I answered properlike. "A Roman statesman and patron of the arts who helped Horace and Virgil."

"Even as you have been helped, Phillis?"

"Yes, sir."

"Who, then, is your Maecenas? Canna you tell us, Phillis? For whom did you write this poem, lass?"

My mouth went dry. "If you ask who helped me, sir, there are many. From my mistress and master, who have been naught but kindness itself to me since the day I was brought here, to the Reverends Byles and Cooper, who, when they came to visit, counseled and advised me. And Master Nathaniel, of course, who first taught me to read."

"Is he your Maecenas, then? Canna you tell us?"

No, I canna, I minded. For I had written the poem to Nathaniel. But neither he nor they would ever know. I would take my secret to the grave with me. "Sir, my Maecenas is likely made up of bits and pieces of all these people."

Reverend Ebenezer Pemberton stood up. He was very fat and the effort of getting out of the chair caused considerable difficulty. His breath was spent. Thus he had earned the nickname Puffing Pem.

"In one of your poems, Phillis, you speak of certain people as being 'the offspring of six thousand years.' What mean you by that?"

I sighed. *This is all too easy, surely,* I minded. "James Ussher, archbishop of Armagh, born in 1581, figured from what he studied in the Bible, sir, that God created the world in 4004 B.C. That would be six thousand years before this year of 1772."

Puffing Pem smiled and sat down.

Now there were more murmurings, more whispers. Then they seemed to arrive at a decision.

It was John Hancock who stood to say that the meeting was over, and would I be pleased to wait outside in the hall?

I sat alone on the bench in the great hall, staring down at the marble floor, shivering. I admired the rich wallpaper above the wainscoting. I wondered who the expensively clad gentlemen and ladies were staring down at me from gold-framed paintings. *Whoever they are, they must be dead*, I decided.

They all looked like I felt. Lifeless.

I would have given anything for a hot cup of tea. A clock chimed somewhere in the great house. Then in a while it chimed again.

The door of the chamber opened. John Hancock came out.

"Phillis," he said, "you have done well. They are of a mind that the poetry is, indeed, yours."

He was grinning. He had such white, strong teeth. His handsome face, swooned over by so many women in Boston, was close to mine.

He took my hand in his own. "You have *won*, Phillis," he said. "You have won. For your race. There is no doubt now that the African species of man can create formal literature. And master the arts and sciences."

I felt tears in my throat. "I did well, then?"

"Well? They are fair to fainting from your responses. We are ready to draw up a paper saying the poetry is yours. We will all sign it. My signature shall be the largest. And written with the most flourish. I'll send Nathaniel out to sit with you."

And with that, John Hancock winked at me and went back to sign the paper saying my poetry was mine.

Chapter Twenty-six

We whose names are under-written, do assure the World, that the Poems specified in the following Page, were (as we verily believe) written by PHILLIS, a young Negro Girl, who was but a few years since, brought an uncultivated barbarian from Africa, and has ever since been, and now is, under the disadvantage of serving as a slave in a Family in this Town . . .

Signed, this seventh day of May, in the town of Boston, province of Massachusetts, in the year of our Lord, 1772.

Thomas Hutchinson, governor
Andrew Oliver, lieutenant governor
Councilmen Thomas Hubbard, John Erving,

James Pitts, Harrison Gray, James Bowdoin,
JOHN HANCOCK
Merchants Joseph Green, Richard Carey
Reverends Charles Chauncy, Mather Byles,
Ebenezer Pemberton, Andrew Eliot, Samuel Cooper,
Samuel Mather, John Moorhead,
Nathaniel Wheatley, signing for her master,
John Wheatley

"Those dear men. I am so gratified." Mrs. Wheatley dabbed at her eyes with a handkerchief.

"I'd be considerably more gratified if they hadn't taken on so about Phillis being a *slave*," Mary said angrily. "In heaven's name, what's wrong with Hancock? He knows we don't refer to our servants as slaves!"

It was late afternoon. Nathaniel and I had just returned from the governor's mansion with the signed paper in hand.

Nathaniel was triumphant. I was dazed. It had started to rain outside. Aunt Cumsee had just served tea. The paper was passed around and digested with the tarts Aunt Cumsee had taken from the beehive oven.

When it came into my hands, I could scarce believe it. There it was, the richest of vellum, with the blackest of ink. All those signatures saying my poetry was mine!

"Couldn't you have had some say about the *wording*, Nathaniel?" Mary asked. " *'Under the disadvantage of slavery'*? This paper must go to London! What will people think?"

I knew what I thought. That I would like to get up and throttle Mary, despite the fact that she was balancing four-month-old John Lathrop, Junior, on her knee and was already two months in circumstances with her next one.

Did she have no idea of what I had been made to endure this day? Could she have stood up to such questioning?

"We're wearying Phillis." Mrs. Wheatley got up, reached for a shawl, and put it around my shoulders. "We must think of her welfare. She isn't that strong."

"I'm fine, ma'am," I said.

"I still think that Nathaniel should have insisted on having the wording changed," Mary said. She was determined today, to give the devil his due.

"No matter, Mary," her mother said.

"That was not Nathaniel's duty," her father said. "He was acting in my stead. If not for this gouty foot I'd have been there myself. By heaven, I missed it! No! Nathaniel acted as I would have done. He acquitted himself well. Now I will hear no more of it."

The matter was finished.

"Nathaniel, fetch my Madeira. By heaven, I will have a toast!" My master set down his cup.

It was done. Nathaniel poured some for himself and his father, who held up his glass. Toasts were made.

They toasted the committee. Then John Hancock. Then Mrs. Wheatley. Finally, Mr. Wheatley held up his glass to me. "To Phillis," he said, "for you do us proud."

"Hear, hear," Nathaniel said.

"And now, I have an announcement." Mr. Wheatley still held forth his glass. "I am retiring. An advertisement saying such will appear in all the papers tomorrow. Nathaniel has done so well running things that I feel assured in leaving everything in his hands."

Everyone cheered.

"And another announcement. Within the year, Phillis will have to set sail for London. Mrs. Wheatley has been in correspondence with the Countess of Huntington, who will sponsor her there. She will travel under the protection of Nathaniel, on our own ship."

"Nathaniel is going to *London*?" Mary was full taken aback.

I almost felt sorry for her. Mary knew she would never go abroad.

"He must," her father said. "Our mercantile business has grown so that we must set up an office in England."

There was much kissing and hugging all around.

Nathaniel was congratulated by his father. His mother embraced him. Mary offered her cheek for a kiss.

"London!" Mary whispered snidely to me later in the hall as I held little John so she could put on her cloak. "Well, just remember who you are. Remember your place."

"How can I not," I returned, "when others are constantly speaking of it?"

She turned away. I could not dismiss her remark out of hand. It cut like a knife. But I was numb. Numb with joy. I was, after all, going to England. My work would come out in a book there. I was being sponsored by a countess.

But more than all else, I was going with Nathaniel.

Chapter Twenty-seven

In the next year it seemed that everyone of my own race felt it incumbent upon themselves to give me advice about my trip to London.

"Remember yourself," from Aunt Cumsee. "Don't hold him in higher esteem than he holds you. Or it will come to grief."

"Do not let Nathaniel dally with you," Obour wrote. "Remember to lay aside money from the earnings of your book. Do not garner expensive habits in London. And remember, they may be sending you to London, but they are still playing with you. Find some way to make a living for when they leave you to your own devices."

Sulie became outright hostile. I swear that woman lay awake nights thinking of ways to plague me.

She would serve me cold tea. Or make the water

extra hot and spill some on my hand while pouring it.

She would scorch a dress of mine when ironing it. Mrs. Wheatley had Aunt Cumsee take my measurements, so her own mantuamaker could fashion me a new wardrobe.

Sulie was to deliver them. She changed the measurements. Three new gowns, fancier than I'd ever possessed, made of silk with lace trim, had to be ripped apart and made over to remedy the matter.

Once she sent bad meat to my room on a tray. Mrs. Wheatley, realizing she could no longer trust Sulie, had Prince bring my food up to my room when I was working.

I was glad for it. I hadn't seen much of Prince of late.

"You happy, Phillis?" he asked me one day after he delivered my noon meal.

I assured him I was.

"Then how come you look like they gonna take you out an' shoot you at sunrise?"

I could never lie to Prince. "I was just pondering."

" 'Bout what?"

"Mrs. Wheatley wants some poems left out of the book."

He scowled and set the tray down. "Which poems?"

"The one I wrote on the death of Chris Seider.

And the one I wrote about the arrival of the British ships of war."

Prince had read all my poems. In secret. The family still didn't know he could read and write. But when I'd come back from Newport, after finding this out, I had managed to slip all my poems to him. "What about the one on the massacre?" he asked.

"That, too. She says they're too anti-British."

To my surprise, he didn't object. He commenced to pour my tea. "You want words from me on this?"

"Yes, Prince."

"Sure 'nuf, then, here's the way I see it. Seems to me they wouldn't be likin' those poems over there in England, those people with the red coats. And the mistress knows this. Plenty of time to get those poems published here in America. After."

"After what?"

"Plenty of time," was all he would say.

I nodded, waiting. Surely there would be more.

There was.

"You gotta think on the important things now."

I waited again.

"You know this Jonathan Williams they're out visitin' today?"

"Only as a neighbor."

"His uncle-in-law is a man named Benjamin Franklin, who is colonial agent for Pennsylvania over in London."

I felt something coming. I looked up into Prince's lean, dark face.

"Mrs. Wheatley, she wants to fix things so as you meet Mr. Franklin over there. Franklin has influence. Mr. Nathaniel, he isn't so fond of Franklin."

"Why?"

"He's from Philadelphia. A Quaker."

"I never heard Nathaniel speak ill of Quakers."

"Reason Mr. Nathaniel doesn't like him got nuthin' to do with religion."

"Why then?"

"Think on it, Phillis. It will come to you. You smart enough to go to London, you smart enough to figure it out."

Before he left the room, he paused. "If Benjamin Franklin calls on you over there, you see him, Phillis. Even if Mr. Nathaniel don't like it. Promise."

I promised. But for all the world, I did not know what pledge this was that I had given.

Two weeks later Scipio Moorhead, the Negro artist, was drawing my likeness in his studio. The Countess of Huntington, to whom my book would be dedicated, had written saying a likeness of me should appear in front of the book. Mrs. Wheatley had commissioned Scipio to do it.

"You be free in England. You know that, don't you?" Scipio did not mince words.

I sat at a desk in front of a large window in his studio. In a far corner of the room Scipio's wife, Sarah, was painting in lacquer on glass.

"How can that be?"

"Didn't they tell you? No, I suppose not."

"Tell me what? Don't play with me, Scipio. What is there that I should know?"

"Just what Lord Mansfield said a year ago in London."

"Who is Lord Mansfield?"

"A judge. You know. The kind what wears a long white wig, with all those curls? And black robes?"

"I know what a judge *wears*, Scipio. What did he *say* that has to do with my being free in London?"

"Scipio," Sarah warned, "you got this job from the Wheatleys. And we need the money. So don't go and ruin it."

"Hush, Sarah. What's the harm in telling Phillis what to expect in London?"

"The harm is that she'll go home and tell the Wheatleys. And they'll never commission you to do a sketch again. Or recommend you to their friends."

"Then Phillis won't *tell* the Wheatleys. Will you, Phillis?"

"I know when to keep a still tongue in my head."

So he told me then. "A year ago this British judge, Lord Mansfield, handed down a decision. And there it is, written plain as the nose on your face. 'As soon as a slave sets foot on the soil of the British islands, he becomes free.' "

I turned to look at him. "He never did."

"There you go turnin'. You know this is a profile, Phillis. Now you sit properlike."

"I'm sitting properlike."

"What happened is," he explained, "this Jamaican slave, name of James Somerset, was brought to England by his master. No sooner he gets there, he sues in court for his freedom. Judge Mansfield ponders on it and says, 'The air of England has long been too pure for a slave, an' every man is free who breathes it.' "

"Women, too?"

" 'Course."

"Then why didn't he say so?"

"You know how these judges like to talk in riddles. Makes them seem smarter than the rest of us. So you just remember, when you get to England, you breathe some of that pure air. And you get yourself free."

"But how will I do that, Scipio?"

"You just keep your mouth shut and your ears open. And sooner or later someone will tell you how. You'll see."

Chapter Twenty-eight

APRIL 1773

"So we're going to England, Phillis," Nathaniel said.

"Yes."

"Together. On the *London Packet.*"

"As your mother wishes."

"And you don't?"

"I want to go, but I'm afraid of ships."

"You have better things to fear. The ship is sound and smart. She's a three-masted schooner merchantman. I'm engaging a woman to travel with you. A Mrs. Chelsea from Boston. She's joining her husband in London. She brings two servants. I'm giving her an allowance of milk from the cow Mother is sending aboard. And fresh eggs from the chickens. In exchange for having one of her servants assist you. And for her companionship."

"Companionship?"

"Yes. You two and the servants will be the only women aboard. Because you will be the object of considerable attention, I expect you to spend most of your time in your cabin and behave with the utmost decorum at all times. People will be watching."

"How will they be watching me if I'm in my cabin?"

"It's a very commodious cabin, with everything you need."

"Will I have my own bed?"

"Of course, but it's called a bunk. You were on a ship before. Didn't they call it a bunk?"

"When the sea was calm, I had a small corner on deck. With a canvas over me."

"Yes, of course. Well, you will be permitted to stroll on the deck at certain times. If the sea is calm, you and Mrs. Chelsea will be invited to dine with me and the captain."

"And if it isn't calm? Where do I dine then?"

"If it isn't calm, you won't feel like dining."

"Oh."

"If anyone asks, you are traveling under my protection. You are not my servant. And you are not to behave like one. Neither are you to tag all over with me on the ship."

"Why should I want to do that?"

"Yes. Well, you'll have your work to do, going over the poems. And I have my work. I just thought

I'd make mention of these things. We have to keep matters seemly."

"Yes," I said, "seemly."

"We clear Boston Harbor on the eighth of May. The voyage will take five weeks. Captain Calef makes this trip often."

"Does he have a first mate?"

"Of course. Why do you ask?"

"I just wondered."

"We have a full hold, lumber from Vermont, cases of smoked salmon, crates of candles, stacks of woolen fabric, pelts of beaver, and at least fifty-eight pipes of rum. Don't look at me like that. I'm not engaged in the triangular slave trade. When we get to London, you will not enter into any discourse on politics. Or go about spouting any Patriot folderol. I have gone out of my way to remain neutral in the current unpleasantness. And I am about to expand our mercantile interests in England. Do you understand?"

"Yes, Nathaniel. I understand."

I lay in my bed, which I must remember to call a bunk, dying.

We were both dying, I and Mrs. Chelsea. It had been so for the whole first week at sea. I was more wretched than I ever recollected, though I was waited on hand and foot and covered with velvet and propped up against lace pillows.

The *London Packet* pitched and heaved. And I pitched and heaved with it. As did Mrs. Chelsea in her own bunk.

Her two servants, Susan and Passy, held porcelain bowls for us to vomit in, cleaned us, and attempted to spoon broth into our mouths.

I did not eat for four days. Dimly, I was mindful of Mrs. Chelsea on her feet, having recovered. Why didn't I?

Because I was plagued by my old cough, is why, the one that claimed me every winter, that gave Mrs. Wheatley a regular fixation of worry about me.

Now she was not here. And the cough raged. I got over my seasickness, but I developed a fever. Soon I was in delirium.

Mrs. Chelsea was young, blond, and possessed a sense of humor that served her in even the most dolorous situation. She could joke at her own seasickness. And once well, she took charge.

I was somewhat aware that she was having the cabin scoured all around me. But I did not care. I was too busy—not dying now, but trying to live and breathe without gasping for air.

I heard Nathaniel's voice. "Mother sent along this remedy. Just in case the cough came."

"Bless your mother," Mrs. Chelsea said. Then she pushed a spoonful of the familiar hateful stuff between my lips.

I swallowed and slept.

I awoke drenched with sweat, and coughing. Every cough sent drums through my head, like the ones held by the Negro drummers the British had once sent to Boston.

Was I in Boston? Where was I? The place was pitch dark, except for a small candle hanging overhead. It cast shadows. I heard fearful creakings. There was nothing solid under me.

I was on a ship.

Then I smelled vinegar. The crew had just washed the stench from below, yes. Where the slaves were shackled.

From the upper bunks came breathing. Was I belowdecks? Shackled? I moved. No, I was free. But where was Obour?

"Obour!" I yelled for her.

Someone was leaning over me.

"Do you want to be thrown to the sharks? Do you want to be flogged?"

It was Captain Quinn's voice.

Next thing I knew he was forcing food into my mouth and yelling, "Eat!"

I thrashed in my bunk. I pushed the spoon aside. "I want my mother!" I yelled. "Don't throw her overboard. She did nothing! Mother!"

"Bring the lantern closer," I heard a man's voice say. I knew the voice, but I could not name it.

"I want my friend Obour!" I yelled. "I will eat, and I will tell her to eat, if you leave us both unshackled. I promise!"

"Dear child," a soothing woman's voice said, "what have they done to you? What have you suffered? Nathaniel, you will not believe it, but I was in the room when she dressed. She has a brand on her hip!"

Nathaniel! No, she must not tell him that. I had told no one.

"Your friend is here," the woman said. And a cold cloth was laid on my forehead. "Your friend is here." I felt a hand in mine.

I clenched it and opened my eyes. The lantern glowed above me, held by one of the servant girls.

"Phillis? Are you all right, child?"

The voice and the hand belonged to Mrs. Chelsea.

And sure enough, the man hovering over me was not Quinn but Nathaniel. I struggled to sit up. They helped me.

"You must eat, Phillis," Nathaniel said. His brow was furrowed. He looked frightened. He took the bowl of soup from the serving girl and sat on the side of my bunk. "You must get well, or my mother will kill me."

I took a spoon of the broth. It was too salty. I pushed the spoon away.

"You must eat, Phillis," Nathaniel said sternly, "or you will never reach London alive."

"It's too salty."

"What would you like?" Mrs. Chelsea asked. "Tell me, and I'll see to it that you get it."

"I want pudding," I said of a sudden. "I'm hungry. We have a cow. And two goats. I want pudding. Like Aunt Cumsee makes."

Mrs. Chelsea looked up at Nathaniel. "Can you get me into the galley?"

"At this hour of night?" He was incredulous.

"Yes. I'm a good hand at cooking."

"All right." He stood up, took some paper from the desk, wrote a note, and gave it to one of the serving girls.

Mrs. Chelsea and the girl left.

The door closed after them. Nathaniel stood leaning against it. His face was as white as his ruffled shirt.

"Your mother was thrown overboard?" He could scarce say the words.

But I did not answer.

"Cover her," he said to the serving girl. "She must stay warm."

She did so.

"Please take some broth, Phillis," he begged.

I took some, to please him.

He nodded and backed out the door. But he never

took his eyes from my face. And his own face was ashen.

The sea calmed. Yet not so much that we languished without wind in our sails. Recovered, I spent about an hour a day on deck, getting some sunshine and exercise. Mrs. Chelsea accompanied me.

Sometimes Nathaniel did, too. And he was very solicitous. When we strolled on deck he took my arm, as he would that of a white woman.

"Shall I hold an umbrillo over you to protect you from the sun?" he asked one hot afternoon. Indeed, he had one in hand. And we both laughed at the significance of the word.

It seemed that he had forgotten all his stern admonitions to me from before we sailed. Or else my near dying had frightened him.

Or mayhap he felt guilty now that he was sensible of what had happened to my mother. At the captain's table he was especially courtly.

Still, I obeyed his rules. I did not tag after him on deck. I did not make a nuisance of myself. I let him seek me out.

As much as I disliked the voyage, my instincts told me that I should enjoy this time on the sea with Nathaniel, and the comfort our mutual history gave, so far away from home.

Once we got to London, I would lose him. My instincts told me that, too.

Chapter Twenty-nine

JUNE 1773

London!

The first morning I awoke in the rooms Nathaniel had rented in the Bath Hotel in Picadilly, I rushed to the large ceiling-to-floor windows and opened them to gaze down.

Never had I seen such color and excitement! The streets were wide and clean. The squares of green neatly stitched with colorful flowers. People rushed by intent on some important missions, as if life were moving too fast for them and they had to catch up. Never had I seen so many luxurious coaches!

"Phillis, you must dress." The maid came in, bearing a silver tray of breakfast. "You must eat."

I turned from the window. My room itself filled my eyes with awe. It was done in blue and gold, the carpets were soft, the mirrors large. Our rooms were really an apartment with a kitchen and parlor. Nathaniel had engaged a cook and kitchen maid as well. He had his own coach and footman.

The maid handed me a note from Nathaniel.

"I await your presence in the tearoom at one. We go first to Vauxhall Gardens, then to a festival of music by Handel. Work on your poems this morning. I have a business meeting. This afternoon, wear your pale green with the lace shawl collar."

The maid's name was Maria. She cared for my clothes, helped me dress, fussed with my hair. She was white and spoke with a slight cockney accent. In one day we became friends.

She was comely and rounded and always smiling. She and her sister were supporting their invalid mother. She knew London, the shoppes, the bookstores. "Ask your master to let me take you about," she said that first morning. "I know where to go to get the loveliest gowns. Especially if you are to be presented at Court. You must have a hoop, ruffled cuffs, and a lace cap with two white plumes. Also, pearl pins for your hair."

Every morning a note came from Nathaniel with my breakfast, telling me where we were expected that day and what to wear. After a week of begging, he finally let me go with Maria for new finery. At first it was difficult for him to allow me such friendliness with a maid, but then Maria told him about the proper dress for Court and he relented.

She took me, forthwith, to the mantuamaker's where her sister worked. And I was fitted for a gown of white silk with a train, for Court. Of course, we got the hoop for under the skirt. And the required lace cap with two white plumes and pearl pins for the hair.

I even purchased a straw hat for everyday wear. Maria said it was worn by ladies in Virginia.

"I was lady's maid for a while to Hannah Philippa, wife of William Lee. They're from Virginia. You should be glad you weren't sent there. I can tell you, they would not be buying you such frocks."

It was all she ever said about my being a slave. She never spoke of it again.

Satisfied with my purchases, Nathaniel then allowed Maria to take me out some afternoons, as long as we stayed in the neighborhood. There was much to see. Elegant shoppes displaying all kinds of frippery I had never seen at home. Bookstores and, of course, the park, where we would buy ices and sit and watch the people go by. Or I would sit and read while she did her needlework.

One day we heard a great fuss. Dogs barking, people gathering and shouting, soldiers on horseback.

"Is it a riot?" I asked Maria.

She smiled. "No. This is not Boston, this is London. We don't have riots. It's the Countess of Effingham, likely on her way to see the queen. See? There is her carriage."

All that fuss for a countess, I thought. *What must they do for the king and queen?*

We were expected everywhere, Nathaniel and I.

At the pleasure gardens at the end of the city. At musicals. At Westminster Abbey. At the theater to see *Othello* and *Macbeth.*

At the home of Lady Cavendish for a wonderful supper. At the Royal Observatory at Greenwich. At a Bach concert at Covent Garden. At the Hill Street home of Baron George Lyttelton, a distinguished English statesman and man of letters who was ailing.

Lyttelton sat the whole time in a large wing chair while we and his wife and other guests sat at the table. He could not leave the chair. But afterward, he bade me come sit beside him. And in a voice weakened by some terrible sickness, he told me that I was "God's little poetess."

It brought tears to my eyes. Nobody had ever put it in such a light before.

"Where do you go this afternoon?" Maria said, leaning over me to set a lace mobcap on my head.

"The Tower of London. Nathaniel is taking me. I can't wait to see it."

She shrugged. Like most Londoners, she had never been inside the Tower. "Just a pile of old rocks," she said.

"How can you say that? Anne Boleyn was imprisoned there."

"People make their own towers," she said.

In three weeks we had come to know each other well enough to have exchanges of conversation I would never dare to have with a serving girl at home. Maria knew a lot, though she'd had no formal schooling. She had a whole set of opinions and quirks all her own.

"What do you mean by that?" I asked her.

She smiled in that secretive way of hers. "We build walls around ourselves. We imprison ourselves with longings."

I fell silent.

"Your master is handsome," she said then.

"Yes."

"And very much in demand."

Nathaniel was very busy of late. He had joined the Royal Exchange. And the Haberdashers, an influential guild. He had made friends with Stephen Sayre, an American merchant; the Earl of Chatham; and Lord Dartmouth, who was a stepbrother of Lord North.

"It's no wonder that Mary Enderby is making a fool of herself over him," Maria said.

My ears perked up. Mary Enderby? I had heard the name. "Who is she?" I tried to keep all feeling from my voice.

"Oh, the Enderbys are one of London's foremost merchant families. And Mary is their only daughter. Your master has business with the family. He spends many mornings there. Didn't he ever tell you?"

I did not ask how she knew. "Of course," I said.

It turned out that Maria knew more than she let on. Was she preparing me?

That morning Nathaniel's note disappointed me.

> *I find I cannot accompany you to the Tower this day. You must find your own amusements. You have been looking peaked of late. I suggest you stay inside and rest. We have supper tonight at the home of Lord Lincoln.*

The bright July day stretched before me. Then, about midmorning, the Reverend Granville Sharp came to call. Nathaniel summoned me to his apartment.

"Reverend Sharp wants to take you to see the Tower." Nathaniel's voice and manner were distant. He did not offer Sharp any refreshment. I immediately sensed some dislike on his part for the man. Did he want me to say no?

"I would wait until you can take me if you so wish, Nathaniel," I said.

"No, no, go, by all means. I find I'm busier than I thought. Maria will accompany you."

Indeed. His maid and butler were laying out a lunch of cold chicken, fresh fruit, and champagne. "I am expecting guests," he said.

He did not look me in the eye when he said it.

So, then. He had broken his promise to me for these guests. I did not have to ask who they were. I knew in my bones that one of them would be Mary Enderby.

All the while, the noodleheaded woman setting the snare for him had been here in England, not in America.

There was no way I could say no to Sharp, of course. I felt Nathaniel wanted to be rid of me. I ran to tell Maria we were going to the Tower.

Sharp took us not only to the Tower of London but to the place they called the zoo, where they kept lions and panthers and tigers.

I shivered in fear, standing with Maria so close to these fierce beasts, with only iron bars to separate us. At home in Senegal we had wild beasts. But we kept them at bay. My father hunted them. We did not bring them close and cage them behind bars.

"What do you think? Aren't they beautiful?" Sharp asked.

"Yes," I said, "but I feel sorry for them. They should be free."

It was not until we were returning to the Bath Hotel in his carriage that he asked me, "Do they know of me in America, my dear?"

"We have heard your name," I said. "For some reason I cannot recollect."

He smiled. "Three years ago I raised a fuss. I ridiculed the Americans for claiming rights to liberty when they keep thousands upon thousands of Negroes enslaved. No better than those lions and tigers we just saw, whom you wished free."

I felt uncomfortable that we should be having this conversation in front of Maria. Then I saw she was asleep.

"I am considered a dissenting clergyman," Sharp said. "I took issue with none other than your Benjamin Franklin on the subject."

One thing about these Britishers. I might be Negro and a slave, but they all considered me American. He was *my* Benjamin Franklin. "And what does my Franklin say on the matter, then?"

"He said we have no right to raise a finger at Americans while we enslave our own laboring poor. Have you met Franklin yet, my dear?"

"No, I have not had the honor."

He smiled. "At first he would not come out in public and condemn slavery as a moral evil. Then, last spring, Anthony Benezet, leader of the abolitionists in America, wrote to Franklin of the horrors Negroes endured on the passage from Africa to America. Franklin immediately sent a letter to our *Chronicle* and attacked slavery as an outrage against humanity."

I had the feeling this was more than idle conversation meant to fill in the gaps on the long ride back to my hotel. And the zoo had been more than just a place to see the animals.

And I knew now why Nathaniel did not like him.

Chapter Thirty

JULY 1773

"There is a small group of people here in London," Nathaniel's note read, "who support us in our troubles against the Crown. We dine at their home this evening. Lord Dartmouth will be there. Wear your best."

Our troubles against the Crown? I smiled and put the note in the sleeve of my morning gown so Maria would not see it. Nathaniel walked a fine line between the American Patriots and the Crown. He cozied up to both sides. All merchants had to do this or perish, he said.

I could have argued the point with him. I knew that some merchants in America had taken sides. But I was at peace with myself and the world this morning, this first week in July.

Two days ago Nathaniel had sent a present to my

room, wrapped in black velvet. It was a ring with my initials, P. W., on it.

"You can use it to imprint the sealing wax on your letters," the note said.

He had purchased it at a jeweler's near Fleet Street. I had not yet seen him to thank him properly. I would do so tonight.

To add to my gratification of spirit, this morning's edition of the *London Chronicle* carried a poem of mine, "A Farewell to America."

I'd written it before I left. Mrs. Wheatley must have sent it on the very next ship bound for London after we departed.

For the third time since I'd sat myself down to sip my morning chocolate, Maria had brought flowers into the room.

Flowers from Benjamin Franklin, who said he would soon call.

From the Countess of Huntington, along with a note saying my poems were even now being printed into book form. "I am seventy-one years old this summer," she wrote. "I look forward to welcoming you and your guardian to Trevacca, the Methodist missionary school I support here on Talgarth, my estate in South Wales."

Flowers from Lord Dartmouth. He also sent five guineas: "Purchase, in my behalf, the whole set of

Pope's works," he wrote. "Until this evening, I remain—your servant."

This was heady stuff for a skinny nigra girl the color of ashes, with next to nothing for a bosom and a brand saying she belonged to Timothy Fitch on her hip.

On my bed was a new gown of lemon yellow muslin. And this evening I was to be the guest of honor at a supper. Nathaniel would escort me. I had not been out with him of an evening in over a week. He had been busy. Political dinners.

In London, women did not go to political dinners.

I fingered the ring on my hand, sipped my chocolate, and for the tenth time, let my eyes linger on my poem in the paper.

My life was complete.

Nathaniel was late coming home from the Royal Exchange, so he sent a note around. His carriage would take me to the home of Reverend Richard Price, another dissenting minister. Lord Dartmouth would be there.

Lord Dartmouth, who "had the best disposition toward the colonies; who wished, sincerely, for their welfare," as Nathaniel had described him, was there himself, waiting for me at the door. He escorted me inside.

"I have been asked by my friend Nathaniel Wheatley, who has been delayed, to introduce America's first Negro poetess," Lord Dartmouth said. "Ladies and gentlemen, the honor is all mine. I present Phillis Wheatley, whose poem you all read in the *Chronicle* this morning."

The party was held in the good reverend's garden, behind the house. Lanterns were strung from trees. Flowers scented the air. The elegant ladies and genteel men clapped. I stood on the walk next to Lord Dartmouth and made my curtsy.

My muslin gown billowed around me. Overhead the stars twinkled. From somewhere in the scented darkness a violin played. Handel. Perfect. Glasses tinkled. Delicious food was being set down on flower-bedecked tables.

Dissenting ministers here live grander than Congregationalist ministers at home, I minded.

I thought my heart would burst with joy as Lord Dartmouth escorted me around and introduced me to everyone. My head swam with their compliments.

One elderly lady with sparkling eyes and white hair piled high on her head reached out a bejeweled hand. "My dear, we have a mutual acquaintance. I understand my brother dined at your house in Boston."

"So many people have," I said.

"Surely you must know him. Your guardian,

Nathaniel Wheatley, acts as foreign exchange agent for him. His name is Aaron Lopez."

My smile froze on my face.

"Your brother?" I asked stupidly. "Aaron Lopez?"

"Yes, he is a Newport merchant well known in the colonies."

"I met him." My ears were buzzing. I felt light in the head. "You say Nathaniel is his agent?"

"Yes, dear. Nathaniel handles all his affairs here in England. Imagine that we should meet like this." Her smile was fixed. I saw it as a glaring death's head.

I wanted to hit her in the face.

Nathaniel? Agent for Lopez? The slave trader?

For a moment I thought I would be sick. I felt a cold sweat break out on my forehead. My hands went icy, my thoughts jumbled. My head went addled. I could think of nothing to say. It was as if someone had moved the very ground under me.

At that moment he appeared. Nathaniel. He came through the flowered archway at the end of the garden, from the side street. One by one people recognized him.

"Here he is now," Lord Dartmouth said. "Thought you'd never arrive, old chap. What's detained you? Or shouldn't we ask?"

Everyone laughed. Then they applauded.

They applauded Lord Dartmouth's remark. And they applauded the woman on Nathaniel's arm.

She was the most beautiful creature I had ever seen. She was a vision. And at the same time, she was a nightmare.

Her gown was lavender silk, barely clinging to her shoulders. It molded itself to her body contours, then splashed out in folds of swishing silk and lace. Her hair was spun gold. The curls spilled down, barely contained by the elaborate fixtures placed in her hair to hold them up.

Around her neck she wore pearls. Her arms were white and slender and shapely.

Her bosom almost spilled out of the front of her gown, sculptured to perfection.

I thought I would die from shame. At my own dark skin, my spindle arms, my short hair, which no lace mobcap could hide, my scrawny neck and flat bosom.

My face flamed in shame. I shrank back from Lord Dartmouth's side. Thank goodness, he did not notice. Nobody noticed.

Once Mary Enderby came into the room, how could anyone pay mind to anyone else? She was the sun arrived on a wintry day. Everyone knew her. Everyone spoke to her. And Nathaniel never once released her from his arm. He had eyes for no one but her.

I no longer existed. I did not want to exist. I wanted to run away and die.

This was no mean feat, in a garden full of people.

But I managed part of it. I just slipped backward, step by step, into the darkness. It was not difficult.

After all, I had come from darkness, hadn't I? I would return to it now. And welcome it.

I slipped back, past servants carrying trays of food. Then I turned and ran around the house to the front gate, where Nathaniel's carriage waited.

"Take me home," I told Nathaniel's startled footman.

"What's that you say?"

"I said take me home. I'm ill. Master Nathaniel requests it. Now."

All the way home, I gazed out of the carriage window at London's dark streets. And the voice I heard was from another July day so long ago.

It was the voice of John Avery in the auction yard. *Meanest cargo I ever saw.*

He was right, I decided. What ever made me think he wasn't right? I was part of the meanest cargo he ever saw and nothing could make me any different, not learning to read and write, not my poetry, not anything.

What they require of you in this world, if you are a woman, is that you be beautiful. That you have a bosom and wear silks and have hair touched with gold. This is all the men want. Poetry means naught to them. It is nothing.

As am I.

Chapter Thirty-one

"I tried to tell you," Maria said, holding a vinegar-soaked cloth on my throbbing head, "didn't I? Didn't I tell you how we imprison ourselves with longings?"

"Go away," I sobbed.

"You get a fever and Master Nathaniel will throw me out into the street. I don't care much about *you*, but me mum needs the shillings I bring home." She said it with mock severity.

"Open the windows. I need some air."

She went to do my bidding. Then the hour struck in sonorous tones from some cathedral clock. Midnight. I heard the rumble of carriages on the cobblestone street.

"Do those carriages never stop?"

"Londoners come home at all hours," she said, coming back to dip the cloth in vinegar again. "What they don't do is leave when the festivities are in their honor."

"Take that filthy cloth away! I hate the smell of vinegar."

She obeyed.

I sat up. "What am I going to *do*?"

"About what?"

"Nathaniel. You should have *seen* him with that woman. How can I face him?"

"Have you had any supper?"

"Is that all you can think about? Food?"

"Me mum says food helps even in the most dolorous situation. I'll send to the kitchen for a tray."

She had given me a powder for my head and I lay back against the pillows and dozed. Images paraded before my eyes. Aaron Lopez's sister and her death's-head smile. Lord Dartmouth's snide remark to Nathaniel. The compliments I'd received from so many on my poetry.

Faces leered. I heard cackling laughs.

I saw Nathaniel. My Nathaniel, as he'd moved across the room with that woman on his arm. I knew what the expression on his face meant. *Look at me, everyone, I've done this. I've caught the fancy of this lovely lady.*

It was the same expression he'd worn the day he'd told his parents I could read. And countless other times.

I knew his walk, the look in his eyes. I could read those eyes. I knew by the set of his shoulders what he was thinking.

I ought to. How many times had he walked across my heart? His voice was part of me, directing, coaxing, scolding, cajoling, teasing, encouraging, pushing me when I stopped.

Now all that was finished. I wanted to die. *I belong in the Tower of London*, I minded. *Buried behind those damp, slimy rocks. I might as well be. There is nothing left for me now.*

The clock chimed one. It was a knell, drawing me awake. Moonlight flooded the room. Maria sat dozing. Her eyes flew open. "I brought a cold supper, but I didn't want to wake you."

"Tea," I said. My mouth was parched.

Thankfully, she had it, a pot still hot. "I never tasted anything so good in my life," I said.

"You Americans do love your tea."

"I'm a slave, Maria."

"You're still American. I'd give the world to be."

"Maria," I said. "I've decided I must go home. There is nothing else for me now. Will you come with me?"

At that moment the door of my room opened and Nathaniel stood there. "Why in God's name is it so dark in here? I heard you two talking. Light candles."

Maria jumped up to do so.

"Now get out," he ordered.

She fled.

"You have disgraced me!"

I stared up at him. He looked like a madman. He had flung aside his tricorn hat and was now taking off his frock coat and loosening his stock. "Who do you think you are?"

"No one, apparently."

"Don't give me that drivel. You may get away with those scenes in Boston, but they don't tolerate them here in London. London received you, you little fool! These people, my friends, opened their arms to you! Made a place for you! This supper tonight was given by people who support the colonies! They saw you as a product of what those colonies, given the liberty they so desire, can do!"

I got up. I slipped off the bed and stood facing him, toe to toe. "What do you care about the colonies? You cozy up to both sides!"

"That is good business."

"Oh, and I suppose it's good business to act as foreign agent for a slave trader, too!"

His eyes darkened with a fearful blackness. "What mean you by that?"

"Aaron Lopez. You seem to forget his sister was there tonight. 'We have a mutual acquaintance,' she said to me. How *can* you! How can you act as foreign agent for that flesh dealer? And then stand here and upbraid me!"

I burst into tears. He could not abide my crying. It was a dreadful sound, he had said on more than one occasion when Mary had tormented me.

Now he made no move to console me. He just stood there, taking my measure, preparing his next onslaught.

"Phillis, there is nothing for it. You have disgraced me tonight." He said it plain. His voice had a deadness to it.

I stopped crying.

"But, more, you have disgraced my mother, who did so much for you. Who worked so hard to mold you into what you have become."

"What have I become?"

"You know better than I. Don't fish for compliments. You'll get none from me this night."

"I'm nothing," I flung at him. "I'm a Negro slave. My skin is dark. I'm skinny and ugly. My hair is like wire. People pay me mind right now because I'm an amusement for them. And they are all bored, these Londoners, looking for more amusements every night."

"You dishonor them. They think much of you and your poetry."

"They think so much that they ceased to know I

existed the minute your Mary Enderby came into the room!"

I saw the understanding light his eyes then. "So that's what brought all this about, is it? Mary Enderby?"

I kept a still tongue in my head.

He eyed me, perplexed. "Phillis, what is it that you want me to do for you?" he asked plaintively. "I have done all for you that I can. But it is beyond my power to make you look like Mary Enderby."

"Who wants to look like *her*?" I asked. "She looks like a doxy on the street, her and her lavender gown!" I walked to the open windows. I needed some air.

In two steps he strode across the space that separated us, grabbed my arm, and whirled me around. There was pure hatred in his eyes.

"Phillis, I swear to you, all that keeps me from striking you at the moment is that I promised my mother when I was a child that I would never strike a servant."

Then he released me and walked to the door.

But he had struck me. Couldn't he see? I reeled under his words.

"A servant?" I yelled it at him. "I'm still a servant to you?"

He turned. "You always will be, until you learn not to act like one," he said.

I stood open mouthed, reaching for a reply, something to hurt him. No, to mend things. I could think of nothing.

"Mind this, Phillis," he said sadly. "Mary wanted to personally compliment you tonight on your poetry. She couldn't wait to meet you. She wanted to tell you how she'd give anything to be able to do what you do."

A great heaving sadness surged inside me. *Oh, Nathaniel,* I wanted to say. *Oh, please*. But I could not get the words out.

"For the remainder of our stay here, I shall find someone to escort you around," he said quietly. "There are many dependable scholarly souls who would be glad to do so. I shall be busy with my business dealings anyway. Except for the visit to her ladyship the countess. I'm afraid we can't beg off that engagement. We'll muddle through it somehow."

I wiped my face with my hand. "Nathaniel, don't you recollect what you told me once a long time ago? *Omnia vincit amor, et nos cedamus amori*. Love conquers all things. Let us yield to love."

"No, Phillis, I'm sorry. It won't work anymore. There are some things love cannot conquer. This night you have made me grievous sore. And undone yourself."

"I'll make my apologies to your friends for leaving. Can't you tell them I was ill?"

"No, Phillis," he said again. "It's what you said about Mary that can't be remedied. You see, this night I became betrothed. Mary and I are to wed. In November."

Chapter Thirty-two

For the next two days I did not see Nathaniel at all. I moped in my chamber; I went over some last-minute changes in poems sent to me by the printer for that purpose. I turned down two invitations. And I cried.

Two or three times I heard his footsteps in the hall as he passed my door on his way out. Once those footsteps paused and I held my breath. But there was no knock. He went on. I ran to the window to see him getting into his carriage and then being driven away. To some assignation with Mary Enderby, I supposed.

Likely, I would have perished if Benjamin Franklin hadn't come to call the day after that. It was dismal and raining. All of London seemed to be weeping for me.

Midmorning, Maria brought a note from Nathaniel

summoning me to his apartment. My heart pounded. *He has forgiven me.* I rushed down the hall and knocked on his door.

His footman ushered me down another hall to Nathaniel's bedroom and study.

He was in a dressing gown, writing at a desk in front of the hearth, where a low fire burned. He did not look up.

"Mr. Franklin has come to call on you. He is in my parlor. I wish you to extend my regrets."

Something was amiss. Benjamin Franklin was colonial agent for Pennsylvania and a very important personage. He was in demand in all the high-placed salons, at political gatherings, and at country estates on weekends.

"You mean you haven't received him?"

"No. Surely you can negotiate that now, can't you?"

He had not forgiven me, then.

"But—"

"Yes?"

"What will he think?"

"Mr. Franklin will think what he wishes to think. Thus far, not George the Third, Parliament, nor Lord North have been able to influence him. I certainly can't expect to with my meager talents."

"For you not to come with me is a slight to me. But more so to him, Nathaniel."

"I hardly think it will affect the constitutional relationship of the colonies to the mother country," he said. Then he bent his head to his work.

I left the room hearing Prince's voice. *If Benjamin Franklin calls on you over there, you see him, Phillis. Even if Mr. Nathaniel doesn't like it. Promise.*

Mr. Franklin stood as I entered Nathaniel's parlor. He smiled as I curtsied, and he took my hand and kissed it.

"The little black poetess," he said.

"You honor me with your visit, sir."

"And where is your protector?"

"He begs your forgiveness, sir. But he is tied up with matters of business."

He sat down heavily. "Americans always are. In England I am deemed too much an American. And in America too much an Englishman. I sometimes think I belong nowhere."

"I can appreciate the feeling, sir."

He took my measure. "I can only ponder on your dilemma. Toasted here in London, and at home in bondage."

"My people are good to me, sir."

"So am I good to my slaves."

I was pouring his tea and near dropped his cup. "*You* have slaves?"

"Yes. Though my wife cares for them as if they were her own children. And she has helped me become uneasy about holding them in bondage. She visited a school for Negroes in Philadelphia and sent one of our servants to the school. He is doing admirably."

I nodded.

"Slavery is senseless," he went on. "It drains the economy more than it replenishes it. However, I came late to condemning it as a moral evil."

"You attacked it as an outrage against humanity in the *Chronicle*," I said.

"Ah, someone has seen to the finer points of your education. Always mention something flattering about a visitor."

"I need not flatter you, Mr. Franklin."

He nodded and sipped his tea.

Now I heard Scipio's voice. *When you get to England, you breathe some of that pure air. And you get yourself free. Sooner or later someone will tell you how. You'll see.*

That person was sitting here now in front of me.

Prince had all but told me when he said Nathaniel did not like Franklin. Scipio had all but told me in his tale of the slave Somerset.

I held my breath and waited. I made small talk. "Do you miss America?" I asked.

"I have violent longings for home, which I cannot subdue but by promising myself a return next spring or fall."

"But you have many good friends here."

"Yet I am fearful that some infirmity of age may attack me before I get the opportunity to return home."

A quiet moment passed between us. He smiled and my spirit quickened to some gentleness in him, some benevolent concern.

"I love the English summer," he went on. "Parliament has adjourned and left me free to wander. I spend long weekends on country estates. Lord Dartmouth invites me often. He is a good man and sincerely wishes a true understanding with the colonies. But he does not seem to have strength equal to his wishes."

"Nor do any of us," I said.

He set his teacup down. "What do you wish, child?"

Tears came to my eyes. "To be free," I said.

He was not surprised. "Do you know that you are free here in England? By virtue of simply setting foot on its soil?"

"Is that what you have come to tell me?"

"I felt it my bounded duty. I speak of Judge Mansfield's decision."

"I have heard tell of it."

"Who told you?"

"A Negro friend back in Boston. But I would not know how to secure this freedom. I am dependent upon Master Nathaniel. I cannot move a step to the right or the left except by his leave and under his protection."

"Fetch me paper and quill," he said.

I did so, quickly. There had been a whispered urgency in his voice.

Quickly he scratched something on paper, folded and handed it to me. "This is the address of my house on Craven Street. I board there, but Mrs. Stevenson allows me to think of it as my own. If . . ." He paused. ". . . *When* you are ready to announce to your master that you wish to take your freedom, send a note around to me. Mrs. Stevenson will always receive you and attend to you if I am away."

I took the folded paper and thanked him.

"I have a niece, Sally, living with me. She is from the English side of my family and nineteen. And I have seen to the education of my grandson, William. He is twelve. He goes to school in Kensington. I shall be happy to avail myself to you in any way that I can."

"Oh, thank you, sir!"

He got up and waved away my thanks. "I come late to speaking out against the evils of slavery," he said.

Then he was gone.

Sooner or later someone will tell you how, I heard Scipio say, *you'll see.*

"Is that what you truly want, Phillis? Are you sure of it, then?" Nathaniel's face was ashen as he turned from his desk to look up at me.

"Yes," I said.

Sighing heavily, he tossed aside the letter he was reading and for one long and dreadful moment said nothing.

I waited, expecting the ax to fall. It had taken me full two weeks to approach him and tell him I had decided to take the freedom that was mine simply for the taking. Those two weeks were not without anguish.

It seems I hadn't slept in all that time, but lain awake listening to the carriages rumbling along on the street outside. I had much to ponder.

Nor had I taken sufficient nourishment. Maria had threatened to tell Nathaniel I wasn't finishing my meals.

"Clear the air for me, Phillis," he said, sounding bored. "Are you telling me you wish to stay here? And not return home? To my parents who have done so much for you?"

"I have pondered it," I said.

"And?"

"The thought of not seeing them again has sore afflicted me. I would have you write and ask them to free me when I return home."

"And? If they refuse? Then you will stay here? And consider yourself free? Simply by virtue of breathing the pure air of England?"

His sarcasm cut me. I said nothing.

"So, then, this letter of mine carries not only a request. But a threat."

"No threat is intended, Nathaniel."

"Well, well." He gave a short laugh. "The little black poetess has been doing more than receiving accolades here in London. She has been plotting, is that it?"

"I have not been plotting, Nathaniel. Just thinking."

"Not alone, though, I take it. Surely someone has been tutoring you in your rights. Do you care to tell me who that someone was?"

I bowed my head and kept my silence.

"It was Franklin, wasn't it? I smelled a rat the day he came to call. Damned upstart Franklin. He does more harm than good. Disgusting old man. Isn't he content with meddling in politics? And bringing us to the brink of separation with the Crown? Must he meddle in personal lives, too?"

I raised my head. "Nathaniel, I knew about Judge Mansfield's Somerset decision before I came to England," I said softly.

His eyes narrowed. "Yes, but Franklin must have cleared the path for you. What has he done, offered you asylum?"

I shook my head no.

"Don't flummox me. What would you do if I gave you leave to go this day? Where would you go?"

I felt a shiver of fear. "This day?"

"Ah. Not prepared for that, are you? Freedom is a juicy morsel to contemplate. But it makes for meager fare on the plate and cannot sustain you."

"I would make my way," I said with dignity.

"There's no profit in pride, Phillis." He got up and began to pace. "You can't eat it when you're starving. It will not warm you when the winds blow cold."

"I can live from the proceeds of my poetry. You always said I would someday be free by the fruits of my pen."

"I see." He went to look out the window. "You can live from your poetry here. But not at home. They will still not accept you at home."

"I shall manage."

"In Boston as a free woman, you'll not be wearing any fancy frocks such as the one you have on now."

"I seek things more suitable to the immortal mind."

"How laudable. I have underestimated you. You pretend to be amiable and demure, but you are an independent, ungrateful little baggage."

I said nothing.

"Why do I get the feeling you are doing this to punish me because I am marrying Mary Enderby?"

I faced his back. "You do underestimate me, Nathaniel."

He turned from the window. "Regardless of your reasons, it will come to ill, this freedom of yours. Mark this day that I have said it. You play with fire. You and the colonies."

"The colonies?" I gaped. "You liken me to the colonies?"

"Yes."

"All thirteen? Or just one?"

"Don't be saucy. You think I haven't minded all the metaphors of iron chains in your poetry? And wanton tyranny? Boston is a hotbed of sedition. Living there has addled your brain."

"My brain has never been clearer, Nathaniel."

"Yes, well then, you will understand when I say that I cannot predict the outcome of this freedom with the colonies. But I can with you. It will be the death of you, Phillis. Your ruination."

I felt a knell in my bones.

"Nevertheless, it is my place neither to give it nor to refuse it. It is the place of my parents."

"Then you will write in my behalf?"

"I shall pen Father a letter this day and mail it. Or would you prefer to take it to him yourself when you sail on the twenty-sixth?"

I gasped. "We're leaving? But we haven't seen the countess yet. And I am to be presented to the king and queen as soon as the Court of Saint James reopens with the new season."

"You are leaving, not I." He sat down and began to write.

I felt something ominous in the air.

He finished with a flourish. "George the Third and Queen Charlotte will have to muddle through somehow without meeting you. My mother is ailing. I had a letter on the seventeenth. She requests you home. Unless you wish to stay until my father sends your free papers. In that case you will not see my mother again. I strongly suspect that she is dying."

Chapter Thirty-three

SEPTEMBER 1773

I knew something was wrong when Prince did not meet me at Long Wharf in Boston. The Wheatley carriage was there, all right, looking old and in need of repair in comparison to the fancy gold-trimmed coaches I'd seen in London.

But no Prince.

A nigra man met me. Name of Bristol.

"Sulie's husband," he told me.

"I didn't know Sulie had wed."

He smiled at me. *Why*, I thought, *he's all puffed up with himself.*

"Lots of things you doan know. Been away awhile, haven't you?"

"Four and a half months."

"Things change in that time."

I did not like him. He knew things that I didn't.

And he acted superior about it. "Where is Prince?" I asked him as he commenced to pull away from the wharf.

Everything was wrong. For one thing, Boston looked smaller. What had happened to it? For another, I had a sense of dread.

"Prince gone."

"Where?"

He shrugged. "Been messin' wif those Sons of Liberty. Gone." It was all he would tell me.

Sulie opened the door. "So you's home. Good thing, too. I'm tired."

The house seemed seedy and in need of a good cleaning. Where was Aunt Cumsee? I looked around. No one made a move to take my bags. I had to carry them upstairs myself.

My mistress lay in bed, looking wan. She held her arms out to me. "Phillis, child, come to me."

I ran to her and knelt down beside the bed. She smelled of sickness. I noticed a stain on the front of her bed gown. Never would she have allowed such in the past.

"Where's Aunt Cumsee?" I asked.

"Oh, Phillis, we were both taken with the fever at the same time. She's so old, you know. We had to send her to her sister's. We have only Sulie now. She and Bristol run things."

"They aren't doing a very good job of it, from what I can see."

"Hush, dear, they're doing their best. Now, tell me all about London."

That night, as a cold September rain slashed outside the dining room windows, I left Mrs. Wheatley sleeping and went belowstairs to seek out my master. In the pocket I wore around my waist was the letter Nathaniel had penned asking for my freedom.

But I had something to attend to first. I stood in the kitchen. "There's no more wood for the mistress's fire."

Sulie was spooning some soup into a bowl. "Then get some. Or did you forget? It sits right outside the door there." She turned to face me.

So, then, I minded, *this is how it is to be.* But I would not chide her. She was waiting for me to do that. She had been waiting a long time to put me in my place.

I just stared at her stonily.

"Oh, I forgot." She cocked her head and put one hand on her hip. "You was supposed to see the king and queen. Well, we can't have you fetchin' wood now, can we? Wouldn't be seemly. Then suppose you bring this to the master in the liberry. And I'll get the wood."

I put the soup on a tray, sliced some bread and cheese, and fetched a glass of Madeira. I found Mr. Wheatley at his desk before a meager fire, scribbling by the light of a lone candle.

"Phillis!"

I set down the tray.

He got up and hugged me. Then he wept.

I comforted him. The sight of him weeping like that undid me. He looked so different, so old. His hair was thin and white; there were sagging lines under his eyes. His hands shook.

"You find me not at my best. My gout has been plaguing me. How was your voyage? Won't you sit and sup with me?"

"You sup in here?"

"Sulie says why bother with the dining room when I eat alone anyway? It saves lighting the hearth in there."

"Sir, forgive my asking, but are we suffering a shortage of funds?"

"Of course not!"

"Then why do I find you and my mistress in such mean circumstances?"

"We're as we always were, Phillis. Mayhap your sojourn in London has made your blood too rich for our simple tastes. Speaking of which"—and he took a sip of the soup—"go fetch a bowl and sup with me. There are more important things we must discuss."

"Things are not good," he said, after inquiring after my health and telling me how proud and happy I had made them. "Governor Hutchinson is walking around saying that any union between the colonies is pretty well broken. And I'm afraid it is true. The nonimportation agreement turned us against each other. New Yorkers call Boston the common sewer of America. The *Boston Gazette* describes Rhode Island as filthy, nasty, and dirty."

He would talk politics. And I must listen.

"The king now pays the judges himself. No more are they receiving their salaries from the General Court of Massachusetts. So they now act without regard to the wishes of our local officials."

"Sir, have you become a Whig, then?"

"I? No, Phillis. The Whigs are scattered. People are tired of riots and rabble in the streets. But now we hear that in order to save the East India Tea Company from bankruptcy, the Crown is giving it the monopoly on the American market. We must now buy only what tea is sent to us. No more smuggling in Dutch tea. The merchants are terrified. Suppose the Crown does this with Madeira? Or shoes?"

"Where do your sympathies fall, then?"

"With Englishmen of liberty everywhere," he said solemnly, "here and abroad."

It was a vague answer, I thought, from a vague man. He did not seem to know what he was about. He seemed confused. Yet he pored over notes and newspapers on his desk as if he were Benjamin Franklin.

We talked for a while. He inquired after Nathaniel. I felt the letter in my pocket. Before I had a chance to speak, he smiled at me. "Ah, Phillis, it's so good to have you home. We need you here. Now things will get back to the way they used to be."

"Yes, sir," I said weakly.

Then he said he must get back to work.

"What are you doing?" I asked.

He smiled at me triumphantly. "I am proposing myself as a consignee to sell the tea when it arrives from England. Only certain shoppekeepers are being selected to sell it. And will make the profit."

"But you said the merchants are terrified of this tea."

"Yes, but everyone trusts me, you see. I had a respected merchant house for years. We can't allow the Hutchinsons to be selected. And they are putting themselves forth for the job."

" 'We'?"

"We're all giving the Hutchinsons a run for their money. I, John Hancock, Will Molineaux, and John Rowe." He went back to his scribbling.

"But you have no more shoppe," I reminded him.

"I'll sell the tea from my front parlor if I must." He winked at me. "Nathaniel isn't the only merchant in the family. There's life in this old boy yet. I'll show him."

So that was it. He had nothing to do with himself; Nathaniel had taken everything over. My master had no more life's work. He sat in this dimly lighted house with his wife sickly upstairs, pushed around by Sulie, lonely, ailing, and confused by the changing world around him.

"Sir," I asked, "where is Prince?"

"Prince?" He considered the matter for a moment. "He's taken up with the Patriots in Newport. While you were away he made a trip there and became involved in luring a royal schooner into shallow water, then boarding and burning her. I couldn't have that, Phillis, not with my son a London merchant. I gave him his freedom and let him go."

"You freed Prince?"

"Why, yes. I had to. Loyalists were after his hide. I could not have him connected with this house."

I felt for the letter in my pocket.

"And he'll come to no good. There are some people who just don't know what to do with this freedom. He'll end up on the end of a rope. Mark what I say."

Chapter Thirty-four

I did not give him Nathaniel's letter. I could not do it in the face of the trust those two dear people had in me.

I tore it up.

There was too much to be done now for me to concern myself with freedom. Freedom, for white people, was there in the air they breathed the day the good Lord first gave them breath.

Freedom, for a nigra, was something you got when your master and mistress were finished with you.

The Wheatleys were not finished with me yet.

For the next three weeks I settled in to making things right in the house. I cooked special delicacies for my mistress. I bathed her and kept her in fresh bed linens. Nobody asked me to. I just did it.

One golden afternoon the third week of September, I was rushing home from a visit to Aunt Cumsee, across town at her sister Cary May's house. My spirit was sore. My head ached. It had taken every bit of mettle I had to hide my sadness from Aunt Cumsee.

That woman might be in the last throes of life, already talking to the angels, but she could still read my thoughts.

"How did you leave Nathaniel?" she'd asked.

"Parting sore afflicted us," I lied.

Her breath was shallow. "So he dallied with you, then."

"Of course not!"

"Sweet talk is all it was."

"He never sweet-talked me. Don't you remember how we used to fight?"

"Sweet talk has different voices. Does he know you're smitten?"

"Aunt Cumsee, I'm not smitten. Never was. And he doesn't know. I'd die before I'd tell him."

"Find yourself another, child. You're only a slave to him. Chattel."

"I don't want anyone, Aunt Cumsee. I don't need anyone."

"There's that nice John Peters who has the greengrocer stall at North End Market. He saves the best oranges for Cary May all the time. Said he could get us tea even though they don't let the fool ships unload when they come."

Her words echoed in my mind as I hurried through the September dusk. Of a sudden, a gang of young urchins came running toward me on King Street. We near collided. And a bunch of broadsides they were carrying fell to the ground.

"Oh," I said. "I'm sorry."

One especially ragged urchin handed me a broadside. "Take one home to your mistress," he said. "We gotta post the others." And off he ran.

I stared after him. I hadn't seen urchins running together like that since the time of the massacre. Then I noticed at least three groups of men gathered on corners, engaged in lively discourse.

At the same time I minded the smell of pine-knot torches and heard some names. Molineaux. Adams. Hancock. There was a tremor of excitement in the dusk. It passed through the air like Benjamin Franklin's electricity.

Boston is enlivened again, I thought. *For the first time since the massacre.* I hurried along. The town watch passed me, crying something about a meeting at Faneuil Hall. *I must pay mind,* I decided. *I must not let my own concerns blind me to what is happening.*

But my own concerns did blind me. There was no help for it.

A few days later my book came out in London.

The only reason I became sensible of it was because Mr. Bell wrote to Mr. Wheatley and enclosed advertisements for it from three London newspapers.

The day we received that intelligence, I'd spent the morning making a chicken broth for my mistress.

Sulie had not given me an even time of it in the kitchen. She considered it her domain, though she allowed me to work there if it lessened her duties.

I heard Mr. Wheatley come through the front door and go into his library. *He'll want some cold meat and cider*, I thought. Then, after a moment, I heard the library door open and he called my name. I hurried, wiping my hands on my apron. A sense of foreboding went before me, along with my shadow.

"Your book has been published, Phillis."

"Oh." I put my hands over my mouth in disbelief.

"You will soon be receiving three hundred copies." But he was not smiling.

Something was wrong.

"There is a matter of grave importance that has been brought before me." He cleared his throat. "Do you know what these are?" He was holding some papers up before me.

"No, sir."

"Reviews of your work, Phillis. They are most complimentary. At least a dozen newspapers and periodicals took note of your book. Here, let me read you part of one review."

He commenced reading. " 'Youth, innocence, and piety, united with genius, have not yet been able to restore her to the condition and character with which she was invested by the Great Author of her being.' "

He looked at me, waiting.

"I do not understand, sir."

"Well, then, mayhap you will understand this one. 'We are much concerned to find that this ingenious young woman is yet a slave. The people of Boston boast themselves chiefly on their principles of liberty. One such act as the purchase of her freedom would, in our opinion, have done more honor than hanging a thousand trees with ribbons and emblems.' "

He set down the papers and sighed. "Do you understand now, Phillis?"

"Yes, sir."

"They chide us for keeping you in bondage."

I said nothing. Was he angry?

"Do you wish to be free, Phillis?"

I could not speak. My heart was hammering so that I had to put my hand on my bosom. I felt weak.

He drew forth some paper, a jar of ink, and his quill. He commenced writing.

For several moments all that could be heard was the scratching of the quill on the paper. Then he signed it and sprinkled some sand on it, folded it, and held it out to me.

I could not move.

"It is not that we do not have honor, Phillis. It is that we considered you as our own. And not as a slave."

I nodded mutely.

"Do you know what I have just done?"

"No, sir."

"I have hung a thousand trees with ribbons."

"Oh, sir," I said.

"Take the paper, Phillis. Tomorrow I shall register it with the courts. You may hold it close for tonight."

I stepped forth and took it.

He got up. "I must go and pay a visit to my wife. You have been taking good care of her, Phillis. I hope you will stay with us. At least as long as my wife lives. Now that you are free, I hope you will not feel the need to leave."

"I will stay," I murmured.

He patted my shoulder and went out of the room and up the stairs. I minded his shuffled gait. He was old.

I stood alone in the room, clutching the paper against me. I was free!

Why did I feel no joy? Why did I only feel pain? Still, I must tell someone. I ran into the kitchen.

"I'm free," I told Sulie. "The master freed me." I showed her the paper.

She was turning a roast on the spit. She glanced at the paper. "Well, now, so what do it do for you?"

"I'm *free,*" I said.

She laughed. "Tha's nice. You is still black as me. Ain't gonna make no difference. But you always was one for fancy notions. You'll learn someday. Inna meantime, if it ain't too much to ask, could you get some taters from the larder? We still gots to eat."

She was right, though I'd die before I told her.

Free made no difference in my life. Nothing changed. No one took note of it. Mr. Wheatley registered my free papers with the General Court. All that meant was that he had to give fifty pounds to the town treasurer to ensure I would not become a public charge.

My life went on much the same except for the excitement over the arrival of the tea ships in late November. Mr. Wheatley was not one of the consignees and he was beset by that. To mollify himself he joined the citizens' night watch, which served to guard the tea ships so that the tea wouldn't be unloaded. It also served to beset his wife.

Her health was no better. But for an hour each day I got her out of bed and sat her in front of the fire in her room.

"An old man," she fretted one day, just as I'd gotten her settled in her chair, "out there in the cold. Has my husband gone daft?"

"He must do something," I told her. "He wants to still be part of the merchant community. It makes him feel useful."

She allowed that I was right.

I did not tell her the citizens were now armed. And that post riders had spread word to neighboring towns that the tea must not be landed.

My concern was that we would no longer be able to get tea. And she loved her Bohea tea. It seemed to restore her. What would I do? Our supply was dwindling fast.

In mid-December, when the wind howled around the house and the darkness descended early, the Patriots in Boston did their work. Hundreds of them disguised as Indians boarded the tea ships at Griffin's Wharf under cover of darkness and threw crates of tea into Boston Harbor.

Some held that it was a foolish move. Others celebrated. I didn't know what to think. The common folk were making themselves heard again. But to what end? What would be the profit?

I'm common folk. What's the profit in my freedom? Nothing has changed. I am still skinny and black. Sulie still mocks me, has more to say about how things are done around here than I do, and never lets me forget it. I cannot make my mistress well.

Yes, my book came out in London. But did Nathaniel write and say he was proud of me? No. Mr. Bell wrote. All about how my friends were having parties to celebrate. But this was not London. Here people scarce took note. All they could talk of was the fool tea.

I knew what my friends in London would say about that. *What harm would it do to pay the threepence a pound tax on the tea?* they would say. *It is cheap enough. Parliament has reduced the price from twenty shillings a pound to ten. You Americans don't know how precious good we're being to you.*

As far as I could see, the only thing to come from this tea party was that we would no longer have tea.

I made our supply last as long as I could. Mr. Wheatley preferred chocolate. And I drank it, too. But Sulie had an inordinate fondness for tea, so I hid our last tin from her.

Sulie had an inordinate fondness for many things, I minded. She sent Bristol to the North End Market every day. And if he did not bring back the best cut of meat, the fanciest imported chocolate, she sent him back again. It seemed they were always asking the master for money and complaining about prices. Several times when I came upon them at their evening meal, I was taken with the lavishness of their board.

Well, I had enough to mind with the tea. I made our supply last until the beginning of January.

Then two things happened.

Three hundred copies of my book were shipped to me from London. And that nice John Peters, the greengrocer who had the stall at North End Market, came knocking at our door.

Chapter Thirty-five

JANUARY 1774

The day was bitter cold. Snow was falling. I was returning from the office of the *Boston Gazette and Country Journal*. They were going to publish my poem on the death of the Reverend John Moorhead, Scipio's master. I had taken up my poetry writing again, though I had not much time for it.

"What's this?" Sulie stood in the kitchen, waving a wooden spoon at the crate.

In the middle of the floor was a large wooden crate. It was addressed to me. I threw off my cloak. "It's my books! Arrived from London."

"Well, get 'em outa my kitchen. Now."

"I can't move the crate. Where's Bristol?"

"He's got better things to do. Master's got friends comin' for supper. An' I got enuf to do without worryin' 'bout trippin' over that box. Move 'em or I'll set 'em out in the snow myself."

At that moment the door knocker sounded. I opened it. A nigra man stood there, grinning at me. He had the whitest teeth I had ever seen. And his eyes were kind. I wasn't above noticing the broadness of his shoulders, either.

"Yes?" I asked.

"You Phillis Wheatley?"

"I am."

He pulled off his hat. "I'm John Peters," he said. And he handed me a package.

I took it and invited him in. Gingerly he stepped over the threshold. "I couldn't help hearing"—and he gave Sulie a quizzical glance—"I'll move the crate if you like. Just tell me where to put it."

"Oh, I couldn't prevail on you," I said.

Sulie laughed. "Prevail on him. Just get it outa here. Hello, John. You ain't never delivered any groceries for me."

"Hello, Sulie. This is different."

"Why?"

"Cary May sent me."

Sulie *hmph*ed.

Peters gave me a little bow. "I'm honored," he said, picking up the crate, "just to be handling the books of the famous Phillis Wheatley."

For a moment I stared. Then I came to life. "Bring them right in here," I said. And I led him into the back parlor.

He set the books down, then took a knife from his pocket and pried open the crate.

There they were. My books. My name on them. Handsomely bound.

John Peters picked one up, opened it. "Your likeness," he said.

"Yes."

He stood up, book in hand, and walked over to the window for more light. He read. Then he looked at me. "You know what they call you in the street?"

"No."

"The little Ethiopian poetess."

"I didn't mind that they called me anything."

"Oh yes. We should celebrate."

" 'We'?"

He smiled and there were those even white teeth again. And that gleam in his eye. At once familiar and sassy. His hair was short and kinky. His face was round and strong. "You got someone else to celebrate with?"

"No."

"I feel as if I know you. I do know you. Heard enough about you from Cary May."

"You're the one who gave her the fresh oranges for Aunt Cumsee."

"Yes, and she sent me with the package."

"Oh! The package! I forgot. How rude of me." I set down my book and grabbed up the package, opened it, and exclaimed, "Tea! Oh, tea." I opened the lid and sniffed. "Good Bohea. Oh, thank you. My mistress will love it. But where did you get it?" I was babbling and he knew it. He was watching me with a warm gaze, taking my measure.

"I have my connections. And I can get more for your mistress. Also"—he lowered his voice and crossed the room to close the door—"you should tell Mr. Wheatley to have the groceries delivered directly to the house. And let you pay for them."

I did not take his meaning. "Why?"

He gestured his head toward the door. "She's cheating him."

"How do you know?"

"It's my business to know."

"But who would deliver them?" I asked.

He grinned. "Me."

"Will your master permit it?"

"I've got no master, Miss Ethiopian poetess," he said. "I'm free."

And so it was that that nice John Peters came to our house three times a week with the groceries. And Mr. Wheatley, on hearing my reasoning, gave me the responsibility of ordering them and paying.

Sulie rebelled, of course. But there was naught she could do. Mr. Wheatley might be old and addled, but he could conjure up his old firmness when the occasion warranted.

John came of an evening, after he closed his stall. One cold night in February when he delivered our vittles, I was distracted. I spilled hot cider while pouring some for him in the kitchen. I overpaid him.

"Things weigh heavy on your mind," he said as he put two shillings back in my palm.

I flushed. "My mistress is getting worse. And then there are the books. I must sell them myself, if I am to make a living. And I don't know how."

"Then why not ask someone who does?"

"You?"

"I sell things all the time."

"Books aren't sides of bacon."

"It's the same thing. You have a product the public wants, you must get the product out where the public sees it."

I was less than enamored, having him compare my books to three hundred sides of bacon, but I listened.

"I know Mr. Cox of Cox and Berry. Likely he'll take ten volumes. What do they sell for?"

"Mr. Bell sold them for two shillings in London."

"Ask three shillings fourpence."

My eyes went wide. "That much?"

"You'll get it. People have money to spend now. Wait for the war and they won't."

"What war?"

There was that insolent grin again. "The war that Sam Adams and the rest of the Sons are pushing for. Where you been keeping yourself, Miss Ethiopian poetess? Don't you know what's going on out there? The Crown is angered about the tea. There's talk Boston has to pay for it. You think they will? I heard there's five hundred barrels of gunpowder stored in Boston and Charlestown right now."

"Talk," I said. "There will be no war."

"The House of Representatives is going to impeach Chief Justice Peter Oliver for high crimes and misdemeanors against the people of Massachusetts Bay."

"You know a grievous lot for a grocer."

"People talk when they buy; I listen. Some of them work in the houses of important men. What plans do you have for the rest of your books?"

"None."

"What friends do you have outside of Boston?"

I thought for a moment. "Obour Tanner in Newport."

He pondered. "There are about twelve nigras who can read in that town. Anybody else?"

"Reverend Occom in New London, Connecticut. And Reverend Sam Hopkins in Princeton, New Jersey. But he hates poetry."

"Isn't he the one who's raising funds to educate two African slaves?"

"Yes."

"Write to him. He is soon going to develop an inordinate fondness for poetry."

"How so?"

"He needs your name."

"My name?"

"Yes"—and he grinned again. "You were a slave. Look what you accomplished with some education. Write to him."

"You playin' wif fire, cozyin' up to him."

I turned from the back door, having just let John out.

Sulie stood there in the shadows. I felt a shiver. And it was not from the cold draft of February air the door had let in. "If you have anything to say, Sulie, say it plain."

"I gots nuthin' to say to you. You wouldn't listen anyways, Miss Fancy."

"Say it! Or keep a silent tongue in your head."

She poured herself some cider. "All right. I'll say it. He's a ne'er-do-well. A bounder."

"How dare you?"

"Full of charm. Especially wif the women. But there's nuthin' behind it."

"He's hardworking. And he has intelligence."

She sipped her cider. She drained the mug dry, then set it down and sashayed away. "Knew you wouldn't listen. Only warnin' you, though doan know why I should. You'll learn."

Then she was gone. I stood in the empty kitchen. The fire flickered low on the hearth. *She's jealous because John has such charm,* I thought. *And Bristol is so morose. And she's still angry because we found out she was cheating Mr. Wheatley.*

Chapter Thirty-six

MARCH 1774

Aunt Cumsee died the last week in February, and my mistress on the third of March.

Two women, one nigra and one white, whose voices were part of me, whose hands had comforted, soothed, and taught. One a pine-knot torch and the other a scented beeswax candle against the darkness of my ignorance and fear. Both gone.

Where? I believed in Aunt Cumsee's Jesus and in Mrs. Wheatley's God of Deliverance, but I was hard put to say how either one of these ladies was now occupying her time. Unless Jesus had a side of mutton that needed turning on the spit. And God had any little nigra girls running around who must be taken in hand.

How could people be here one moment and gone the next?

I was not there when Aunt Cumsee died, but I was notified the next morning. I was at the bedside of my mistress. Mary and Nathaniel were not. Mary was in childbed. Mr. Wheatley was in attendance but of no earthly use. The poor man was so addled he had all he could do to pace and wring his hands.

It was me, her little nigra slave girl, she wanted.

I knelt beside her.

"You must make me a promise."

"Yes, ma'am."

"You must write no elegy for me, no poem."

"Oh, ma'am. How can I not? I am known for my elegies. To not write one for you, the woman who gave me so much!"

"Christian humility dictates that I forbid it. The Author of all good works knows what I have done. Do you think you can best Him at saying it?"

"No, ma'am."

"Another thing." She paused, resting. "That letter you wrote to Reverend Occom."

"What letter, ma'am?"

"Silly girl, did you think you could keep it a secret from me? The one on freedom. And the hypocrisy of Christian slaveholders. He wrote to me of it and how he wants to get it published. But you said no, until after my death."

"Ma'am, I didn't wish to disgrace you."

"Do you think so little of me, then?"

"Oh no."

She smiled weakly. "Well, you may publish it now. I wish you to. Do it with my blessing."

She died that night, with her eyes fully open and her hands reaching outward. "Come, come quickly!" she shouted. "Oh, I pray for an easy and quick passage."

There was a parade of mourners at her funeral. Boston prides itself on gala funerals.

Mr. Wheatley did not go.

Before we were to leave, I found him gazing out the window of the front parlor. "Sir, I have your heavy coat. The sun is warm but the wind is brisk."

He turned and eyed me quizzically. "Is there to be another riot, then? There is a crowd outside. Are the Liberty Boys gathering? Has the news arrived from England how they will punish us for the tea?"

Dear God, I thought, *he has taken refuge in idiocy.* He'd been doing a lot of that of late. Times his mind was sharp as a saber. Other times he could not remember your name.

I sat him down in his favorite chair. "You wait here, sir. Your friends will wish to know where to find you." I fetched his paper and called to Sulie to bring him a pot of chocolate.

"You're a good girl, Phillis. Where are you off to?"

"I've an errand to run. I'll be back shortly. I'll send Bristol with another log for the fire."

All I could think of, as I wound along Boston's cold streets with the procession of mourners, was the day so long ago when the skinny little nigra girl, crawling with vermin and wrapped in a scrap of rug, was carried into the Wheatley mansion by Prince to meet the fair-haired goddess of a lady in her gray gown with rose fluff on it.

All I could think of was her eyes. And how they looked like she was just about to tell me something wonderful. And how I'd wondered what it was.

So long ago now, I thought, with a pang of sadness for Nathaniel and his boyish kindness. For Mary and her girlhood giddiness—Mary, now a married woman, so worn down from bearing child after child that she could not even be here today. I thought of Mr. Wheatley's quiet power and dignity, now ground down to muddleheaded confusion.

White folk don't have it any easier than we do, I minded. *They just think so. We all die in the end. That of itself is not so grievous to me. It's what comes before we die that gives me the quivers and quakes.*

Nigras know what comes. White folk never do. It always takes them by surprise.

So, then, why is it I am fear quickened of a sudden? Because inside I've become white. They've treated me white. I've trusted their soft words. I've been coddled by everyone.

Except Nathaniel. Nathaniel knew. He always knew I was still nigra, would always be nigra. Aunt Cumsee knew, too. So did Obour. But I fought them all.

So here I am now, come to a pretty pass—white on the inside, where nobody can see it, and nigra on the outside, where it's all anybody sees. Free, yes. Oh, I'm free all right. But all that means is that I must now earn my own bread.

A melancholy took hold of me as we passed through the gates of the Old Granary Burial Place on Tremont Street. Mary's husband, Reverend Lathrop, was saying prayers.

I looked into the yawning grave and was frightened. *My mistress and only protector is gone. What will happen to me now? Mr. Wheatley is half daft. War is coming. There is no telling what the British will do to punish Boston for the tea. I have three hundred more books coming in May and I must sell them in order to live.*

Who will buy them? Who will care about the poems of a little nigra girl if there is war?

The sun, which had been milky weak, disappeared behind a cloud. A gust of wind blew some old leaves around. *I'm one of those leaves,* I thought, *discarded, of no more use to anyone.*

Reverend Lathrop finished his prayers. We turned to leave.

Then the sun came out again. Or was it just the fact of John Peters standing there waiting for me at the cemetery gate?

The next day, Mr. Wheatley passed me in the hallway. "Phillis, where is my missus?" he asked of me.

"She is with the Lord, sir. We buried her yesterday."

Tears gathered in his eyes as my words took hold. He blew his nose.

"Why wasn't I told so I could go to the funeral?" he asked petulantly. "You must tell me these things, Phillis. I count on you to do so."

"You were told, sir. We decided it was best for you not to brave the raw March air. She would have wanted it that way."

"Oh yes, of course. She was a true Christian, Phillis."

"Yes, sir."

"I have a letter from Nathaniel. He plans a trip home soon. This is his house now, you know."

I felt something coming. I nodded.

"We shall prevail upon him to let us stay." He winked at me. "Else I shall have to remove to Mary's. I don't think I would care for that. Do you think he will permit us to stay?"

"I'm sure he will, sir," I said.

He patted me on the shoulder and went on his way. And I thought, *He is warning me, in the only way he can. I must plan. What if Nathaniel does not let me stay? What will I do?*

Chapter Thirty-seven

MAY—JUNE 1774

But I did not plan. For I did not know how. A bat-eared fox could probably plan better than I. Added to which was the distraction of everyday life.

I had to sell my books. I had to sort out my mistress's things. I had letters to write. A thank-you to Reverend Hopkins, who had purchased twenty of my books. A refusal to John Thornton in London, from whom I'd had a communication asking me to become a missionary in Africa.

Then there was my master. I had to see to his everyday needs. Though he went out of the house each morning, turned out as if for a session in the General Court, I suspected he met friends at coffeehouses just to pass the time. When he came home he expected me to dine with him. And listen to him.

There was more poetry to write. I had decided to

bring out a second volume. So I wrote. And I waited. I was confused.

Why, I did not know. But everyone in Boston seemed of the same mind. On the street, people who had always nodded hello to me now walked by with bowed heads.

"They're waiting," John Peters told me.

"For what?"

"To see what the British will do to us."

"Why should people mistrust me? I'm not British."

"They trust no one."

"I think it's pure nonsense. I think the British will do nothing." But I did not really believe that. I was saying the words because I was frightened.

"They're hoarding food," he told me. "At my stall and others, my customers buy more than they need. They're laying aside. This is always a bad sign."

Then spring came. And with it, on the tenth of May, the news of how England planned to punish us for the tea.

The Port of Boston was to be closed. Our waters were to be blockaded. Nothing would get in or out.

They would starve us. Their own brethren.

The House of Commons called Boston "a nest of locusts." London's *Morning Chronicle* said Boston was "a canker worm in the heart of America, which, if suffered to remain, will inevitably destroy the whole body of that extensive country."

On the eleventh, three hundred more copies of my book arrived from London.

On the thirteenth, His Majesty's ship *Lively*, only seven weeks out of Liverpool, dropped anchor, bringing the newly appointed military governor of the Province of Massachusetts, Thomas Gage. And four regiments of his military force.

Governor Hutchinson was going back to England, relieved of his duties. I felt sad. His name was on the paper that said I had written my poetry.

I remembered his blue eyes. And how he loved his home. And how he'd told his children that I wrote like an angel.

Boston was in turmoil once again. If we opened the windows we could hear the noise of the troops drilling. At night we could hear them brawling. The people met in Faneuil Hall in a great coming together to decide what to do.

What they decided was that they did not know what to do. So they did what Bostonians do in such an event. They got down on their knees and prayed.

Parliament made Salem the capital of the province. And Plymouth the seat of customs. Armed schooners appeared in our harbor. People began to leave town.

But Gage had not yet closed off the Neck. So I

scrambled to pack my books and ship some to Obour in Newport for sale. And while I was doing that, John Peters was scrambling to bring food in.

Quintals of fish, casks of olive oil, bushels of corn and flour, boxes of candles, cured sides of meat, even half a dozen live sheep that he purchased from an old Indian fighter named Israel Putnam of Connecticut.

In the early hours before dawn, disguised as a fish peddler, John Peters came down King Street with his cart. Yes, he had fish. But underneath it were the supplies he brought us, to be stored in our larder.

It was I who greeted him at the back door in the sweet, wet June mornings when the soldiers were still sleeping off their debaucheries of the night before. In the hushed, rosy-dawned stillness I brewed him coffee and we drank it together and talked.

"The world has gone mad," I said to him on the twenty-ninth of June.

Boston's port was closed now. The town was shut down.

"The world always was mad," he returned. "You just weren't sensible of it, Phillis."

That was John's way. He never missed an opportunity to remind me that I moved in a world of my own. We could argue the point, but this day I did not feel like arguing.

"I think of my English friends," I said. "Lord

Dartmouth, who was so friendly to the colonies. John Thornton, Archibald Bell, the countess. Do they not have a care for us?"

"Not a care," he said.

"I don't want to believe that."

"You always were too trusting, Phillis. You'll learn."

There it was again, the familiar bone of contention between us. "Why must I learn?"

"We all must, if we are to survive."

"Are we two separate peoples now, the British and the Americans?"

"Yes."

He was so certain of it that I was fear quickened. And willing to listen to him. For, differ as I did with him, he made sense.

"I'm muddleheaded, John. I feel myself part of them in England. And part of us here in America."

"And part white," he said, "and part nigra. Poor Phillis, you're split into four pieces."

We laughed. But there were tears in my eyes.

"One good thing has come of all this," I said. "Sulie sings your praises now, because you bring us food."

"Then it must be worth having our harbor shut down, if it makes me pleasing in the eyes of Sulie."

That was another thing about John Peters. In the

most dolorous situation he could see humor. I was beginning to note more and more good things about him every day.

On the last day of June a knock came on our door. Since Sulie was busy in the kitchen, I went to answer it.

Two British officers stood there, resplendent in their blue coats and white breeches.

"Are you looking for someone, gentlemen?"

They took off their tricorns. The silver hilts of their swords glinted in the sun. "May I please present myself," the taller one said. "Lieutenant Thomas Graves, of His Majesty's navy."

"Graves?" I asked. And my heart quickened. Just this morning Vice Admiral Graves had arrived in town. Guns had boomed and boatswains' whistles had blown all morning to welcome him. But surely *this* young man was not the admiral.

He smiled and bowed. "I'm the admiral's nephew," he said. "And this is Lieutenant James Rochefort. Is your master home?"

"He's at business this morning."

"Business, yes," young Graves said, smiling. "You people are always at business. Well, your mistress, then."

"She is dead."

He bowed again and lowered his eyes. "This is the Wheatley mansion, is it not?"

"Yes."

Young Graves took my measure. "And you must be Phillis Wheatley then, the young Negro poetess?"

"I am."

"Charmed." He bowed again.

"How may I help you gentlemen? Did you wish to purchase one of my books? I can offer you refreshment. Mr. Wheatley will be home soon."

"Books?" Rochefort smiled sardonically. "I hardly think so."

They were casting their eyes about to the rooms beyond the wide hallway.

"Most commodious," Graves said.

"Many luxurious appointments," from Rochefort.

I felt fear—some foreboding, nameless, but real. "My master has lived here many years," I said.

"May we inspect it?" Graves asked.

"*Inspect* it?"

"Yes." And he took a paper from his pocket and thrust it at me. "We invoke the old Quartering Act of 1765. It has been newly extended. You can see that yours is one of the private homes there on the list, suggested as possible abodes for royal officers."

My hands were trembling. I looked at their haughty, if handsome, faces. "I do not know of this Quartering Act. Mr. Wheatley never made mention of it to me."

Graves sighed with impatience. "I told my uncle,"

he said to Rochefort, "that we should have sent a liaison ahead. But no. We do not have the men for such niceties. Well, Rochefort, what do we do now?"

"Inspect the house," Rochefort said.

"I'm not going to force myself in like a bounder," Graves said. "My brother was here in '70. I know full well how fast a bloody ruckus can start."

"Do you have a maidservant?" Rochefort asked.

"Yes."

"Then we'd be most appreciative of some cold meat and bread and claret. Given that, we'll wait for your master. We have rights to come in and take up abode, you see, but since we're going to be living here for quite a while, I think we ought to start this thing off as amiably as possible. What say you?"

What could I say? What could any of us say? They waited for Mr. Wheatley, and when he appeared, instead of invoking the Quartering Act, they praised his house and his town as if he himself had laid it out and planned it. They laid claim to having met Nathaniel in London.

Mr. Wheatley had been so long without male guests at his board that he fell prey to their charm and warm assurance. They sensed this immediately. And played to all his needs.

He came alive. It had something to do with the pouring of Madeira, the talk about trade, the pipe smoke. He gave Bristol orders to move his things out of his own bedroom to accommodate the soldiers.

They moved in. Things changed.

The house came to life. They had their own food brought in and Sulie cooked it. There was no more need for John Peters to sneak around the back door and bring us eggs, flour, or meat.

But there was need, or so John thought, to put a lock on my door. Nights, when their bootsteps wakened me, I was glad of it, of course. Or when their drunken laughter sounded belowstairs. By day they were most discreet. They turned the front parlor into a study. There were papers and maps all about. Mrs. Wheatley's good cherry table was constantly strewn with the remains of chicken pie or ham or buttery scones.

And tea. They had their own. The finest Bohea.

Their fancy blue coats with the epaulets were draped over chairs. They demanded hot water for shaving, their boots to be polished, their wigs sent out to be repowdered. Sulie and Bristol were kept on the run.

I should have hated them. But, spineless wretch that I am, I didn't. I was hungry for the sound of the English voices, their impeccable manners. All of which bespoke my days in London.

They knew I had been in London. And that I was

hungry for news of it. So at night when they supped with us—or more precisely, we with them—they spoke of it. Of that world of ordered gentility, of culture, leisure, receptions, lavish entertainments, and constant amusements.

But more than that—oh, so much more—Lieutenant Graves had served on the *Edgar*, recently off the coast of Africa. One night, long after Mr. Wheatley left the table, he kept me enthralled with his impressions of my homeland.

The candles burned low as he spoke. "It is an Eden," he said. "The soil is inexhaustible, the harvests rich, the flowers like none I have ever seen."

Was he being artful? There was no need for it. He was speaking the truth. I felt tears in my eyes as the scene before me in the dining room fell away and I saw the flowing streams, the soft retreats, the ripening harvest, the verdant plains.

That night I burned my own candles late in my room, writing a poem, "To a Gentleman of the Navy." And it wasn't until morning that I minded that I'd gone to bed and forgotten to lock my door.

I knew I was spineless and weak. But John Peters told me so anyway.

"You wrote a *poem* about him?"

"Yes. It's going to be published in Joseph Greenleaf's *Royal American Magazine*."

He spit into the fire on the hearth in the kitchen. "Are you daft, woman? He's the enemy!"

"I don't see him as such."

"Well, you'd best start. Our warehouses are empty, our port shut, our people hungry. They've done away with the town meeting, they've forced themselves into your house. Even old Mister hasn't got the rights of a slave when they're around."

"They've been naught but polite and amiable, John. Methinks you're jealous."

He was staring into the fire. "Jealous! Of those dandified fops?"

"Yes."

"You never did know what you were about, Phillis," he said. "They flatter you. It's all you require."

"How dare you! I need no praise, from them or anyone."

"You need it to live."

"Well, I get none of it from you, do I?"

He set down his mug of cider. He turned from the hearth. "Your head is addled, Phillis. It isn't your fault. You're still struggling to figure if you're white or nigra. And now you don't know if you're British or American. It's time to decide."

"Why must I be one thing or the other? I feel as if I am a part of many peoples. What's wrong with that?"

"Such feelings are not abided these days."

"Poets don't meddle with politics."

"You just did in that poem you wrote about the lieutenant."

"I'll write what I please, John. No one has ever told me what I can and cannot write."

"I've no desire to do that. I don't know poetry. But I know you. So mayhap it's time I say what's on my mind."

"You always do. Why stop now?"

"You need steadying. I can steady you."

"Now what is *that* supposed to mean?"

He took my wrist in his big hand. I pulled back, but then his voice gentled me. "I would take you to wife, Phillis. I would protect you. Marry me."

Chapter Thirty-eight

"Patrick Henry saying 'I am not a Virginian but an American,'" Nathaniel said angrily. "Now, God in heaven, what does *that* mean?"

It was his first night home after a near-disastrous two-month voyage at sea. He had come alone, thank heaven, without his wife. October 2. Outside a cold rain slashed against the windows. Inside candles glowed in sconces on the dining room table. He was older, handsomer, and richer. And though I knew he was foreign agent for a slave trader and we had fought bitterly, the sight of him still benumbed me.

Months we had been parted. Yet the span of his shoulders was still familiar to me, as was his walk, the tilt of his head, every nuance of tone. *Of what shallow stuff,* I asked myself, *is the heart made, then? And does it never forget?*

"Phillis, pass the buttered beans to Lieutenant Graves," Mr. Wheatley said.

I did so. The board was set lavishly. You would never have known that Boston's port was closed. Where did these British officers get their supplies?

"I am afraid," said Graves, helping himself to buttered beans in great plenty, "that when you people find out what it means, it will be too late."

"Too late for what?" I asked.

Nathaniel glowered at me. I paid no mind.

"For conciliation," said Graves.

"There never should have been a Congress in Philadelphia," Nathaniel went on. "Now the fools in our very own county introduce the Suffolk Resolves. Has anyone heard what's *in* them?"

No one answered. Graves and Rochefort were too busy devouring the side of mutton, roasted apples, sweet ham, and Sulie's muffins.

"They call for every town to form a strong militia," Nathaniel recited. "They call for acts of Parliament to be disobeyed and all taxes to be paid not to Britain but to the treasury of a provincial independent government. By God, it's a declaration of war for Congress to countenance such demands."

"Don't forget the call to cease all trade with Britain," Graves said between bites.

"Madness," Nathaniel said. "Why, more than seventy members of Parliament own plantations in the

West Indies. They have large interests in colonial goods. They will be ruined."

"It will never be enforced," Mr. Wheatley said.

Everyone looked at him. He was lucid this evening. Nathaniel's return had done wonders for him.

"The reason being," he explained, "that the southern colonies have scarce any market, beyond England, for their rice and tobacco."

"Pray so, Father," Nathaniel said, "pray so. Good Lord, what have I come home to? Everything is in a shambles."

He was in such a befouled humor that I dreaded his summons, yet I knew it would come. And come it did, the next morning.

It was still raining. The eaves dripped. The house was chilled, and Bristol went about tending the fires. Graves and Rochefort had gone out to attend to their business. Mr. Wheatley was out, too, meeting friends.

"Who is this John Peters?" Nathaniel asked. He sat before a cheery fire in his room, taking a late breakfast.

"A greengrocer. He has a stall in North End Market. Before the officers came, and after the port was closed, he supplied us with food. Else we might have perished."

"Where did he get this food?"

"I did not inquire."

"Did it never occur to you that you should have?"

"No. We were in dire need. Would you have your father starve?"

He took a mouthful of fish and eggs, reached for a scone. "You've lost none of your sauciness, I see."

"Should I have?"

"I hear tell he's asked you to marry him."

I let my breath out, slowly. Sulie. She listened at doors. How else would he have known? I had told no one. "Yes."

"Has he pressed his suit with Father?"

"We have not spoken of it to anyone yet."

"And why? Does he think you're some scullery maid to be dallied with?"

"We haven't dallied, Nathaniel."

"You are a ward of this family."

"I am free," I said. "Your father freed me."

"Ah yes." He took a long draught of chocolate, set his cup down, and wiped his mouth with his linen napkin. "So you have what you desire, then. Freedom, which cures all ills. Does it pleasure you, Phillis?"

"I've not had time to notice."

He laughed. "Welcome to freedom. To say it has its constraints is not to do it justice. The colonies will learn."

I said naught, not wishing to anger him further.

"You are still writing, I see."

"Yes."

"I saw your poem about Graves in the *Royal American*. Do you think that was wise?"

"I did not consider the wisdom or the stupidity of it. I just wrote it," I said.

He sighed. "Don't try to flummox me, Phillis. You have become nothing if not an artful jade."

My face flushed. "How so?"

"You use people. You got your friend Obour and Reverend Occom to sell your books. To say naught of poor Reverend Hopkins in Princeton, who loathes poetry."

"I was as helpful to him as he was to me," I said.

He waved aside my protest. "You are demure with clergymen because you need their backing. You wrote to John Thornton, the rich philanthropist, claiming that the freedom my father gave you was perhaps the deserved wages of your evil doings. When all you ever wanted was freedom. You know how pious he is, and that he might think you vain and un-Christian if you said otherwise."

"How do you know all this?"

"You carry my name," he said. "It would be remiss of me not to know how you are using it."

"I have used it to no ill, Nathaniel."

"Not yet, but you will."

"How can you say such?"

"Then you wrote that letter condemning Christian ministers who have slaves," he went on quietly, "and waited until two weeks after my mother died to publish it."

"She urged me to publish it."

He got up and went to the window and stood looking out at the rain.

"I am a free nigra woman, Nathaniel," I said to his back. "I must do everything I can do to exist."

"Do you wed this John Peters for a roof over your head, then?"

"I have not said that I will wed him."

He shrugged. "It matters little to me if you do," he said, "but I feel it incumbent upon myself that I tell you I do not like him."

"You scarce know him," I pointed out.

"I know of his kind. He cannot support you, Phillis. He cannot keep you in the way you have been kept here."

"It is not my desire to have any man keep me. I shall make my way on my own. Freed by the fruits of my pen. Remember, Nathaniel?"

"Don't use old memories on me, Phillis. They no longer suffice. The world has changed and so must we. Or we will not survive."

"You've become hard, Nathaniel," I said.

He turned from the window. He picked up his coat and put it over his arm. "As I must, to exist in the world. And as you never can be. Which is why I predicted once, a long time ago, that free, you would perish."

"Thank you for your confidence in me," I said.

He gathered up his hat and some papers that he put in an oilcloth bag. "I must go out." He walked by me to the door, then turned. "You may stay in this house as long as you wish, Phillis. Don't wed John Peters because you think you must go."

He was staring at me intently, and for just one flicker of a moment I thought I saw some of the old Nathaniel, my old friend and mentor.

"Thank you," I said.

"I would, of course, be much gratified if you would look after my father. His mind is going."

So, then, the reason for his kindness. But I know I saw something of my old Nathaniel there, something he quickly wanted to hide. "I was not planning to leave him," I said.

He nodded briefly. Then he was gone.

I felt myself split in two. I collapsed in a chair, crying for the effort of not betraying my true feelings for him. I plunged into the depths of my soul, sitting there, such depths as I never knew existed.

Chapter Thirty-nine

SPRING—SUMMER 1775

I kept my promise to Nathaniel. Seven months later, John Peters and I delivered Mr. Wheatley to the door of the Lathrops in Providence, Rhode Island.

War had come. A month ago things had blown up between the colonials and the British in Lexington. We could no longer stay in our house with the British officers, no matter how amiable they tried to make things.

John Lathrop had left the pulpit of Old North in March, taking Mary and their one child to Rhode Island, where he was asked to fill the pulpit of the First Congregational. Three of their four children had died in the last year, of a malignant fever.

There was no place in Boston for ministers who defied the Crown. And no place in Boston now for us.

It had naught to do with being Tory or Patriot. Mr. Wheatley still considered King George III his sovereign. It had to do with lack of food and candles, with living surrounded by soldiers in the streets, and with all our friends having fled.

It had to do with the fact that at any moment Boston might explode into a million pieces, and I had to get Mr. Wheatley out.

The first thing Mary's husband did was ask John Peters to stay. "We cannot pay you. My salary is but a pittance. But we can offer you a roof over your head. Mary is in circumstances again and we shall need help with my father-in-law. He is failing."

"A roof I could use," John said. His stall at North End Market was gone, of course. I'd sewn money inside his coat pocket when we fled. British sentries at the Neck had searched everyone. We were not allowed to take money or food out of Boston.

John Peters cast a look in my direction. "But there is something you should know, Reverend."

"What is that?" Lathrop asked. "You're not planning on joining the British, like Sulie and Bristol did?"

John Peters grinned. "No, they did it for freedom. Which I wager they'll never see. I've asked Phillis to marry me. Do you think it seemly I live under the same roof?"

Lathrop's thin, ascetic face broke into a smile. "Splendid! I think that is splendid. Did you hear that, Mary?" He turned to his wife.

She shrugged. "That was months ago, Phillis said. And she hasn't said yes."

"Well, then, you must talk to her, Mary. You must tell her there is no better state than a good Christian marriage, despite all grievances."

Mary only smiled. "Come, let's go in to supper. We are all tired and must get settled. Phillis and I will take up that question another day."

I fell into the rhythms of the Lathrop household. I made myself useful. With another child coming, Mary certainly could use any help she could get.

John Peters stayed.

Should I marry him? I deferred the question. War was coming. In June, John Peters left to help dig the trenches on the hill above Boston where the Americans fought off the British. A thousand British regulars were killed. Charlestown was burned.

I was in a fit of terror until John returned, dirty and grinning and sassy as ever. That summer an army was being formed in Cambridge with a Virginian, George Washington, at its head.

"I'll sign on with Washington if you don't marry me," John said.

"I won't be bullied into making up my mind. Anyway, Washington isn't taking nigras."

"Yes, he is. Free nigras are joining."

But he did not go. He was badly needed in and around the parsonage. The hot summer days melted, one into another. I dragged myself around, once again waiting. For what, I did not know, but after Bunker Hill everyone else seemed to be waiting, too, for some decisive action, some shift in the wind.

One hot July day I sat in the garden with Mary. Little Thomas was just put down for a nap. The men were all out. We were both sewing.

"Is there no better state than marriage?" I asked her.

She smiled. "I did promise to take up that question with you, didn't I?"

"Yes."

"I love my John. But marriage is hard labor and sorrow and crosses of every kind."

That was no answer. I waited. Surely she would say more. But she continued darning.

"I don't know what to do," I confided. "My John is sweetness in itself. I know he wouldn't ill-use me."

"What else is there for a woman?" Mary asked.

"I have my poetry," I said.

"Ah yes." She sighed. "You are a woman accustomed to her independence, Phillis. You always were.

Look how you went to England. How I envied you! And now you're working on a new book of poetry! I scarce have time to read."

"I can't support myself, Mary," I said. "It would be nice to have a husband to look to for that."

She nodded. "He's a good man."

"But he knows nothing of my work. He never reads it."

"Does he object to your doing it?"

"No."

"Then you have no complaint. Most husbands want their wives to do nothing but sew a shirt and make a pudding."

"I fear marriage, Mary," I said.

She went on darning, not looking at me.

"I lie awake nights, thinking on it. I keep asking John to wait. Then I ponder, how long will he do that before he runs off to war and gets himself killed?"

"Do you love him?" she asked.

I thought for a moment. "Yes," I said. And I was surprised to realize that it was true.

She smiled. "I always thought you loved another."

I just stared at her. Had she been sensible, then, of my love for Nathaniel? I could scarcely meet her unblinking gaze.

"Prince," she said. "I always thought you loved Prince."

I was flooded with relief. Tears came to my eyes. I nodded. "He was a good friend. But my spirit never quickened to him in that way."

"Then what do you fear?"

"I fear what will happen to me and John if we get this independence. How will nigras fit in? If I marry John, I'm his wife. I must live his life. If I don't, I'll always be accepted by whites because of my work."

"Then you must do something so the Patriots will embrace you as their own," she said, "and your husband with you. For we shall have this independence. My John is sure of it."

I stared at her with new appreciation. She was no silly girl anymore. She had substance now. When I'd first come, she'd embraced me warmly, as if there had never been any girlhood animosity between us. And I'd watched her these last weeks in her role as the parson's wife. She was a true helpmate to John, running the house with the help of only one hired girl.

All this alone should have been enough to convince me of the merits of marriage, I minded.

"That would be good, Mary," I said. "But what could I write?"

Her smile had some of the old mischief in it.

"Why not write a poem in honor of our new commander-in-chief?" she said. "Why not write a poem to George Washington? I hear he is quite a man."

I did not act on it right away. Not until John Peters told me about this Washington who had taken command of the army.

John had been to Cambridge. He was helping again, bringing food in from the farmers of Rhode Island, for the army.

"You should see him, Phillis," he said.

"Oh? And you did, I suppose?"

"I did. I saw him riding through camp. So tall he is. And so solemn. The army is a shambles. The camp is thirty miles long. The men loll about and pick fights with each other. The Southern men hate the Yankees. The Southern riflemen refuse to take orders from anyone. All they do is show off with their long rifles and waste ammunition. They need food, clothing, shoes. Mischief abounds. But when Washington rides through, they all come about and take notice. You should see him, Phillis, as I did."

"Tell me, John."

"They call him the Fox Hunter."

Everything about me came alert. "The Fox Hunter?"

"Yes."

I thought of my father. I had not thought of him in a long time. I saw him suddenly, standing with his musket in his hand, about to go to the edge of the village and hunt the black-legged mongoose. I felt my father's presence as if he were in the room with me.

"A silence falls over everyone when Washington rides by on that white horse of his," John was saying. "They stop what they're doing, stop their fighting and lolling. They snap to attention. They know he's not hunting foxes now. The roughest Kentucky rifleman stands tall. At the same time everyone gets becalmed. He looks at you and you cringe. Like you would if God looked at you. But there is kindness, too, in that face. Oh, Phillis, I tell you, this is a man who will do good things for us all."

"The Fox Hunter," I said again.

"Yes, that's what they call him."

"I would like to see him," I said.

Still, I did not write the poem. And then, in October, the British burned the town of Falmouth in Maine, laying waste to wharves, houses, shoppes, leaving people without shelter. A Captain Mowat, who led the shelling, said he was ordered to destroy all the coastal towns. And said Portsmouth would be next.

Here was wanton savagery. Englishmen burning the village of other Englishmen. Everyone was in a panic. And no one had doubts anymore as to what side they were on.

I wrote the poem. And a letter. John Peters personally delivered both to Cambridge. By now he knew some officers there. They got my correspondence into Washington's hands.

At the beginning of December I had a letter from General Washington himself, inviting me to Cambridge to meet with him.

Chapter Forty

DECEMBER 1775

John Peters sat erect and proud on the wagon seat as we drove down the main road of the camp at Cambridge.

It had snowed a bit the night before, but this afternoon the sun was out in a sky that was a blue bowl overhead. And the sun was warm.

The scene around me made me cower close to John.

For as far as the eye could see were men, rough men in shirtsleeves. I heard curses, shouts. Some, in leather leggings and shirts, seemed fierce and raw. They spit tobacco. They wore all manner of things slung on their persons, everything from powder horns to slabs of bacon.

Some were drilling. Others cooking. They had no uniform but wore all manner of clothing—red worsted caps, hats of beaver, tricorns of black with clay pipes stuck in them. Some wore uniforms from the French war. All carried guns. Some of the guns were seven feet long. Others were ancient flintlocks.

John Peters knew his way around. He pointed things out to me. "We're at the foot of Prospect Hill. That two-story farm house is called Hobgoblin Hall. It's headquarters for Charles Lee. He commands the left wing of the army. Artemas Ward has the right. Israel Putnam, the old Indian fighter, has the center. He's fifty-six years old."

"Who are those young men drilling there on the green?"

He laughed. "Yale students."

Drums were throbbing, men shouting orders. I could smell wood smoke and gunpowder. Men were bending over steaming camp kettles, waving smoke away from their faces. I heard some fifes in the distance. And there were flags everywhere, flags of different sorts, snapping in the breeze.

I felt very small and lost, riding on the wagon next to John. Like all my concerns and worries were of no account. Like all my life I'd been thinking only of my own needs, while these rough-and-tumble men were thinking of the good of us all.

Something was happening here. Something grander than I could ever conceive with all my fancy words. Something outside my ken.

"I feel lost, John," I said.

"Don't worry, we're here." He drew the horse's reins up in front of a large house with shuttered windows. "This is Craigie House, Washington's headquarters."

Immediately we were surrounded by young officers wearing blue and buff. The reins were taken from John's hands.

"State your business," one young officer said.

John gave him Washington's letter. The officer read it and looked up at me, then helped me down. "Move this wagon. Get it out of sight. Supplies are coming in," he ordered.

John clucked to the horse and drove away. I stood watching him, a helpless, strangled feeling in my throat.

I was once supposed to be presented to the king and queen of England at the Court of Saint James. I do not know how I would have abided the glittering court, the pageantry.

This house was no court. By English standards it was a rude country home. But my heart hammered inside me nevertheless. Things were happening here. There was an air of purposefulness, even power.

Inside, all was aflutter. Dozens of people, some of them officers, seemed to be moving things about. Two were carrying a heavy clothespress up the main stairway. Two others were bringing in a pianoforte.

A man stood at the back door with an armload of evergreens. Behind him someone was unloading a cart of firewood.

The officer and I stood outside a closed, polished door. "The general is busy at the moment," the officer said. "We'll just wait here."

It was drafty in the large hall. I shivered and looked up. On the landing a man was fastening evergreens to the fat cherry banister.

"Are they preparing for Christmas?" I asked.

The officer smiled. "Yes. And for the arrival of Mrs. Washington. They expect her coach tomorrow."

Washington had slaves. John Peters had told me that. How would he receive me, then? Had he ever met a free nigra woman?

The door opened. I held my breath. A tall, broad-shouldered man in full dress uniform came out. I made ready to curtsy.

The officer put a restraining hand on my arm. "That's General Greene," he said.

I watched the general walk down the hall. Then the officer stood in the half-open door for a moment and, having been acknowledged, went inside.

I heard his boots walking across the wooden floor, heard murmurings, then a man's voice raised in surprised pleasantry.

Again the footsteps; and from behind the half-open

door, the officer nodded to me. "He'll see you now," he said.

The room was large and welcoming. A fire burned in the hearth. The wainscoting was seasoned and burnished, the rugs somewhat faded, the desk piled with papers. It was an old house and it had that look of solid, even shabby comfort that was the watermark of so many New England homes. No fancy furbelows like in England.

There was pleasant clutter, candleholders, books, maps. I felt in familiar surroundings, as if I'd come home.

And there was the man at the window, framed in its light.

The Fox Hunter.

"Ah, Miss Wheatley."

For a moment I was taken aback. *He had called me Miss.* No nigra woman was *ever* addressed as "Miss," be she bound or free. It just was not done.

This man had done it. Lightly, with no effort. Yet the knowledge of what he had done was there in his eyes.

I felt things falling into place inside me. And for the first time in a long while everything seemed of a piece.

I was whole for the first time in my life. I felt becalmed in his presence, with a peculiar sense that everything would be all right.

His voice was as it should be, deep but with a tone of rich amusement. And the eyes—oh yes, they were hunter's eyes.

They were like my father's, missing nothing.

I curtsied. I moved across the Persian carpet. I moved like words across a page, hoping he would read me as I had written myself to be.

He did. "I thank you most sincerely for your polite notice of me. The poem, I mean."

"It was my pleasure, sir."

He gestured that I should sit. I did.

"Everyone wants to notice me these days, it seems. They come here just to gawk. I hear I am the topic of conversation in every common room from Maine to Georgia. But your elegant lines were written without seeing. Though I am undeserving of your praise."

"You are head of our army, sir, a task that befits your talents."

"I'm the head of an army that has neither food, gunpowder, nor clothes."

"Supplies, sir. They can all be procured. What can never be procured, and what you bring, is leadership. The men all rally around your name."

He nodded approvingly. His eyes took in every aspect of my appearance. I was glad, of a sudden, that I had not accepted Mary Lathrop's offer of her one good velvet frock. My own neat linen and cotton seemed to please him.

"How long have you been in this country?" he asked.

"Since I was seven years old."

"Are you still in bondage?"

"My master freed me."

He sat in a satin-tufted chair. He was a very tall man, I minded. "Would you do the honor of pouring us some tea?" he asked.

I did so.

He took a cup. "There's some gingerbread there. Mrs. Greene sent it. She's always sending things for my comfort. The general has a good woman for a wife. Are you married?"

"No, sir, but I could be if I wished."

He took his tea and a slice of gingerbread. His movements were graceful, in spite of his size. "I miss my Martha. She's due tomorrow. We must have women about. Their presence gives the army civility. Otherwise the men are a pack of hounds braying for the kill."

He smiled at me. "You understand this, I see."

"My father was a hunter."

"Was he?"

"Yes, sir. Where I come from, which is Senegal on the Grain Coast, he was known as a great hunter."

"What did he hunt?"

"The black-legged mongoose." I told him about

it then, how it seemed tame and children would try to catch it. And get bitten.

He was much interested, so I elaborated.

"It's very crafty. It lives in termite hills. And it attacks our poultry."

He nodded slowly. "Crafty like our fox. I would like to hunt such a creature."

I told him then how my father also hunted the bat-eared fox, and so then he would know all about the bat-eared fox, too. I told him.

"You miss your father," he said.

Tears came to my eyes. "Yes."

"I was eleven years old when my father died. My half-brother Lawrence saw to my upbringing. He was older by fourteen years—like a father to me, but also my best friend. I would have been schooled in England if I hadn't lost my father. You have been to England, I hear."

"Yes, sir."

"I have never been there. But in my youth I called England home."

"I have many friends there," I told him.

"But we have become a different people. So now it is up to us to find our destiny in our own way."

"That frightens me, sir," I allowed.

"It frightens us all. But we do it because we must. As we Americans have always done things because we must. I have many an uneasy hour when all around me are wrapped in sleep. I pace alone, reflecting on my situation and that of this army."

"You, sir?"

"Yes. But then I think we Americans have always found our own way. And sometimes we must sacrifice to break new ground for those who will follow. I think that is our destiny. Do you know, the volunteers from Virginia and Carolina said they would not fight with free Negroes? I insisted the Negroes remain. And Congress has supported me."

"I was told you had Negro soldiers," I said.

"Yes. We break new ground every day. There is nothing to fear."

His gray-blue eyes met mine. I saw a peace in them, a fatherly concern, a tranquil assurance. And in that quiet moment, while the fire crackled and muffled sounds came from the far reaches of the house, I knew that it was right that I be here this day, that I meet this man, hear the quiet dignity of his words, bear witness to his subdued strength.

I had come for the wrong reasons, written my poem for the wrong reasons. But all that did not matter now.

All that mattered was that I met him.

"When one cultivates the affections of good people and practices domestic virtues, there is nothing to fear," he said again.

We spoke more. He told me of Mount Vernon and

how he missed it, of how he never separated his slaves from their families, and someday he would find a way to free them all. Of how he wanted to have my poem about him published, but then it might be considered a mark of his own vanity.

He asked me who my admirer was, whom I might marry if I chose. I told him about John. And my doubts.

"May I give some advice?" he asked.

"Oh, sir, I would be honored."

"Do not look for perfect felicity before you consent to wed. Love is a mighty pretty thing, but like all delicious things, it is cloying. It is too dainty a thing to live on alone, and ought not to be considered more than a necessary ingredient for that happiness that results from a combination of causes. None of which is of greater importance than that the object of your devotion have good sense, a good disposition, and the means of supporting you."

"Thank you, sir," I said.

"The sun grows weak." He stood. "I would talk more, but duty calls," he said.

I stood.

"I am happy to meet a person so favored by the Muses. I wrote poetry when I was young, you know."

"Did you, sir?"

"Yes. To girls. It was grievous bad."

We laughed. He took my hand. "Good-bye, Miss Wheatley."

"Good-bye, General."

"Nature has been liberal and beneficent in her dispensations to you. Use them well."

I did not walk back across the carpet. I floated.

Somehow I found my way out of the house. Somehow, in the confusion of men and officers moving about, I found John, with the wagon, a little way down the hill.

He was grinning at me. "I don't have to ask you how the interview went, Phillis. I can see it went well. Am I right?"

I got into the wagon. I drew my cloak around me. "John," I said, "I can only quote what the Queen of Sheba said on meeting Solomon."

"Very well, Sheba, I'm listening."

" 'The half was not told me,' " I said.

I married John Peters. Did I do the right thing? Times I think yes, other times no. But I know this: I am no longer afraid. Always, you see, I recall what the Fox Hunter was trying to tell me that day.

Love is a mighty pretty thing. And too dainty a thing to live on alone. But just an ingredient for that happiness that results from combined causes.

It was what my own father would have told me, I am sure of it.

If I never got the combined causes all of a piece, the fault was mine. It wasn't the Fox Hunter's fault. He tried to tell me.

I think of him often, and what he said to me that day when I and the country were so young and unformed and hopeful. And he was right.

We Americans sometimes must make sacrifices. And break new ground for those who follow.

Author's Note

After the British troops left Boston in March of 1776, Phillis returned, to find devastation. The Wheatley mansion was hit by cannonballs that had been sent across the bay by American soldiers on Cobble Hill in Charlestown. She lived alone, no one knows where, until April of 1778, when she married John Peters.

Just a month earlier, her master, John Wheatley, died. He bequeathed the bulk of his estate to Nathaniel. Phillis was not mentioned in his will.

Although Peters has been described as "a respectable colored man who kept a grocery store in Court Street, very handsome and well-mannered, wearing a wig, carrying a cane, and acting the gentleman," soon after they were married he failed in business.

Phillis kept on with her writing. But she had no

real moral support for her work. Mary Wheatley died in 1778, at age thirty-five. Phillis's Tory friends had deserted Boston once the Americans regained it. All the Wheatley relatives were doing their best to get along in the war, dealing with inflation and shortages.

By 1778, half the men who signed the paper attesting to the fact that Phillis wrote her poems were dead. Others were scattered and doing their best to survive.

Some people say that John Peters failed in business because he would not stoop to do jobs that he considered beneath him. Having failed, he was thrown into prison to relieve himself of debt.

Yet others say that he became a lawyer and took up the cause of Negroes in court. Indeed, Josiah Quincy, a renowned lawyer in Boston at the time, remarked that he recalled seeing Peters in Boston courts of law.

Both these reports about the man could be true. Perhaps Peters "read law," as was done in those days, and tried his hand at it.

At any rate, the marriage flourished in the beginning. Reports say that John and Phillis lived on Queen Street, a fashionable part of town. And even had servants.

In 1779 Phillis found herself "in circumstances," the eighteenth-century term for carrying a child. As she was preparing to give birth, she was also preparing proposals for her second volume of poetry, which she hoped to dedicate to Benjamin Franklin.

She was doing what Mrs. Wheatley had previously done for her, putting proposals for subscribers in the newspapers. She planned to publish thirty-three poems and thirteen letters in this book. The price was to be "twelve pounds, neatly bound and lettered, and nine pounds if sewed in blue paper."

Her first book had sold for two shillings and six-pence. The new price was set by John Peters, but it was not out of line, considering the inflation of the day.

The proposals for Phillis's book ran for six weeks in Boston newspapers. Nevertheless, once again Bostonians rejected her work. It may not have been prejudice this time, but simply that people were too busy with the war to care about something as frivolous as poetry.

In her letters to friends, Phillis never complained about her husband or his inability to support her. Actually, there is speculation, by some, that the marriage failed because Phillis was raised to be a spoiled poetess and could not cope with the realities of everyday life. This may be true. The Wheatleys certainly did not prepare her with any real-life skills. They may have helped her, raised her out of poverty, given her every opportunity, coddled her, and eventually freed her, but I cannot help feeling they regarded her as a plaything, a possession to show off to their friends.

Which is exactly what I have Aunt Cumsee and Obour telling her in my narrative.

Obour also felt, and wrote, that "poor Phillis let herself down by Marrying." For some reason their correspondence dropped off. In 1779 Phillis wrote to Obour, hoping to revive their communication. But that is the last letter she wrote to her friend.

Obour died in 1835. Upon her death she gave her letters from Phillis to the wife of Reverend William H. Beecher, who in turn gave them to the Massachusetts Historical Society.

Sometime after 1780, Phillis and John moved out of Boston to the small town of Wilmington, Massachusetts. No reason is given. Here Phillis did not flourish. It was a small remote village, not cosmopolitan like Boston. Research tells us that she suffered much, sometimes from want and sometimes from just plain hard work.

Phillis was the mother of three children when she moved back to Boston to live under the care of Mrs. Elizabeth Wallcutt, a niece of her old mistress. Phillis earned her keep by teaching at a school run by Mrs. Wallcutt. But after six weeks, John Peters came by to take them away.

In the spring of 1783, Nathaniel Wheatley died in

London, leaving a wife and three daughters. He was wealthy and happily married. He left Phillis nothing in his will.

Somewhere in these years, Phillis lost two children. In this time she also made thirteen attempts to solicit subscribers in Boston's papers for her second book of poetry.

She never succeeded.

While Peters languished in debtor's prison, she lived for a while in a "colored" boarding house in a bad part of town. Her health was failing. Several of Mrs. Wheatley's relatives, having heard nothing from her, sought her out. They found her living in filth and poverty, she and her remaining child both "sick unto death, in a state of abject misery, surrounded by all the emblems of squalid poverty."

Henri Grégroire, a French historian who wrote of colonial Boston, said, "The sensitive Phillis, who had been reared almost as a spoiled child, had little or no sense or need of how to manage a household, and her husband wanted her to do just that; he made his wishes known at first by reproaches and followed these with downright bad treatment, the continuation of which so afflicted his wife that she grieved herself to death."

Is this what made Phillis grieve herself to death? Or was it grief at not being able to publish another volume of poetry? Or at the loss of her former life, friends, and status?

At any rate, help came too late. Phillis Wheatley Peters and her last child died on December 5, 1784. A grandniece of Mrs. Wheatley's, who was passing up Court Street, saw her coffin being borne to the Old Granary Burial Ground.

She was, by my calculations, thirty years old.

After her death, when Peters was released from prison, he placed a notice in a local paper, asking the person who had borrowed Phillis's manuscripts to return them immediately, as all her works were to be published.

Phillis had left her manuscripts with Mrs. Wallcutt. She returned them to Peters. Obviously in need of money, he went about selling Phillis's gift books, books that had been presented to her in her celebrity days by famous and well-placed people.

A copy of John Milton's *Paradise Lost*, for instance, with the inscription on the flyleaf reading, "Mr. Brook Watson to Phillis Wheatley, London, July 1773," is now in the Houghton Library at Harvard University. Watson was former lord mayor of London.

Or Peters may have tried to sell Phillis's complete set of Alexander Pope's *Works* (thirteen volumes) that were given to her by Lord Dartmouth (and are now at the University of North Carolina).

Although a grandniece of Mrs. Wheatley's saw Phillis's coffin being borne to Old Granary, no one really knows where she is buried. Her grave went unmarked.

In today's world, Phillis would have been a celebrity, talking on morning shows, reading her poetry at presidential inaugurals, touring, and speaking. In eighteenth-century Boston, there was no place for her. She died in poverty and obscurity. Yet, more than two hundred years later, she remains what she was meant to be from the day she was sold on the auction block next to Avery's Distillery in the South End. America's first black poet.

As in all my historical novels, I will attempt to tell my readers what and who in the book is real and what and who was invented for the sake of story.

Perhaps, where characters are concerned, it would be simpler to tell which ones I made up. They are Aunt Cumsee; Sulie; Bristol; Mrs. Chelsea, who traveled to London with Phillis; Kunkle, the first mate on the *Phillis* (although there were many like him); Maria, her maid in London; and the lady Phillis met who was a sister to Lopez the slave trader. All the other characters really lived and played a part in Phillis's life.

However, I took risks with this book, in that I

created my own Phillis, as I created my own Harriet in *Wolf by the Ears*.

"Don't tell me someone is finally going to put flesh on that girl," an African American librarian and friend said when I told her I was writing this book. "It's about time."

This is what I have attempted in my novel, to flesh Phillis out. All the books written about her at present are scholarly, concerned with the dry facts of her life or her classical poetry.

We are told that Phillis was modest, shy, reverent, gentle, and unpretentious. *Yes,* I thought, *that may have been her public persona, but what was she really like?* So I set out to discover her.

Phillis Wheatley presented herself to me as I read between the lines of all the scholarly work. My Phillis is vain, confused, silly, and at times conniving. She has moods. She falls in love indiscriminately. These are the watermarks of most teenagers. Imagine a teen given the celebrity, the adulation, that Phillis was given, yet held on the tether of slavery, sometimes given some slack and other times drawn in.

I made Phillis real. Not in accordance with the speculation of the scholars. Because then I would have one more scholarly book. I did not set out to do that.

So, then, my Phillis falls in love with Nathaniel. I developed relationships between her and the Wheatleys, between her and Mary, Prince, Obour—

indeed, everyone who crossed her path. This is the job of the historical novelist. I took the facts and I ran with them.

Research tells us that Mrs. Wheatley tutored her. Yet in *The Collected Works of Phillis Wheatley*, edited by John Shields, we are told that likely it was Nathaniel who tutored her in Latin and Greek and the classics. "Given the wealth and status of the Wheatley family," we are told here, "it is likely Nathaniel attended Boston Latin School through the sixth form." Mrs. Wheatley did not know Greek and Latin. Nathaniel did. Although she may have had additional instruction from learned ministers, I went with Nathaniel as her tutor.

It is speculated that Phillis came from Senegal, West Africa. So I created a background along that line and recounted the middle passage as best I could, after considerable study concerning that terrible experience. Captain Quinn really did bring her over on the *Phillis*, and it is thought that Obour did come with her. However, nowhere is it mentioned that her mother made that voyage. This is my invention.

As to how and when she wrote her poems, I adhered closely to the schedule of production. As for the poetry itself, it is very scholarly, very eighteenth century. It relies heavily on Greek and Roman mythology. It would not be understood or enjoyed by my readers. For this reason, I have not quoted it at any length.

Her meeting and "oral exam" in front of the distinguished men of Boston did happen, although no one knows the questions they actually asked her.

Mrs. Wheatley did take her about Boston to meet important personages, to display her, and have Phillis recite. She was accruing a support group to get the first book published.

Phillis's trip to London is written much as it happened. She went under Nathaniel's protection, saw and did all the things I have portrayed, with the exception of the scene in which Nathaniel walks in with Mary Enderby. (Although he did court Mary Enderby on this trip and married her that November.)

In London she was received, celebrated, and coddled. And Benjamin Franklin did call on her. Nathaniel would not receive him, however. It is believed that was because of the recent Somerset Decision, which pronounced Negroes free, "simply by breathing the free air of England." And because Franklin was antislavery.

When Phillis returned to America she did nurse her mistress, and later cared for her master. He freed her in October of that year, after London reviews of her book criticized the fact that she was in bondage.

Scipio Moorhead did draw her portrait.

Hundreds of other parts of this book are true. I

cannot name them all here. A perusal of the scholarly books on Phillis Wheatley will bring them to light.

As for Phillis's meeting with George Washington in Cambridge in December 1775, it did happen. I saw the meeting with Washington as the high point of her life. From that moment on the war worsens and so does Phillis's condition. It steadily goes downhill.

I saw no reason to elaborate on her troubles after marriage in this book. I wanted my readers to see her in the prime of her creativity, in her girlhood, touched by the wand of the Wheatleys' kindness and generosity. That wand, as I see it, was a double-edged sword, in that they lifted her out of poverty and servitude, educated, and nurtured her. Yet at the same time they kept her in silken fetters.

One can interpret their treatment in two ways. Did they use her for their own enjoyment, then cast her aside, unprepared for what would follow? She was constantly referred to as "Mrs. Wheatley's Negro girl who writes poetry."

Or did they rescue her from terrible circumstances and give her the opportunity of a lifetime, an opportunity that her own willfulness brought to a bitter end?

Did they prepare her for life? Or make her so dependent on them that she could not function when left to her own devices? Was it fair to educate and encourage her to be a poet when the world was not

Bibliography

Alderman, Clifford Lindsey. *Rum, Slaves and Molasses: The Story of New England's Triangular Trade*. New York: Crowell-Collier Press, 1972.

Bowen, Catherine Drinker. *John Adams and the American Revolution*. Boston: Little, Brown, 1950.

Grzimek, Bernhard. *Grzimek's Animal Life Encyclopedia*. New York: Van Nostrand Reinhold, 1975.

Hogendorn, Jan, and Marion Johnson. *The Shell Money of the Slave Trade*. London: Cambridge University Press, 1986.

Johnson, Charles. *Middle Passage*. New York: Penguin Books, 1990.

Robinson, William H. *Phillis Wheatley and Her Writings*. New York: Garland Publishing, 1984.

Wheatley, Phillis. *The Collected Works of Phillis Wheatley*. Edited by John C. Shields. The Schomburg Library of Nineteenth Century Black Women Writers. New York: Oxford University Press, 1990.

White, Anne Terry. *Human Cargo: The Story of the Atlantic Slave Trade*. Champaign, Ill.: Garrard Publishing, 1972.